Praise for Terry Lynn Thomas

'I was gripped from page one … An atmospheric
read which I really enjoyed'

'Wow! … You won't be disappointed'

'Gripping and enthralling … Wonderful'

'Fantastic! … Such an amazing read!'

'An entertaining and engrossing read,
highly recommended'

'A suspenseful, compelling plot that kept
me up late reading'

'Brilliant book … Brilliant author'

'Fast-paced and gripping'

TERRY LYNN THOMAS is the *USA Today* bestselling author of six historical mysteries. *The Betrayal* and *The Witness* are the first two books in the Olivia Sinclair series, Terry's foray into the world of domestic suspense. When she's not writing, Terry likes to spend time outdoors with her husband and her dogs.

Keep up with Terry on Facebook (https://www.facebook.com/terrylynnthomasbooks/), Twitter (@TLThomasbooks), Instagram (@terrylynnthomasbooks) or via her website at www.terrylynnthomas.com.

Also by Terry Lynn Thomas

The Cat Carlisle series
The Silent Woman
The Family Secret
House of Lies

The Sarah Bennett series
The Spirit of Grace
The House of Secrets
The Drowned Woman

The Olivia Sinclair series
The Betrayal

The Witness

TERRY LYNN THOMAS

ONE PLACE. MANY STORIES

HQ
An imprint of HarperCollins*Publishers* Ltd
1 London Bridge Street
London SE1 9GF

www.harpercollins.co.uk

HarperCollins*Publishers*
1st Floor, Watermarque Building, Ringsend Road
Dublin 4, Ireland

This paperback edition 2021

1
First published in Great Britain by
HQ, an imprint of HarperCollins*Publishers* Ltd 2021

Copyright © Terry Lynn Thomas 2021

Terry Lynn Thomas asserts the moral right to be
identified as the author of this work.
A catalogue record for this book is
available from the British Library.

ISBN: 9780008364823

Printed and bound by CPI Group (UK) Ltd, Croydon CR0 4YY

This book is dedicated to all the writers I've met along the way. You rock.

Prologue

Thirteen-year-old Ebby Engstrom wanted to die as he rode his bike home in the cold December night, his thighs on fire as he pedaled faster and faster. His lungs burned, but the pain caused by the physical exertion was an instant panacea to his broken heart. No matter how hard he tried, he couldn't shake the image of Mary Beth slow dancing with a seventeen-year-old high school student. Granted she was drunk – Ebby had the vomit stains on his new sweatshirt to prove it – but even that knowledge didn't take away the pain. He let the hot, salty tears run down his cheeks, hoping he'd cry himself out before he got home. His mother could not see him crying, especially over a girl.

Stopping at the bottom of his drive, Ebby looked up at his family house, the lights in the windows a welcoming beacon. His dad had died this past June, six months and three days ago, to be exact. The sight of the home and the lights on in his dad's study just made Ebby's heartache worse. How he longed to share the crappy evening and Mary Beth's betrayal with his dad, who could be counted on to say just the right thing to soothe Ebby's broken heart. Ebby's mother wasn't nearly as understanding. She was strict, uncompromising, and took great pride in running her house like a tight ship. Ebby had to leave his broken heart at the door, or his mother would take one look at him and know something was wrong. If she knew that her youngest son was a mess because of a girl, she'd wave off the emotion as unimportant, and tell him to buck up and be a man.

As Ebby wiped his tears with the back of his sleeve, the rain started. He rushed up the driveway, eager to take a hot shower and wash the events of the past two hours down the drain. Maybe he could get Allegra to make him hot chocolate with extra marshmallows. If not, he'd make his own. Take it to bed. Maybe he could fall asleep and forget today ever happened. Maybe he could sleep like Rip Van Winkle and wake up in a hundred years.

The rain turned torrential as he got close to the house. It pelted on his head and shoulders and quickly soaked through his heavy sweatshirt. Ebby jumped off his bike and let himself into the house, hoping he could sneak upstairs without seeing anyone. If he tiptoed, he could scoot past the office door and his mother wouldn't see him. Someone was in there with his mother, arguing. Ebby could sense the tension, even though he wasn't in the room with them.

Creeping down the hallway, careful to avoid the floorboards that creaked, Ebby paused outside the office. Something made him stop when he heard the two voices in the office. No longer worried about his mother noticing him, he tried to peek into the room and see who was with her. He only caught a quick glimpse of his mom and another person who had his back to the door. Ebby tried to catch a better view of the person, who seemed familiar, but he couldn't even tell if it was a man or a woman from that angle. The mysterious visitor placed their hands on the desk and leaned close to his mother, hissing words born of fury.

His mother didn't back down. She leaned even closer and spoke. Their bodies became shimmery as Ebby strained to hear what they were arguing about. He'd never seen his mother so full of indignant anger. Try as he might, he couldn't understand their words. It seemed as though they were being spoken in slow motion. When his mother turned her back and fiddled with something on the credenza behind her, Ebby watched in horror as the stranger picked up the bejeweled letter opener that had sat on his parents' desk for as long as he could remember. He couldn't take his eyes away as his mother turned around, and the stranger raised the letter opener high in the air and plunged it into his mother's chest. Up and down the arm holding the letter opener went. Ebby registered the sound of labored breathing and red cascading blood that splattered, its metallic tang assaulting Ebby. And even though he was far away, he felt it drench his shirt.

But how could that be? How could he be covered in his mother's blood? He was tucked safely out of the way in the alcove in the hallway. He wasn't in the office. Something wasn't right. Ebby's chest became tight, as though an elephant were sitting on it. He couldn't breathe. And then he felt his knees give way as everything went black.

* * *

When Ebby opened his eyes, it took him a couple of seconds to orient himself. It was 2015. He was forty-three years old. He was sprawled on the heavy rubber mat in the kitchen of his restaurant, The No Name Diner, a pile of Caesar salad scattered all over the floor around him. Lettuce clung to his chef's coat as he rolled onto his back and met the gazes of his chef, Javier, his sous chef, Alex, and his waitress, Belle. All three of them stood over him, various degrees of concern etched on their faces. He had suffered yet another – Ebby didn't know what to call the phenomenon – flashback, hallucination, whatever, to that night thirty years ago. The name didn't matter.

3

"It's okay, Ebby. You just fell." Belle squatted down and put her cool fingers on Ebby's forehead.

He tried to sit up but immediately felt woozy. Javier, dependable Javier, took charge. "I got this, guys," he said.

"I'll make another batch of salad," Alex said.

"You sure you'll be okay?" Belle asked, her eyes filled with worry.

Ebby managed to sit up on his own. Despite his clothes smelling of garlic and anchovy paste, he didn't appear to have hurt himself. At least not this time. "I think I'm coming down with something. I'll just have Javier drive me home, if you two don't mind being alone for half an hour or so?"

"We'll be fine," Belle said, as she and Javier helped Ebby to his feet. "You just take care of yourself, okay?"

Ebby and Javier didn't speak until they were in Javier's car riding up the twisty road toward Ebby's cottage. When the tension between the two men became unbearable, Javier pulled his car off to the shoulder and turned to face Ebby.

"What are you doing?" Ebby asked.

"I'm not driving an inch farther until you tell me what's going on. What the hell was that, man? That's the second time that's happened. I know you aren't coming down with something. You passed out cold. Face-planted on the kitchen floor and were out for a good three minutes."

"I don't know what's happening—"

"Ebby, I love you like a brother, man. You know that. We've been friends for a long time. And I know you're going to get mad at me for saying this, but you need to go back to the doctor. You need a psychiatrist to help you."

"Javier—"

"No. Listen to me, you're slipping. You look like hell. It's hard for me to stand by and watch you destroy yourself, all because you want to remember some horrific thing that happened thirty years ago. It's been four months since you stopped taking your meds, right? Have you remembered anything specific? I can tell by the look on your face that you haven't. This has got to stop, Ebs. Today you were lucky enough to knock over a large bowl of lettuce. Have you thought of what would happen if you were handling a knife or a skillet of hot grease? As your friend and as the manager of your restaurant, I'm telling you that you need help. Find a doc you like, someone you can trust."

Embarrassed, Ebby felt hot tears prick behind his eyelids. In his heart, Ebby knew Javier was right. How he longed to spill his guts, to tell his friend that he was remembering the night his mother was murdered. What a relief it would be share the burden of his past and his fear of the future with a trusted friend. But he couldn't tell anyone, not even Javier. Not yet. Not until he knew … But Ebby needed to tell Javier something. For now, his friend would have to be happy with a sanitized version of the truth. "You're right. I need help. And I'm going to get it."

Javier let out a long sigh, his relief almost palpable. "I'm sorry, Javier. I'm not ready to say anything else. Not yet." Javier stared out the window, while Ebby silently prayed he wouldn't push for more details.

"When you are ready to talk, I hope you'll come to me." Javier put the car in drive and they started once again up the wooded road that led to Ebby's cottage. "You know I'm here if you need me, any time."

"I do," Ebby said. "And I appreciate it."

After Javier left, Ebby didn't go straight into his cottage. He ducked into the woods and headed to Elodie's Airstream. The clean air and the walk went a long way toward restoring Ebby's strength. By the time Elodie's trailer came into view, he had resolved to confide in his aunt. After all, she was the only person he would trust with this horrible secret. Her Airstream, a giant silver behemoth resembling a spaceship, was nestled among the trees near Ebby's cottage. Ebby and Elodie had shared this trailer from the time Ebby turned eighteen until his twenty-first birthday, when he and Javier – with the help of Javier's father who was a builder – had built his cottage.

How happy they'd been in the tiny trailer, which Elodie had remodeled so it was filled with light and warmth. His eyes traveled to the wooden fence they had constructed along the back of the property line. Elodie had drilled holes in the wood and filled them with what appeared to be colored glass. When the light hit, the fence looked like a rustic Tiffany lampshade.

Elodie met Ebby at the door, where she stared at him before letting him in. "You've had another one, haven't you?"

He slid onto the leather booth in the kitchen area while Elodie put on the kettle. Once they were both seated with hot mugs of tea, Ebby explained what had happened at the restaurant. "I saw someone stab my mother. There was so much blood. I was covered in it. I passed out and woke up on the floor."

"Oh, Ebby, you poor thing," Elodie said.

"It was really vivid." He watched his beloved aunt and noticed the flicker of worry in her eyes. "Are you sure you found me in the rain that night, Elodie? Because that's not what I seem to be remembering."

"Of course," Elodie said abruptly. "I found you outside, under the office window, curled up in the rain. You were soaked clear through. I was afraid you would catch pneumonia, so we managed to get you into a warm tub. You aren't *remembering* anything, Ebby; these are just … visions, or hallucinations."

I don't believe her, Ebby thought. And there lay the proverbial rub. Ebby was sure his aunt wasn't telling him the entire story. Although he had no doubt her motivations were well intended, she was keeping something from him, something that related to his mother's murder, and – just maybe – his involvement in it.

Elodie scooted toward Ebby and put her arm around him. "You witnessed something, Ebby, something traumatizing – that's why you lost your memory. But these flashbacks, or whatever it is that you are experiencing, they aren't real. Surely you understand that."

Ebby ran his hands through his hair. He met Elodie's gaze, looking for any sign of deception as he spoke. "I know I saw something that night. I know what happened is completely different from the story you've told me all these years. I've been to the police, but they won't let me look at the files. Not that I blame them. I get it; I'm a civilian. Either that or I was a suspect."

"You were not—"

"Wait, please, Elodie. Just let me finish. What I'm remembering about the night – that night – isn't in keeping with what you've told me over the years. There's blood – so much blood … I don't know what to think." Ebby swallowed the thick lump that had formed in the back of this throat. "Did I kill her?"

"Ebby!" Elodie cried out and once again tried to interrupt.

"I had motive, didn't I? She wanted to send me away to boarding school. She killed my dog and lied about it. That was the end of the world for me," Ebby said, remembering all of a sudden the infuriating pain when he'd discovered the truth about Lucy and the murderous rage he felt toward his mother.

She'd lied to him, told him his dog had been hit by a car, that she had to be put to sleep. "The poor thing was suffering. It would have been cruel to let her live." Later that night, he'd overheard Elodie and Cynthia arguing about the dog.

"The little bitch growled at me when I gave Ebby a spanking," Cynthia had said. "She was vicious and unsafe."

"You're the one who's vicious and unsafe," Elodie had responded. Ebby had never heard his aunt raise her voice to anyone. "Do you ever think that you spank your son too frequently?"

"This isn't any of your concern, Elodie."

"But it is. Ebby is my nephew. You clearly prefer Mark. Do you think Ebby, the son you so obviously don't like, doesn't see that?"

Ebby had peeked around the corner just in time to see his mother focus her attention on one of the papers stacked up on her desk. "Go away, Elodie. You bore me."

Ebby had stepped back into the alcove near his mother's study – what he liked to call his hidey hole – as Elodie stormed out of his mother's office, tears streaming down her cheeks. It wasn't until later that evening, when he was tucked into bed and Elodie – not his mother – came to say goodnight, that he'd realized his mother didn't love him.

The memories of the past faded as he turned to Elodie and said, "I can remember you and my mom fighting after Lucy died, as clearly as if it were yesterday."

"You were very loved, Ebby. Your mother had her rough moments, but at other times she loved you," Elodie said.

"I know," Ebby said. "But there's something in my brain that's coming to the surface. I can feel it. It's dangerous. I can't sit by and not try to figure it out."

"You need to go back to the doctor," Elodie said. "We can find you a good psychiatrist—"

"No," Ebby said. "No doctors. No more tests. No more therapy. No more – and I mean this with all my heart – no more psychiatric interventions. I need some facts. I need the truth. Elodie, I love you, really I do. But I think you're keeping something from me about that night – you and Aunt Fiona both. I want to know what."

"That's nonsense. No one's keeping anything from you. The only thing I've ever wanted to do is protect you." Elodie's expression softened. She reached out and touched Ebby's face. "You're a grown man, Ebby. You own a successful restaurant and you are doing well in life. You suffered a tragedy as a child. You lost your mother. It's a heartbreaking truth. Maybe you're just going through a rough patch. But you have to agree that you were doing much better when you were under the care of a psychiatrist."

"The drugs they gave me were nothing short of poison," Ebby said.

"Then what about regular talk therapy? Just to get you through this rough patch."

"No. This is more than a rough patch. My memory is coming back. I need to let that happen. And before you interrupt, I want to find out what happened that night on my own. I don't want to be told the story, secondhand, by family members." Ebby rubbed his eyes, thinking of the question that threatened to drive him to madness: Did he murder his own mother? Did he stab her? "Tell me, Elodie, what should I do? Because if I don't do something, I swear, I'll go mad."

"Very well," Elodie said. "I've got an idea."

Chapter 1

Olivia

Friday, January 2

I'm in love with Brian Vickery. Olivia pulled her coat tighter against the winter wind as she walked down Magnolia Avenue in the direction of her office. *I'm in love with Brian Vickery, and he's renting an office from me.* Olivia reached her office, surprised to find the door unlocked and the lights on. *I'm in love with Brian Vickery, and he's dating someone else.* She stood outside for a moment, as the sobering reality of the situation pulled at her heart. Eventually this pain would pass. Wouldn't it? Because the entire scenario could be reduced to three bullet points: Brian and Olivia had slept together. Olivia had pulled away. Brian had moved on. Done. End of story. Now it was down to Olivia to act like all was just hunky-dory as Brian signed the lease that would essentially force them to share an office for the foreseeable future.

Taking a deep breath, she stepped out of the January chill, plastered a smile on her face and headed toward the halo of light that spilled out of Brian's office and into the hallway.

"Hey, Brian—" She stopped in her tracks, astonished to see Leanne Stoddard, Brian's new girlfriend, hunched over Brian's desk, her back to Olivia, as she snapped pictures of documents with her cell phone. "Leanne? Can I help you?"

At the sound of Olivia's voice, Leanne turned around, eyes wide, as she stuffed the documents back in the drawer and closed it. "Olivia? What are you doing here?" Leanne placed her palm flat on her heart. "You scared me to death."

"I own the building." Olivia narrowed her eyes, suspicious now of Leanne's reasons for being here. "Why are you going through Brian's papers?"

"I know how this must look. But I wasn't going through his papers."

Liar. Olivia didn't say the word out loud.

"Really. I wasn't snooping. Trust me. I wanted to get a look at Brian's calendar. I thought it would be easier to just take a photo rather than writing down all the days he was free. I was hoping to surprise him with a getaway weekend or a concert, but he's so busy all the time working."

Olivia had learned long ago never to trust anyone who used the words *trust me.* "How did you get in here?"

"Oh, Brian gave me a key. I'm here to pick up his laptop. It's running slow, and I offered to fix it for him. Please don't tell him you caught me here. I wanted to surprise him." Brian's laptop case sat on the corner of his desk. Leanne picked it up, sliding the strap over her shoulder. "I actually wanted to speak to you anyway. I was hoping we could have coffee or lunch one day. Brian considers you a close friend, and I'd like to get to know you better."

In the spirit of getting along, Olivia forced a smile and said, "I'd like that very much."

"Good," Leanne said, smiling back. "Let me know a day that works. Gotta run. Have a good one."

"Can you lock the door, please?"

"No problem," Leanne said.

Once Olivia heard the door shut and the key turn in the lock, she stepped into Brian's office. She didn't believe for one minute that Leanne was looking through Brian's calendar.

Olivia had never liked Leanne, hadn't trusted her from the minute Brian had introduced them. Olivia had assumed her dislike stemmed from jealousy because if she were completely honest, she wanted Brian for herself. They'd met after Olivia had been arrested for the murder of her husband's mistress, and her attorney had hired Brian to prove her innocence. They had struck up a friendship. When the real murderer had burned Brian's house down in a feeble attempt to destroy evidence, Olivia had gladly invited Brian to stay with her until he found a more permanent place to live. She had been surprised at how well the two of them got along, how easy it was to be together and share the simple day-to-day moments that constitute the bulk of a relationship. But they had moved too fast and everything had fallen apart.

Leanne's sudden appearance in Brian's life had taken Olivia totally by surprise. With nothing else to do, Olivia had stepped away, knowing the best course of action was to give him room to navigate this new relationship without interference from her.

There was a part of Olivia – the seasoned litigation attorney who trusted her finely tuned intuition – that wanted to run a simple background check on Brian's new girlfriend, if for no other reason than to lessen her anxiety. She'd only been around Leanne twice, but each time they'd been together, Olivia had felt like Leanne had an agenda, as though she were hiding something. Olivia hadn't yet acted on her suspicions because it wasn't her place and Brian would not be happy if he found out. She wondered if she should do a little digging into Leanne Stoddard's background. No one would need to know. If she found evidence that Leanne wasn't what she seemed, she would tell Brian. He might get mad at her for meddling in his affairs, but Olivia didn't care. She was sure Brian would do the same thing if the tables were turned.

* * *

An hour later, Olivia sipped her coffee and stared out the café window at the Golden Gate Bridge, and the shimmering San Francisco Bay. Across from her, Lauren Ridley added a generous dollop of cream and sugar to her coffee.

"So what don't you like about this woman, other than the fact that she's got her claws into Brian Vickery?"

"I can't put my finger on it. At the risk of sounding more than a little ridiculous, when Brian's around her, it's like she's the predator and he's the prey." Olivia waited for Lauren to smile and tease. But she didn't.

Instead, she put her coffee cup on the aqua blue Formica table and said, "Go on."

"When she came to the office that first time, I got the distinct impression that she was casing the joint. And she's hiding something. I swear, I can smell it." Olivia picked at the flimsy paper napkin on her lap. "When I got to the office this morning, she was already there, going through Brian's desk. She swore up and down that she was taking a photo of Brian's calendar, so she could take him away for the weekend."

"Ouch," Lauren said. "Do you think they're sleeping together?"

"I don't know. Probably. Am I just being jealous? Remember, I'm the woman who couldn't even see my own husband's infidelity. Maybe I'm totally wrong about all of this."

"Stop it, Liv. Just because you didn't see Richard for the jackass he was, doesn't mean you're wrong about this Leanne creature. You're not the first person who couldn't see their own issues."

"If you saw them together, you'd see what I mean. It's like Brian shrinks when he's around her. He literally looks shrunken and weak, like he's ripe to be taken advantage of. When Brian was working my case, he was focused, had a purpose. Game on, if you get my meaning."

"What's different now? You've said he has more work than he knows what to do with."

"The work he has now isn't personal for him. It's professional – corporate background checks and things like that. His heart's not in it. And, despite Leanne Stoddard, he's still mourning his wife in a big way." Olivia sipped her coffee. "There's a particular type of woman who is attracted to men like Brian – widowers, who are coming to grips with their grief. Some men – in my opinion – just want to be married. I think the pain of their loss softens them, if that makes sense. This type of woman wants to provide emotional rescue and save the man in need."

"What's wrong with that?"

"Other than people should save themselves, nothing at all. There's also a sub-genre – for lack of a better word – in this group, the type of woman who likes to swoop in and exploit. I'm pretty sure Brian got a sizeable property insurance payout from his house fire."

"Are you saying you think this woman is after Brian for his money?"

Olivia didn't give voice to her thoughts. "I'm saying I don't like her. And I'm saying – despite my utter lack of judgment as far as Richard was concerned – in this situation I trust my intuition."

"Brian Vickery is a retired cop. He's seen the dark side of humanity. There's not a gullible bone in that man's body. The question here, my friend, is why won't you admit you want Brian for yourself?"

The waitress approached with two plates piled high with food. "Salmon omelets, extra avocado and extra potatoes." She set the plates on the table. "I'll circle back with coffee shortly, ladies. Flag me down if you need anything else."

After the waitress was out of earshot, Olivia leaned forward and said in a low voice so no one could hear, "All right, I admit it. I'm fond of Brian. But he is not over his wife. And I don't want to get involved with someone who isn't capable of reciprocal feelings. I already had a long-term loveless marriage. If I get involved with Brian, it will be when he is good and ready."

"Right. You see what you did there?"

"What are you talking about?" Olivia shook the ketchup bottle and doused her potatoes.

"You're making these judgments and decisions about a relationship without consulting the other party. You should express this to Brian, not to me. It's obvious you're missing him. Why haven't you talked to him? Don't you think you should tell him why you pulled away after your illicit physical … whatever it was? At some point, you're going to have to talk to him, if for no other reason than to clear the air so you can move on. He's renting an office from you, Liv. You're going to be around him. You need to deal with this."

"I know. I know. I need to talk to him. I've tried, really I have. Just the other day we were in the office together, unpacking his work stuff. Every time I opened my mouth to broach the subject, the words wouldn't come."

They ate in silence for a moment before Lauren said, "When the time is right to talk to him, you'll find the words. Meanwhile, what are you going to do about the new girlfriend?"

"I don't know," Olivia said. "Maybe a little background investigation wouldn't go amiss, given what I saw this morning."

"Agreed. But you need to be careful if you go down that road," Lauren said. "I'm sure Brian wouldn't appreciate knowing you're investigating his girlfriend behind his back. And now that you're sharing office space, the relationship is professional *and* personal."

Olivia waited while the waitress refilled her coffee. When she was gone, Olivia said, "My life mantra right now is 'Proceed with caution'. When the time is right, I'll talk to him. But a quiet little background check wouldn't be harmful. Would it?

Leanne's a nurse. I could start by looking up her record at the California nursing board. They have a website. No harm there, right?"

"Just be careful," Lauren agreed. "On to a new subject. What's the latest on the job front? Last time we talked you were going to start looking for some *pro bono* work?"

"I've gone on two interviews at family law firms in the city. Both times I got into the managing attorney's office, and all he wanted to do was grill me about the situation with Richard and the events of last October. One of the firms didn't want me at all. They wanted me to persuade Richard to come to work for them."

"That's awful. I'm sorry, Liv. Have faith. You'll find something," Lauren said.

Olivia finished the last of her breakfast and pushed her plate away. "From the Olympian vantage point of hindsight, I realize that I shouldn't have been so quick to get rid of my practice."

"But you didn't have a choice, did you? And you could go back to practicing if you wanted to. Can't you just take a case or two, get your feet wet slowly?" Lauren arranged her knife and fork on the right-hand side of her plate and pushed it away. "Take your time and ask the universe what you're supposed to do with your life. I swear, if you ask the question and open your mind, the answer will reveal itself."

The two women had been friends for decades, so Olivia was well aware of Lauren's new-age view of the world. Lauren regularly had her tarot read and she was adamant that no contracts be signed during a Mercury retrograde. Olivia had learned to love Lauren for her quirky way of looking at the world and had always humored her. But now, for the first time, Lauren's words made sense. For it seemed the harder Olivia pushed herself to make some decisions, get a job, just *do something*, the more elusive the joy of a productive life seemed to be. Maybe Lauren was right. Olivia should step back, clear her head, and see what *the universe* had in store for her.

"It'll be okay, Liv. You've got a lot to be grateful for. You're going to be a grandmother, for crying out loud. How is Denny?"

"Doing extremely well. She's still decorating her friend's bed and breakfast in Tahoe. She loves it there so much, she may just stay. The morning sickness has passed, and it looks like she'll deliver on June 16th."

After they paid their check, the pair headed out of the restaurant for a walk along Bridgeway, the shimmering water of the bay on one side of the street and the shops, with the houses nestled into the hills above them, on the other. Olivia realized that although her life was full of uncertainty and that she had no idea what to do with her time or energy, Lauren was right. She did have a lot to be grateful for.

Chapter 2

Olivia

Saturday, January 3

When Brian Vickery had offered to rent a portion of Olivia's office space for his burgeoning private investigation practice, Olivia had jumped at the chance. Maybe, she'd reasoned, being around Brian would inspire her to figure out what she wanted to do with herself professionally. She missed helping the people who came to her with their troubles. Reluctant to admit it, Olivia no longer felt useful. Today she vowed to run the vacuum and feather duster in her office, boot up her computer, and make a list of contacts that might be interested in hiring her for contract work. After that, she would reach out to the Marin County Bar Association and take a few *pro bono* cases.

Happy to finally be doing something to move her life forward, Olivia once again stood in the entrance to her office building, noticing for the first time the desiccated leaves that had accumulated around the front door and the smudges on the front window. Distracted with thoughts of how she had let things slip, she almost didn't notice when Edward Engstrom, known to his friends as Ebby, approached her.

"Olivia?" Ebby Engstrom stood on the sidewalk and stared at Olivia, as if he couldn't place her.

"Yes, it's me, Ebby. I changed my hair." Olivia had stopped coloring her hair in October; where it had once been shoulder-length and a dark brown shade that came from a bottle, it was now cut short and snow-white.

Recognition lit Ebby's face, followed by embarrassment. "I'm sorry. It's very flattering. Do you have a few minutes to talk to me? Or can I make an appointment to see you?"

Olivia had known Ebby Engstrom since he was a child. Her mother and Ebby's aunt Elodie, Ebby's guardian after his mother died, had been very good friends up until the day Olivia's mother had passed away. Both women had grown up in Larkspur and had been friends since grade school. Now Ebby was in his mid-forties and looked like the quintessential California surfer, with his shoulder-length blond curls and a perpetual tan. Ebby owned a restaurant, The No Name Diner, which had been a Larkspur institution for over twenty years. He had started working there as a busboy. When the owner wanted to retire, Ebby had taken over. In addition to serving burgers and fries, he had added his own recipes to the menu and surprised everyone when his innovative food was met with critical acclaim.

Now Ebby looked troubled. His tan had faded; his eyes were bloodshot with dark smudges of exhaustion underneath them.

"I'm not practicing law anymore, but you're welcome to come in," Olivia said. She wriggled the key, finally managing to get the door open.

"I know. I don't need a lawyer, just someone I can trust."

Once inside, Olivia said, "Let's sit out here on the couches. I'm switching offices and don't have a place to sit yet."

Soon they were settled across from each other, Ebby fidgeting with the zipper of his coat. Olivia said, "How's Elodie?"

"She's fine," Ebby said. "Getting ready for her party. You'll be there tomorrow?"

"Her eighty-fifth? Of course I will," Olivia said.

Ebby looked at Olivia with concern. "Actually, she's the one who suggested I come and speak to you."

Olivia waited.

"It's about my mom's murder," Ebby said. He closed his eyes and took a deep breath.

The murder of Cynthia Engstrom and the theft of a respectable number of gold sovereigns from the Engstrom home had startled the Larkspur community in December of 1984, thirty years ago. Thinking back, Olivia remembered the murder occurred the year she graduated from law school. Although she had followed the newspaper accounts of the subsequent investigation, she had been living in Berkeley at the time and was focused on passing the bar exam.

Ebby stood and paced around the room for a second until he wound up at the window, his back to Olivia, his hand in his pocket, jiggling his change. When he turned around, Olivia was surprised to see tears in his eyes. He wiped them with the back of his sleeve. "I've been an emotional wreck these past few weeks. I think I'm starting to remember what happened the night my mother was murdered. It's like I see someone stabbing her, then I'm covered with blood. It's so vivid." Ebby shivered. "Yesterday, I had an episode at the restaurant. I collapsed in the kitchen. Thank God no one got hurt. Anyway, the episodes are happening more and more often. I want you to help me. No, I *need* you to help me," Ebby said.

"Help you how?" Olivia asked.

"I'm worried it was me," Ebby said, his voice barely a whisper.

"What?" Olivia almost laughed. She'd known Ebby as a child and had spent enough time with him to know, without question, he was no killer.

"I'm hoping you can talk to the police, maybe go over the

evidence and look at the case. Maybe we could get the police to reopen the investigation?"

"To prove you didn't kill your mom? Ebby, please don't take this the wrong way, but maybe you need to see a doctor," Olivia said, careful to keep her voice neutral.

"That's what Elodie said. And I'll tell you what I told her: no. Definitely and without question, no. I thought maybe if I could find out what the police know, what they did, some facts, it might help me remember. I've tried over the years to look at the files, but I've always been told that isn't procedure. And before you tell me to ask my family, you should know that I'm pretty convinced Elodie is hiding something from me. I want to know if I was a suspect."

"Are you saying you don't remember what happened that night?"

"No," Ebby said. "I suffered – and still suffer from – a case of what's called dissociative amnesia."

"I didn't know that," Olivia said.

"When Elodie became my guardian, she was more than a little protective. Still is. The fact that she didn't tell you or your mother is a testament to her dogged determination to keep this information within the family. Elodie didn't want me to suffer any more than I already had.

"My mother wasn't exactly well loved, but I had more reason to dislike her than most." After my dad died the previous June, she took my dog Lucy to the vet while I was at school and had her put to sleep. When I came home, she told me Lucy got hit by a car. But Elodie found out what happened, and I overheard them arguing. I felt so betrayed by my mom, so angry with her. Killing my dog gives me a motive, doesn't it? Thirteen-year-old boys become rather attached to their dogs."

Although Olivia's mother had been friends with Ebby's aunts, Elodie and Fiona, Olivia had only met Ebby's mother, Cynthia, a couple of times and had found her demeanor cold and snooty.

"What has Elodie told you about the night your mom died?"

"She's giving me a watered-down version of the truth, I can tell. She's holding something back, and it's infuriating. Can't you just investigate for me? On your own, without the police? You could speak to my family, interview witnesses, things like that."

Olivia hesitated. "You know Brian Vickery, right? He's moving into an office here today. He was a detective at the San Francisco PD. He's doing PI work now. Do you mind if we involve him? He may have some ideas."

"Yeah, okay. I know Brian. He eats at my restaurant all the time. He's a private cop now?"

"Here he is," Olivia said. She caught a glimpse of Brian as he opened the door, and immediately her heart began thumping, her cheeks growing hot. His hair was longer than was fashionable, his eyes full of warmth as they connected with Olivia's just a second more than was necessary.

"Good morning," Brian said before he turned to Ebby and held out his hand. "Ebby. Good to see you." The two men shook hands.

"Ebby needs our help, Brian. Do you have time to speak to him?"

"Sure," Brian said.

Ebby gave Brian an apologetic look before he sat down in one of the guest chairs. "I didn't mean to drop in without an appointment."

"What's going on?" Brian said.

"You recall my mother's murder, in 1984?"

"Only from what I read in the newspapers. I know that a cache of gold was stolen and the murderer was never caught."

"That's true. But what you don't know is that I was at a party at a friend's house. I left and rode my bike home. According to Elodie, she found me under the window of my mother's study, curled in a ball, lying in the rain. They brought me into the house and put me to bed. I woke up the next morning and couldn't remember anything after I left my friend's house.

"Of course, I was seen and evaluated by every pediatric and forensic psychologist in the San Francisco Bay Area. I was diagnosed with dissociative amnesia. The police were desperate to find out who killed my mother, and given where they found me, it was assumed that I witnessed the crime and repressed the memory. I was a minor, so this information was kept out of the papers."

Brian sat in his chair, listening with that stillness and total concentration that was so uniquely his.

"Here's the thing," Ebby continued. "I think I'm starting to remember what happened in bits and pieces, out of order, like a jigsaw puzzle. And the memory that is coming back is not anything like the story Elodie told me. I see someone stabbing my mother, but I'm in the house, in the hallway. And the blood – I am covered in blood." He paused for one heavy moment. "I'm wondering if there's a chance that I killed my mother. It would be just like Elodie to protect me. If I did, I want to know."

"Have you told a doctor about this?" Brian asked.

"No. And I'm not going to. I'm done with psychiatrists. And there's more. I used to have dreams about that night, but now I'm having these hallucinations during the day. The last one happened at the restaurant right before the lunch rush. I collapsed in the kitchen and had to be driven home. I could have hurt someone. It's like I've got something inside me that needs to get out. I don't know what to do, and I don't know who to turn to."

"What about your family? What about your aunt?" Brian asked.

"Elodie? She's eighty-five years old. She's the one who suggested I speak to Olivia. Of course, she's worried about me. I need to find out what happened independently of my family. Elodie is protective. I don't want her involved. She could very well keep the truth from me. I guess I really just want to start with some sort of a plan."

"A plan for what?" Brian's question echoed Olivia's thoughts.

"Any eventuality," Ebby said. "One of these days, I'm going to remember. I can feel it. When that happens, I want to be ready to go to the police and push to get the case reopened. I know my memory won't be considered evidence, but it might persuade the police to take a look at the old investigation with fresh eyes."

"If you killed your mother, do you want the police to know?" Brian asked. Olivia could tell from his tone that he didn't take Ebby seriously.

"Yes," Ebby said. "I want to know what I did. I'll take my punishment. God knows, my life is hell right now.

"Our house had an alarm back then, thirty years ago – one of those deals where you use the key and then you have twenty seconds to enter the code. The one thing I do know about the case was there was no forced entry and the alarm was disengaged, so whoever killed my mother knew the code to the alarm. If it wasn't me, it was someone else in, or close to, my family." Ebby gave Brian and Olivia an imploring look. "Please, I'm asking for your help."

"Do you mind if I speak to Olivia for a minute?" Brian asked.

* * *

They stepped into Olivia's old office.

"What do you think we can do for this kid, Liv?" Brian asked. "He needs psychiatric help."

"You and I both know he didn't murder anyone. And he's a grown man, Brian. He wants to know what happened to his mother. We have to help him," Olivia said.

"You see a grown man. I see a thirteen-year-old boy who is still haunted by tragedy and may have a fair share of psychiatric issues. Amnesia? This is really a matter for the police or a psychiatrist."

"He's suffering. There's got to be something we can do."

Brian leaned against the door and crossed his arms over his chest. "There's no way the police will let us look at their files.

That just doesn't happen. But if you've got your heart set on this, there might be other ways we can dig a little. We could interview witnesses, read the old newspaper articles, things like that. At least we can look at the facts of the case, prepare a written report, give the kid something to cling to. But here's the thing: if Ebby didn't murder his mother, someone in that family likely did, especially given the no-forced-entry issue. Despite your valiant efforts in your own case last October, this is different. Civilians – like you and me – have no business inserting themselves in a murder investigation. And I have grave concerns about Ebby's state of mind. If we agree to help Ebby, you're going to have to let me lead."

"I understand that. I don't mind taking direction from you. Let's just start digging. If we don't find anything, we'll let it go. I think Ebby needs us more for moral support anyway."

"Yeah," Brian said, as he pushed away from the door. "I agree with you on that one."

They filed back into the office reception area, where Ebby remained on the couch, an expectant look on his face.

"We're going to help you, Ebby," Brian said.

Ebby exhaled and smiled. "That's a relief. Thank you. Can I ask how?"

"I'm not sure yet," Brian said. "I'd like you to write down everything you remember from the night your mother died. Start with the morning, or even the day before, if you are able. Don't leave anything out. I'd also like you to write down what you are seeing in your hallucinations, if that's not too painful. That may give us something to go on. I need to be clear that we're not making any promises. It's very likely that nothing will come of this. The police will never give us access to the original files, and given the murder took place thirty years ago, it's highly unlikely any new evidence still exists. You need to understand that. I don't want you operating on any false assumptions."

"I understand." Ebby stood. "I'm just relieved to have told

someone what's been happening. Thank you both." He shook hands with Brian and Olivia before he headed out the door.

"I have a feeling this is going to get interesting," Brian said.

"Agreed," Olivia said.

* * *

An hour later, Olivia and Brian were in Brian's office, clearing out more of the junk that Olivia had accumulated during her years of practice and sorting the boxes of papers and old books. Brian picked up a stack of books and put them in one of the empty boxes. "Are you sure you want to get rid of these?"

"Those books are outdated. Plus, I do all my research online these days. I should have tossed this stuff years ago." She threw a stack of old pleadings in a bag for the shredder.

"Liv, I feel guilty taking over your big office. I'll be just fine in the smaller of the two."

"Nope. I need a change." Olivia thumbed through another pile of old pleadings. "And you're the one with the clients, not me." She stood and stretched. "Clients like to think their investigator is successful. Gives them confidence."

Brian chuckled. "Whatever you say."

The front door opened and Brian stepped out in the hall. "We're back here."

Olivia was wiping her grimy hands on her jeans, when Leanne came into the room, dressed to the nines in a forest-green cashmere coat and hat that set off her auburn hair. Olivia guessed Leanne Stoddard to be in her mid-fifties. She was the type of woman who turned heads and knew it. She hurried next to Brian and kissed his cheeks. "You were right. This office is hard to find." She looked around, her eyes registering the chaos but missing nothing.

"Hey, Leanne," Olivia said.

"Hello, Olivia," Leanne said.

27

"This is a nice office. I like the window and all the natural light."

Olivia marveled at how easily Leanne lied, acting as though she had never been in the office before.

"I told you it was nice," Brian said.

Olivia tried to focus on the junk on top of the desk as Leanne snaked her arm around Brian's waist, pulling him close to her and leaning up against him. "I'll just use the restroom and then we can go."

"Down the hall and to the right," Brian said. When Leanne was gone, Brian turned to Olivia, his eyes shining. "I'm glad you like her, Liv. I'm hoping you two can be friends."

"I'm sure we'll be great friends, Brian. If she makes you happy, that's enough for me." Olivia felt like weeping. Instead, she plastered on a fake smile and kept it there until Brian and Leanne left for lunch. She watched them walk out of the office, arm in arm like a couple of teenagers.

Chapter 3

Brian

Saturday, January 3

Brian and Leanne were the only two people sitting outside at The Left Bank. The waitress had seated them under one of the heaters, and they kept their winter coats on to stave off the cold. Leanne pulled some fingerless gloves out of her purse and was putting them on when the waitress approached.

"Let's get a bottle of champagne," Leanne said.

"Okay. Do we have something to celebrate?"

"We do." Leanne ordered a bottle of Veuve Clicquot. After the waitress left she said, "My travel contract has been extended. I'll be at Marin General until at least March."

"That's great," Brian said. He'd enjoyed getting to know Leanne, but as he sat across the table from her, he realized that he had let himself get friendly with her because he knew she wouldn't be staying long. She worked as a travel nurse, and when they had first started dating, she'd told him she would only be in Marin County through Christmas. Christmas had come and gone and now she was going to stay until March. A frisson of worry started at the back of Brian's mind. He didn't want to get serious with Leanne, but he didn't quite know how to bring up the subject with her. Although their relationship was heating up, they had yet to sleep together. Brian knew once that happened, things would get complicated. Fast.

"Why are you so distracted? Aren't you glad I'm going to be around?"

Brian set his champagne glass down and met Leanne's unflinching gaze.

"Oh, God. What's wrong?"

"Nothing's wrong," he said. "It's just that I don't want you to get the wrong idea about – well, about us."

"What are you trying to say, Brian? I hope you don't think I've been too pushy."

"No, it's not that—"

"Is this about Olivia? I swear she doesn't like me. Honestly, I think she has feelings for you. So whatever she's said about me, just keep that in mind."

His heart gave an extra thump at the thought that Olivia could have feelings for him. "Stop, please. Leanne. Let me explain, okay?" Brian reached across the table and took Leanne's hand in his own. "I think you're lovely. I really do. You've reminded me how nice it is to share my day-to-day with someone. But I'm not ready for a relationship." As he spoke the words, Brian felt the tension he had been carrying in his neck and shoulders release. "It's too soon after Maureen. I just don't want you to think I've been leading you on."

Leanne picked up Brian's other hand and kissed it. "Oh, honey, I understand. We just met. Let's get to know each other, build a friendship. That's enough for me. We're in the same boat in a way. My husband died three years ago, but I still miss him. In fact, I only took my wedding ring off this year. My friends are always telling me I need to get out in the world, meet people and embrace life. That's why I took the travel nurse job. A change of scene was needed. Let's start with a friendship, okay? I'm not looking to marry you. Just have some fun." She held up her champagne glass.

Brian raised his.

"To new friends," Leanne said.

"To new friends," Brian repeated. As they clinked glasses and sipped their champagne, Brian's thoughts strayed to Olivia.

Chapter 4

Ebby

Saturday, January 3

The tension was so thick in the Engstrom house that Ebby almost called off the family dinner. But Melinda, his beleaguered sister-in-law, had been so touched by Ebby's offer to cook, he knew he couldn't back out of his commitment. The time had come to tell his family what he intended to do. As he moved around the kitchen prepping the ingredients necessary for the chicken piccata, Caesar salad, bruschetta, and chocolate soufflé he was preparing for his family, he worried how everyone would react. Elodie and Fiona, his spinster aunts who were eighty-five and eighty-seven respectively, would in all likelihood support Ebby in his endeavor to independently discover what happened to his mom. Melinda was too cowed by her husband to form her own opinion. Mark would no doubt blow a gasket. Ebby didn't care. He started to chop garlic, psyching himself up to do battle with his domineering older brother, when Melinda came into the kitchen.

"You're sweet to cook for us, Ebs, but why all the fuss? And don't you want to use the food processor for that garlic? It would be much quicker."

Ebby had a collection of food processors at his home and at the restaurant. When he was cooking for pleasure, he preferred to use his good knives. That way he could have his hands on the food and see it grow and change from separate ingredients into one well-blended dish. "No, thanks. I'm good with the knife."

Melinda filled the kettle with water. Once it was on the stove, she faced him. "Why did you call this family dinner tonight? Does it have to do with what happened at the restaurant? We're worried about you, Ebby."

"Yes, you could say that. I want to tell you all about what happened at the restaurant. But there's no need to worry. Promise," Ebby said, his knife flying as the smell of garlic filled the kitchen.

Melinda moved close to him, leaning against the counter as she spoke in a soft voice. "Ebs, you look like you haven't slept in weeks. Your clothes are hanging off you. No offense, but you look like you're about to have a breakdown. What's going on?"

Ebby sighed, set his knife down and turned to face Melinda. "I'd rather wait and tell everyone at the same time, if you don't mind."

When the kettle had boiled, Melinda busied herself with her teabag, not meeting Ebby's eyes. "You're still going forward with selling the house?"

"There's no change with regard to selling the house. My brother will get his money." Ebby put the chopped garlic into a small glass bowl and set it aside. Then he took half a dozen tomatoes and started to chop those.

The Engstroms' twenty acres, nestled up against King Mountain and the Marin County Open Space, would fetch a king's ransom. Mark was eager to get his hands on enough cash to bail him out of his latest financial debacle. But Ebby, who had built his own cottage on a secluded part of the property, and Elodie, who – against Mark and Melinda's vociferous protestations – lived in her Airstream trailer on her own little parcel of the property, weren't too enthusiastic about selling the land that had been in the Engstrom family for generations. The main residence was over a hundred years old and needed major repairs. One entire wing, thankfully situated at the back of the property and out of view from the street, had holes in the roof and out of safety concerns had been boarded up after Cynthia's murder. Nature had run her course, and now that section of the house was overgrown with ivy and falling down.

Even though Mark and Melinda lived in the house, Mark refused to foot the bill for any of the needed repairs. Even though Fiona had moved out of the family home ages ago, she had offered to step in and pay to at least have the disused wing demolished. Mark had refused that offer as well, and the structure that had housed Engstroms' past and present had slowly become more and more run-down. When a developer had approached Mark with an exorbitant offer, Ebby and Elodie had reluctantly agreed to sell the property. The house where Ebby's mother had been murdered was to be sold. After it was pillaged of its heart-pine flooring, marble hearth, original windows, and vintage fixtures, it would be razed.

"Time to let all the bad memories go, Ebs. You'll be able to buy any house you want. It's time to move on. Your brother is concerned about what's best for you, you know. He's worried that you living here is taking its toll."

Melinda had always been kind to Ebby, even before she and Mark were married. Over the years, Ebby had witnessed the deterioration of Mark and Melinda's relationship, had watched Melinda become a shell of herself. Mark did that to people. Ebby knew his brother wasn't kind to his wife. Many a time he'd caught glimpses of bruises on her arms. After he'd confronted her about them, she'd taken to wearing long sleeves and refused to discuss the matter further. Ebby had encouraged Melinda to report the abuse, but she had changed the subject and made it clear any discussion on the matter was over. Whenever Ebby had threatened to do the reporting himself, Melinda was quick to explain that she'd fallen or bumped into something. At a loss to do anything, Ebby had no choice but to let it go.

There was no mistaking the terror in her eyes when Mark lost his temper, but Ebby stayed out of their marriage, telling himself that if things got really bad, Melinda would leave. But she hadn't. She'd chosen to stay with her bully of a husband. Out of pity, Ebby bit back his anger as he turned to face his sister-in-law. "My brother doesn't give a fig what happens to me. He's after the money, and you know it. I'm not selling the house to help my brother." Ebby needed to face the past. Once he did, he would be glad to get away from the Engstrom house and its horrible memories. But he didn't tell Melinda that.

He put his hands on her shoulders and turned her toward the door. "Go have a rest and drink your tea."

She gave him a playful smile as she pinched his arm. "What time's dinner?"

"When Mark gets back. I've got everything prepped so it won't take long for me to cook and serve."

"Okay. I'll leave you to it."

Left alone in the kitchen, it took Ebby another half hour to pound out the chicken breasts. Once that was finished, he headed back to his cabin to shower and get ready for the evening. As he stepped outside, he took a moment to fill his lungs with the cold January air. Ebby knew how lucky his family was to have this large chunk of property snuggled right up to the public lands preserved for outdoor recreation. Ebby's great-great-grandfather had built the Engstrom house long before Larkspur was an incorporated city. If it weren't for Elodie and Fiona, Mark and Melinda would have sold up ages ago.

Ebby looked up at the old house, taking in the shabby paint and the patched roof. The original plan had been to make the repairs in the spring, but then Mark had received the timely offer to sell and explained his reason for doing so. Ebby would never forget Melinda's look of shock and betrayal, as Mark confessed his staggering losses. He had closed out his commentary by saying, "I can always make more money. That's not a problem. I just need something to carry me through for the next few months." Mark had then gone on to tell them that a Mr. Lucius Sanderman and his wife Adrienne had expressed interest in the property and had offered an exorbitant amount of money for the Engstrom house and surrounding acreage. "He'll let us stay on for three months after the sale goes through, so no one has to hurry to find a place."

The offer had forced Elodie and Ebby to take stock of their situation. Mark, whose eyes had flashed with dollar signs, was ready to sell. Elliot Engstrom had understood the dynamic between his two very different sons, and in an attempt to keep the Engstrom land in the family, he had the foresight to grant Ebby a fifty-one percent controlling interest in the property. For the first time in Ebby's life, he hadn't immediately capitulated to Mark's demands. Instead he had sat down with his aging aunts, who had surprised him by agreeing to sell. Elodie would go and live with Fiona at the beach. Mark would pay off his creditors, leaving Ebby to forge his own way in the world.

But he wasn't going anywhere until he found out what happened on the night of his mother's murder. Mark wouldn't like it, but those were Ebby's terms. His family had coddled him and tried to protect him since his mother's death. They'd seen him through plenty of therapy and support. Ebby was tired of being treated with kid gloves. He was certain that once he remembered everything – even if he implicated himself – he could heal. On a whim, he turned back to the house, coming to a stop at the window of his mother's study, standing in the exact spot where he had – according to Elodie – been standing the night he had witnessed her brutal murder.

The curtains were closed against the darkness, but Ebby stood in the same place where he had been found as a teenager, lying on the ground, curled into a ball in the pouring rain on the night of her death. Now he paid attention to the placement of his feet and reached a hand out to touch the cold glass, willing his subconscious mind to give up its secrets. Taking a deep breath, he waited. Nothing happened.

"What are you doing?"

Ebby yelped as he wheeled around to face his brother.

"Geez, Mark. You scared me."

"Not my fault you're not paying attention. You should be more aware of your surroundings, brother."

Ebby didn't respond.

Mark shook his head, turned on his heel, and headed to the house. Ebby watched him go, wondering not for the first time what he had done to make his brother dislike him so.

* * *

By 6:30 p.m. the mood in the Engstrom house had lightened considerably. Fiona, Elodie, Mark, and Melinda had at least a couple of drinks under their belts, and they could be heard in the living room talking and laughing. Felicity Matthews, the Engstroms' housekeeper, sat on one of the kitchen stools, chopping the lemon wedges that would garnish the chicken piccata. Tonight, Felicity was here as Ebby's friend. Felicity's mother, and grandmother before her, had worked for the Engstrom family. Felicity had always been a part of the Engstrom household. After she had graduated from college, she surprised Ebby when she asked if she could take the job her mother had held before her. Over the years he had asked his aunts why Felicity had taken a job as a domestic when she had a degree and could have struck out on her own. He'd never received a solid answer to this question, and eventually he had stopped asking it. He now considered Felicity one of his closest and most trusted friends.

"I hope your family doesn't mind me being here and sitting at the table for dinner," Felicity said. "Fiona and Elodie won't care, but Melinda's become rather formal lately. She won't take kindly to eating dinner with the help."

"You're not the help, and Melinda doesn't have anything to say about it." Ebby added some garlic-infused stock to the pan. "This is my house, too, remember. You're my guest. I want you here." He poured them each a small glass of wine and raised his glass in a toast. "To friendship."

"Friendship." Felicity sipped from her glass. "Ebby, why am I here? I wish you'd tell me what you've got up your sleeve. I get the feeling you're going to drop some bombshell on us tonight."

Ebby hesitated. "I am. Mark isn't going to be happy – I'll tell you that much."

"And why am I here?"

"For moral support," Ebby said.

"Okay," Felicity said. "I can do moral support. Are you ready to start plating up the food?"

"Yes," Ebby said. "You're here for dinner, not to work."

Ebby had just started to arrange the chicken breasts over pasta, while Felicity added slices of garnish and loaded them on a tray to carry into the dining room, when Melinda came into the kitchen.

"I'll deal with the food. Why don't you start cleaning up in here? And before we sit down to dinner, would you mind putting the laundry in the dryer?" Melinda started to push Felicity away from the counter and take her place there.

"No," Ebby said. "Felicity is here as my guest. She's not on the clock. She's having dinner with me, with the family."

"Ebby, she doesn't mind—"

"You think she'd speak up if she did?"

Melinda turned to Felicity. "Do you feel that way, Felicity?"

"Oh, no you don't," Ebby said. "Felicity is not getting involved in this. This is between you and me. Felicity is my guest. She has kindly offered to help me serve dinner. Now if you'd like to go back into the living room, I'll serve everyone and let you know when you can all sit down."

Melinda gave Felicity a look that said *I'll deal with you later* before she did as Ebby asked.

"I'll pay for that Sunday," Felicity said.

"Why do you put up with her?" Ebby asked. "Is it my imagination, or has she become more cruel lately?"

"It's not your imagination," Felicity said.

"Come work for me. You can manage my restaurant. I'll double your salary."

Felicity ignored him. "Come on, chef. Plate up."

They worked in companionable silence while Ebby served the chicken, garnished it with the buttery lemon sauce, and topped it with capers. Once the food was arranged on the plates, Felicity divvied up the Caesar salad, while Ebby carried the bruschetta to the dining room. Once the dinner was served, Ebby summoned everyone to the table. For a few minutes they ate in silence. On more than one occasion, Ebby noticed Melinda staring at Felicity, a look of blatant hostility in her eyes. The aunts picked up on it too and did their best to lighten the mood with innocuous small talk.

Even Mark was duly impressed. After he cleaned his plate, he said, "Compliments to the chef. This was excellent, Ebby."

"Thank you."

Mark pushed back from the table, crossed his legs, and drank his wine. "Why have you called us here, Ebby? You've obviously got something to tell us. Now would be the time."

Felicity stood and started to clear the empty plates.

"I'll do that, Felicity. Please stay seated." Ebby stood up and faced his family. "I know you've all been worried about me, especially after my episode at the restaurant. It's clear I'm starting to remember what I witnessed the night mom died."

When Mark started to interrupt, Fiona said, "Be quiet, Mark. Let him finish."

Ebby cast his eyes around the table. Melinda, Mark, Elodie, Fiona, and Felicity stared at him with reluctant expectation. He knew once he told them what had been happening and his plan to find out who killed his mother, there would be no going back.

"You poor dear. What can we do for you?" Fiona asked.

"It's time I start to do things for myself," Ebby said. "I called us together tonight because I wanted to let you know that I've hired someone to investigate Mom's murder, have a look with fresh eyes. I feel called to do this. My hope is that you will understand and support me."

Melinda squeezed her wine glass so tightly that it shattered, sending white wine into puddles on her plate. Small drops of blood dripped from her finger onto the white linen tablecloth.

"The hell you will," Mark said, slamming his fist on the table.

"Stop it, Mark," Fiona said. "There's no need for you to lose your temper. If you can't be civilized about this, you can leave."

Historically Fiona was the only person in the family who stood up to Mark when he was angry. Ebby shot her a look of gratitude.

"Carry on, Ebby," she said.

"I want to find out who killed my mother. I've suffered my entire adult life from the effects of that night. Surely you can understand why I would want to find out once and for all what happened, Mark?"

Mark didn't answer. He guzzled the last of his wine and refilled his glass. Melinda put a hand on his arm. He pushed it away.

"I could have hurt someone when I passed out at the restaurant." Ebby sat down, exhausted all of a sudden. "I'm going to do this."

"So who did you hire and how will they proceed?" Mark asked.

"I hired Olivia Sinclair. She knows and cares about our family. Today I met with her and the investigator who works in her office. I know it's a long shot. They were very candid about my small chance of success. Especially because the police aren't likely to share their case files. But they're going to look into it. Best-case scenario, they find new evidence or see something the police missed, and the case will be reopened. I'm hoping that educating myself about what happened the night Mom was murdered will help me remember that night." Ebby looked around the table, making eye contact with each and every person seated there. "I know this is difficult, but I need to do this."

"You're making a mistake," Mark said. "I'm sorry I overreacted. I understand things are difficult for you. But digging up the past now could have a negative effect on selling the property. Lucius is aware of Mom's murder. I had to disclose it to him, but Adrienne – who controls the purse strings – is superstitious. It won't do for her to find out about it. This could put the kibosh on the whole deal. And I need this right now. Seriously. I'm in trouble."

"You've been in trouble before, Mark, and you'll be in trouble again," Fiona said. "Even if your buyers go elsewhere, I promise you people will line up for this property. And don't even think about suggesting that your financial woes are more important than your brother's need to heal himself. Unless, of course, you weren't entirely forthcoming as to the seriousness of your financial situation?" Fiona let the question hang in the air.

Ebby studied his aging aunt, noticing for the first time that her face had an ashen shade to it, and that her hand shook when she lifted her wine glass.

Mark shook his head. "It's not just that. Don't you all remember what it was like after Mom died? We were hounded by reporters. Hounded. For months. Won't that kind of attention make things worse for you?" Mark got up from his chair and walked over to Ebby. Without thinking, Ebby rose, not wanting his brother to tower over him. Mark put a surprisingly gentle hand on Ebby's shoulder. "You're my brother, and I love you. I'll help you – we'll all help you – deal with your memories. I get how important that is. But I'm begging you, don't bring outsiders into our family business. We can go to the police together and ask them what's happening with the case, maybe spark some interest. Whatever you want, Ebs."

Ebby shook his head. "I'm sorry, Mark. I have to do this my way."

Mark stepped away. "Then you can suffer the consequences."

He stormed out of the room. In the distance a door slammed. Melinda threw her napkin on the table and hurried after him.

"Felicity," Elodie said, "are you okay? You look pale."

Felicity stood and started gathering up the plates. "I'm fine. Just tired."

Ebby had been so worried about telling his family that he had hired an investigator, he had all but forgotten Felicity. Elodie was right. Felicity was pale and her eyes had a hunted look in them. As she headed into the kitchen with the dinner plates, Ebby caught a glimpse of her face in the buffet mirror and realized that Felicity was terrified.

"She'll be all right," Fiona said as she pushed away from the table. Once she was standing, she wobbled on her feet. "Oh, I feel a little woozy." Fiona put her hand on the mantel as Ebby and Elodie rushed over to her.

Her face had a grayish tinge and was covered in a sheen of sweat. Ebby thought for a moment she was having a heart attack.

"Fiona, are you okay?" Ebby stepped close and tried to put his arm around his aunt to hold her up, for she looked like she was about to topple.

"I'm fine." Fiona pushed him away. "Really. Found out recently I'm a bit anemic. I'm taking iron."

"Thank goodness it wasn't my cooking," Ebby said, trying to lighten the mood.

Fiona smiled. Ebby was glad to see the color coming back into her cheeks. "Your meal was delicious. I just haven't been feeling well lately."

"Why don't you spend the night at my place, dear?" Elodie said. "You can drive back to the beach after the party."

"That's a good idea," Ebby said. "That way I won't have to worry about you driving home."

* * *

42

Ebby found Felicity in the kitchen, loading the dishwasher. "You don't have to clean up. Let me take you home. I'll deal with this later."

"It won't take long with the two of us." She turned away from him and loaded the last of the plates into the dishwasher. Ebby had been so wrapped up in his dysfunctional family dynamic that he had neglected Felicity. She had hardly spoken a word during dinner. This shouldn't have surprised Ebby. He should have known better than to invite her to sit down with Melinda and share a meal.

"Have you noticed Fiona has lost weight?" Felicity asked. "She doesn't look healthy to me. I'm worried about her."

"I know. I'll ask Elodie about it." Ebby put the dishtowel he was holding down. "Felicity, what's wrong? And don't tell me you're tired. I know what tired looks like. Tonight you're not tired."

Felicity closed the dishwasher and faced him, her eyes snapping. "Why didn't you tell me you'd hired an investigator to look into your mother's murder? I had no business being at that table tonight. I'm not your family. I should have had a choice." Her eyes filled with unshed tears as she pushed past Ebby to get her coat and purse.

"Felicity, wait. I'm sorry."

"You shouldn't have been so thoughtless, Ebby. I was embarrassed tonight. Melinda's going to give me hell tomorrow."

"Then don't come back. Quit. I told you, I'll hire you. I'll even give you a raise."

She sighed, her shoulders slumping in defeat.

"Why won't you let me help you?"

She flung her purse over her shoulder. "You need to be helping yourself before you try to help me. I'm ready to go home." And with that, she walked out of the house.

They didn't speak on the ride home. Felicity sat next to Ebby, her head tilted back and her eyes closed, as though she were asleep. But Ebby knew she wasn't sleeping; she was avoiding conversation. He let her be and thought about the events of the evening. Everything had gone how he'd expected. Mark's anger was a bit much, but Ebby knew his older brother liked to be in control, and the idea of Ebby making plans to solve his mother's murder without consulting him first was likely an unwelcome surprise.

Felicity opened her eyes and sat up as he pulled to a stop at her apartment. "Do you want me to walk you up?"

"No, I'll be fine. And I'm sorry if I snapped at you, Ebs. I understand your need to find out what happened, but I just wish you would have confided in me."

"You're right," Ebby said. "It was insensitive of me. Do you want me to talk to Melinda for you?"

"Please don't," Felicity said. "Trust me, that will just make things worse. See you tomorrow?"

"Yes, see you at the party."

Felicity waved and headed to her apartment. He waited until she was safely inside before setting off home, his thoughts turning back to his mother's murder. In fact, 1984 had been a cruel year for the Engstrom family. Elliot – Ebby's father – had died of a sudden heart attack in June. After his father's death, the family dynamic had shifted. To Ebby, it felt as though his mother had given all of her love and devotion to her eldest son, leaving thirteen-year-old Ebby to fend for himself. During this time, Ebby and Elodie bonded. Then in December, Cynthia had been murdered.

Felicity and her mother, Allegra, had lived with the Engstroms in their own suite of rooms until Elliot died. Ebby had a vague recollection of them moving out of the house after that and getting their own apartment, but he couldn't remember why. Melinda and Mark had been together since high school. Melinda spent so much time at the Engstrom house she surely had come to know Felicity as a child. Why didn't Melinda like Felicity now? More importantly, he didn't understand why Felicity stayed. He knew she had a college degree and she was extremely capable.

Why in the world would she spend all these years working as a servant for a woman who was so cruel to her?

Ebby felt a headache coming on just as he pulled to a stop in front of his cabin. The radio was turned to a classic old-school rock station that played all the songs that Ebby grew up with. He had just opened the door to his car, when "How Much I Feel" by Ambrosia blasted over the airwaves. As though someone had flipped a switch, his breath suddenly came in short gasps as stars floated before his eyes. He felt his body slump in the seat of the car, but he couldn't do anything about it.

In his mind's eye, he felt the rain falling on him as he stood outside the window of his mother's study. The sting of Mary Beth's rejection was fresh and raw and searing. His clothes were soaked through as the scene in the office unfolded before him. Unable to move, he watched as the mysterious figure dressed in baggy clothes came into the room. Helpless to do anything, he watched the now familiar argument between his domineering mother and her murderer, watched as the murderer picked up the silver letter opener on his mother's desk, shaped like a dagger, its hilt encrusted with semiprecious stones. The letter opener gleamed in a surreal, radiant fashion. He waited, certain this time he would get a look at the killer's face.

In the background, he caught a glimpse of his childhood self, a shimmery wavering vision, standing in the alcove just outside the office. In an instant, Ebby saw himself covered in his mother's blood, frantic, as if suspended in time. Just as the would-be murderer slowly turned to the window, everything went black and Ebby slipped into unconsciousness.

Chapter 5

Olivia

Guests had been asked to arrive at Elodie's party for drinks at two o'clock, with the actual sit-down luncheon starting at 3 o'clock. Olivia, who had been attending this annual event for years, was expected to come to Elodie's trailer early for a pre-party glass of champagne, as she had every year since her mother passed nineteen years ago.

Last year, Richard, Olivia's jackass of an ex-husband, hadn't come with her, claiming that he had a mountain of work to tend to, his usual excuse to avoid social gatherings. Olivia now knew that her reprobate of a husband had likely been spending his day bumping boots with his mistress. She didn't care. Not anymore. Slowing as she passed the drive that led to the Engstrom house, Olivia could make out the pointed top of a shining white tent through the trees. A valet parking company had been hired for the occasion. One white-coated man was moving a podium on a dolly, while another was unloading an electric golf cart from a trailer. Keeping her eyes on the narrow twisty road that led to the back of the Engstrom property, Olivia drove past the bricked pillars that graced the entrance toward the main house and instead turned onto a dirt road marked by a brick mailbox.

She followed the winding lane through a group of tall redwoods toward the silvery shine of Elodie's Airstream, mindful of the crater-sized potholes. As she turned the final corner, Elodie's unusual house came into view.

As Olivia pulled in next to a brand-new Volvo, Elodie stepped outside, waving her arms like a teenager and grinning from ear to ear. She was dressed in a bright purple dress, black and purple striped tights, with purple lace-up boots tying her ensemble together. Her silver curls had been piled up on top of her head and secured in place with rhinestone clips.

Olivia grabbed a bottle of Veuve Clicquot with a bow around the neck off the passenger seat and stepped out of the car just as Elodie reached her. "Happy birthday, Elodie. Thanks for inviting me."

"Oh, thank you for coming. Come in. I'm with Fiona. We're having oysters and champagne before we head over to the party."

Olivia wondered if Elodie's flushed cheeks and sparkling eyes were a result of her birthday mood or the birthday booze.

As if reading her mind, Elodie said, "It's my birthday, so I'm going to get a little tipsy, do some dancing, and enjoy watching Melinda fidget. Did you come alone?"

"Brian will be joining us at the party."

"Very well. Fiona and I will take very good care of you until he gets here. You'll sit next to me at lunch and everyone will tell you how much you resemble your mother."

Olivia followed Elodie into the trailer, where Fiona, in complete contrast to her sister, was dressed in a tailored wool dress in subdued navy blue. Pearl earrings hung from her ears, and her thick snow-white hair was styled in a sleek bob at her shoulders. Fiona was gaunt, drawn, and rigid-looking, especially in comparison to Elodie's round and rosy vigor. Olivia watched as Fiona set a silver tray layered with crushed ice and topped with oysters on the half shell on the table. A half pint of Belvedere vodka also sat on ice, along with lemons and what looked to be cocktail sauce.

The inside of Elodie's Airstream always reminded Olivia of a fairy tale. The walls and ceiling were lined with wood veneer in a herringbone pattern. A kitchenette, comprised of a granite counter, a copper sink, and a tiny copper hood over a ceramic stove, took up one wall. The kitchen nook – as Elodie liked to call it – consisted of comfortable built-in seats snuggled around an old table, with cushions upholstered in vibrant purple tones.

"Hello, Olivia," Fiona said, handing Olivia a crystal flute brimming with golden bubbles and joining her at the table.

"Thank you. And hello."

Fiona raised her glass and said, "Before we sit down, I'd like to propose a toast. To Olivia, a trusted friend."

Olivia held her glass up while Elodie and Fiona drank to her. Once they were all seated, Olivia said, "What a spread!"

"Let's not talk about that," Elodie said. "So this is how we do it." She took one of the oysters, splashed a little vodka on it, added a little cocktail sauce, and ate it straight from the shell. "Try it," Elodie encouraged.

"You can use a fork if you wish," Fiona said.

Olivia skipped the vodka and ate the oyster plain. It was clean and delicious and tasted of the ocean.

"Have another," Elodie said. "I've got a dozen more, if we want them."

"Thanks," Olivia said, helping herself. "Won't there be lots of food at your party?"

Elodie opened a fresh bottle of champagne, topping off Olivia and Fiona's glasses before she refilled her own. She giggled when she overfilled her glass, soaking the linen tablecloth. "You may not remember this, Olivia, but in the old days, my annual birthday party would start with a long hike, followed by a picnic dinner outside. Your mother and father both used to come every year. But we all got older and the hikes turned into walks, and when half of us needed walkers, we stopped the walking and hiking all together. You must remember that I always served the same meal after our hikes: lobster, green salad, crab cocktail, crusty French bread and a never-ending supply of champagne. I love eating the decadent food off the good linen on the picnic table under the trees. The irreverence of it suited me."

Fiona patted her sister's hand. "Don't get too upset, Elodie, dear."

Elodie brushed off her sister and kept talking. "This year Melinda offered to see to things, promised to keep the same menu and the guest list small enough to be intimate. I hate big parties where I feel like I have to talk to everyone and have quality time with no one. Anyway, I trusted her. Of course, not only did she change the menu, most of the guests are Mark's friends and business associates. She's got a hundred people coming! One hundred. Can you even fathom that? And she's making them eat beef, which I loathe. To make matters even worse, as I was getting ready this morning, I started thinking of all the friends I've lost." She looked at Olivia and Fiona with sad eyes. "That's the thing about getting old. If you're lucky enough to keep on ticking, you lose everyone you love. I don't even want to go to this party. I'd rather stay here with the two of you."

"That's enough, Elodie. You'll have a grand time and you know it. You're lucky enough to be alive, and we've got these wonderful oysters and this extravagant champagne. And that's nonsense about the guests. Of course Mark invited business associates, but you will know most of the people, and don't even try to tell me you don't like them. You love them. And they love you."

"Okay, okay." Elodie waved off her sister's comments.

When the two sisters glanced at each other in unspoken communication, Olivia pushed her champagne flute away.

49

"We need to talk to you about Ebby," Fiona said.

"I suggested he come to you, Olivia. He's really struggling, thinking he's starting to remember the night his mother was murdered. We're hoping you can guide him through the process."

"He's a sensitive man," Fiona added, glancing askance at Elodie. "I'm not speaking out of turn in saying that, Elodie, so don't look at me like that. It's true, though. Ebby is very sensitive. His father's death was extremely difficult for him."

"How so?" Olivia asked.

Fiona took a deep breath, but Elodie was the one who answered Olivia's question.

"Ebby and Elliot were very close, kindred spirits if you will. Father and son were both artistic in temperament, and despite Elliot's genius at playing the financial markets, his favorite thing to do was be at the beach or hiking in the hills. Ebby's exactly the same. And, as much as I hate to say it—"

Fiona interjected. "After Elliot died, Cynthia made no bones about showing favoritism to Mark. Poor Ebby was a vulnerable little boy, just thirteen years old when his father died. She wanted to send him away to boarding school. If it weren't for Elodie, she would have. Ebby needed love. He needed his mother. I won't bore you with details, but suffice it to say she wasn't kind to the poor child."

"She'd taken the dog and had it put to sleep, if you can believe that." Elodie's voice wavered as she recalled the horrifying event. "Unfortunately, Ebby overheard. After that incident, Cynthia didn't bother to hide her feelings.

"But I loved Ebby as though he were my own," Elodie continued. "And so did Fiona. I was living at the big house at that time, in my own suite of rooms, you know, in the wing that is now dilapidated and tumbling down." Elodie cast a glance at Fiona and added, "We tried to give Ebby enough love and support to make up for Cynthia's shortcomings."

"The poor kid was bound to have some psychological

problems. Aren't mommy issues the root of all evil?" Fiona asked as she spread cocktail sauce and vodka on an oyster and popped it into her mouth.

Olivia ignored the amateur psychological analysis and asked, "So what do you think of these flashbacks he's having?"

"They started out as nightmares," Elodie said. "Night terrors, I should say. The doctors told us after Cynthia's murder that Ebby might have difficulties if his memories of that night came back."

"And he is remembering," Fiona said. "We need to tell her what happened last night. If Olivia is going to help Ebby, she needs to know what's happening."

Elodie gave her sister an imploring look before she downed the rest of her champagne. She spoke as she once again refilled their glasses. "Ebby gathered us all round for a lovely dinner last night. After we were well fed, he stood up and announced that he had taken my suggestion and hired you to look into Cynthia's murder."

"Mark wasn't very happy," Fiona added. "He's had an offer to sell the house and the surrounding property for an exorbitant sum of money. He doesn't want attention focused on the family just now."

"To make matters worse," Elodie said, "the wife of the buyer is a superstitious woman and Mark doesn't want her to discover that a murder took place in the house."

"But you're going to have to disclose that anyway," Olivia said. "I think that's California law."

"Mark has disclosed it to the husband, but they've both come to an understanding and agreed to keep the wife in the dark."

That's got disaster written all over it. Olivia kept her opinion to herself.

"And Mark does like to be in control," Elodie said. "He's always bullied Ebby. Sees himself as the head of the family, reminding us all on a regular basis that he has our financial interests at heart."

"Which is nonsense," Fiona said. "Mark loves money more than anything."

"You're going off topic, Fi." Elodie turned to Olivia and said, "You saw Ebby when he came to you. Didn't you notice a change in him? He's lost weight; he looks like he's physically ill."

"He's grappling with the past," Elodie said.

"That's what he told me," Olivia said. "I encouraged him to see a doctor, but he was pretty adamant that he wouldn't do that."

"My hope, Olivia dear, is that you can encourage him. He needs to be under the care of a psychiatrist. We're hoping you can steer him in that direction," Elodie said.

"I agree with you, and I'll try. Maybe it would help if he found a psychiatrist on his own, if he interviewed potential doctors until he finds one he likes. Maybe I could explain to him that it's like hiring an employee, make him feel more in control," Olivia said.

Fiona poured big glasses of ice water for the three of them. Olivia took a sip of hers, thirsty all of a sudden. "Can I ask you both a question?"

"Of course," Fiona and Elodie said at the same time.

"Ebby told me there was an alarm back then, thirty years ago. Whoever murdered Cynthia knew the code. There was no sign of forced entry or a struggle, at least according to Ebby."

"Yes, that's true. Which is why the police thought one of us did it," Elodie said. "But we all had alibis."

"What do you think?" Olivia persisted. "I won't repeat what you tell me. I just want your honest opinions."

Once again, the sisters looked at each other conspiratorially, communicating in that silent way that sisters do. Fiona was the one to speak. "We think it was a burglar. My brother had a fortune in gold coins in a duffel bag behind his desk, if you can believe that, and they went missing that night."

"But the alarm wasn't tripped," Olivia reminded them.

"Oh, come now, Olivia," Fiona said, her tone imperious and a wee bit condescending. "A professional thief can get past any security system. After Elliot died, collectors came out of the woodwork wanting to buy his coins. He was known for his collection.

It wouldn't surprise me if he told everyone that he kept the coins in the house. He certainly liked to look at them. If a sophisticated thief got wind of that, they could easily get past our alarm."

"Good point," Olivia said.

"And now we should go to my party," Elodie said.

While they got ready to walk through the woods to the main house, Olivia replayed her conversation with the aunts in her mind, unable to shake the feeling that the old women were holding something back.

Chapter 6

Ebby

Ebby slept in on the day of Elodie's party. Waking up with the sheets tangled around his ankles, he gazed out the window at Mt. Tam and the wispy tendrils of fog that curled around her peaks and valleys. Maybe he could pretend he was coming down with the flu and skip the party altogether. No. That wouldn't do. The aunts would come over and make a fuss over him. As he put his feet on the cold floor and then dressed in his running clothes, he decided he would rather smile and pretend all was well than be fussed over by Elodie and Fiona.

Taking his coffee out on the deck, Ebby thought about the time in the near future when he would walk away from this house, with its gorgeous view and easily accessible trails. He'd be losing his backyard paradise, but he would be gaining freedom from the shackles of his family. Ebby didn't know where he would go after his house was sold, but he knew in his heart it was time to be on his own. Grown men didn't need to live on their family's property.

As Ebby thought about his family, he realized that when he moved, he probably would lose contact with Mark. Would he miss the brother who had made a career of bullying him? Not even a little. When Ebby had first taken over The No Name Diner, he had sought his brother's business advice, hoping to build a relationship and earn his brother's respect. Mark had encouraged Ebby to turn a quick profit by exploiting his labor force and making his staff work long hours with as little pay as possible. When Ebby had ignored that advice and hired friends he knew and trusted, paying them a good wage and supplementing their income with cash bonuses when he could afford it, Mark hadn't been happy. "You'll fail within a year," Mark had promised.

His prediction, of course, had been wrong. With one exception – a dishwasher who had to stay home and care for his ailing sister – Ebby still had the same employees he'd started with on the day he opened. They didn't steal from him, and since they were paid a decent wage and given bonuses when the restaurant did well, they took their jobs seriously.

Despite the vivid flashbacks and the unresolved issues around his mother's murder, his life was pretty good. Changes were afoot, as Ebby embraced the idea of writing cookbooks, a logical next step to his career as a chef and restauranteur. He'd deliberately kept the project a secret, only confiding in Felicity. As the process got underway, Ebby found he liked writing, liked translating his love of cooking into words on a page. The first book, which featured the recipes from The No Name Diner, was nearly finished. One of his regular customers was a literary agent. She had encouraged Ebby to write the story of the diner and share his recipes. Ebby had enlisted Felicity's help, and the two of them had worked side by side, Ebby handwriting the recipes, Felicity typing them up and editing them.

The book had been a work of joy. The agent was thrilled with the end result, and several publishers were interested. The future, despite his unresolved family issues, was opening her doors to him.

And then the flashbacks and dreams had started. Now it was all Ebby could do to get out of bed in the morning. Felicity had taken over the cookbook, testing the recipes while Ebby had told the agent he needed more time.

I need to get my head straight. After he finished his coffee, he dressed in warm clothes and headed out his back door directly onto the trail that led up King Mountain. He'd linger over his hike, and plan it so he arrived at the party just as the luncheon was ending.

* * *

Four hours later, Ebby arrived home. The sound of dance music filtered through the trees, an indication the party was in full swing. He showered and dressed, taking pains to wear the blazer Fiona had bought him for Christmas and the tie that Elodie had given him for his birthday. Today he would put a smile on his face and celebrate the aunt he loved so dearly. Since Ebby had little interest in the requisite mingling and small talk, he'd arrive just as the guests were finishing lunch, and stay for the cake and the speeches. As soon as he could, he would leave, claiming an issue at the restaurant.

Since he was skipping the food at the party, Ebby made himself a spinach and mushroom omelet, along with another coffee with steamed milk. He had just sat down to eat, when the hand that held his fork started to shake uncontrollably. White flashes of light cascaded out of the corner of his eyes and the floor beneath him started to roll.

"Damn it," Ebby cried out. Helpless to do anything, he grabbed on to the seat of his chair and prepared for the inevitable flashback. This time, he wouldn't panic. When his vision started, he'd face it with courage and try to see what really happened. For the first time, Ebby didn't resist when he felt himself slump in his chair and slip to the floor.

He came to in the familiar fog and malaise of his visions. *This is so real, surely I'm losing my mind.* Casting his eyes down, he recognized his young body, his favorite Levi's, his San Francisco Giants sweatshirt, the black Converse Allstars that were nearly worn out but were so comfortable he didn't have the heart to throw them away. He was tucked into the alcove of the hallway, his favorite hiding place as a young boy and a safe place to eavesdrop.

The scenario repeated itself, his mother arguing with a mysterious stranger. Voices raised, angry shouting. Taking a deep breath, Ebby pushed away from the alcove and forced himself to step into the office. He was dreaming, wasn't he? But why did it feel so real? How could he feel the thick carpet under the soles of his shoes, smell the lemon oil Allegra used to polish the furniture, if he was just dreaming? In the office, his mother's voice was becoming louder, but he still couldn't make out what she was saying. The person standing across from her was shouting too, but the words sounded like they were being spoken in slow motion. Try as he might, Ebby couldn't understand what they were.

Ebby closed his eyes, suddenly scared. When he opened them, he was standing across from his mother. She was mocking him, telling him how Lucy had died an excruciating death and only a weak little boy would sob over the loss of a dog. She told him she hated him, regretted the day he was born. Ebby tried to pinch himself. But he couldn't because there was something in his hands – the sterling silver dagger with the jewel-encrusted hilt. Unable to control himself, he saw his arm raised high in the air, to his horror, he felt the cold hilt of the knife in his hand as he plunged it into his mother's chest. Her blood, hot and thick, flowed in waves. The floor rolled beneath his feet as Ebby opened his mouth to scream.

When he woke up, Ebby was lying on the floor in his kitchen, curled up in the fetal position. He jumped up, only to find that he was covered in sweat. The realization of what he had seen, what he might have done, pushed away all of his reason. Ebby was sure now: he didn't merely witness his mother's murder. Tears streaming down his face, Ebby bolted out his kitchen door into the cold January afternoon.

Chapter 7

Olivia

Sunday, January 4

The sounds of a jazz trio filtered through the woods as Elodie, Fiona, and Olivia set out in the afternoon chill toward the party. They had stopped by Ebby's cottage and knocked on the door, but there was no answer.

When Elodie had reached for the doorknob, Fiona had stopped her. "Leave him be. He might be in the shower getting ready for the party. If so, he won't appreciate you fussing. Come on, ladies, chins up. It's Elodie's birthday party. Let's get into the spirit of things."

Ebby and Elodie's properties were separated from the main house and grounds by a grove of old redwood trees. As the path led them through the woods, the air grew damp and sweet-smelling, with droplets of water glistening on the undergrowth of ferns.

"We love these woods, don't we, Fiona?" Elodie said.

"Remember when we used to play here as children?" Fiona reminisced. "My father built us a treehouse, Olivia. We used to play in it for hours and hours. Once we took a picnic up there and used the family china. Mother was furious."

"Remember when I fell out of it and broke my arm?" Elodie said. Both women laughed.

The trail was wide enough for a car to drive on, and consisted of compacted dirt and duff from the pine trees. The aunts each took one of Olivia's arms and they walked side by side, arms entwined, a united front.

The guests were arriving in throngs as the three women stepped out of the woods and onto the lawn surrounding the main house. A large tent had been set up in the corner, one side of it open to allow plenty of fresh air and sunshine. Inside, people mingled and sipped champagne while the jazz trio played the standards that Olivia's parents had listened to and that she still loved. Ten round tables had been situated throughout the tent. White-coated waiters moved among them, setting out silverware and filling up water glasses.

"Dear God," Fiona said. "Melinda's really outdone herself for you."

"Not for me, I'm afraid." Elodie sighed. "But she did a lovely job, so I'm going to be grateful and enjoy myself. Look, there's Fred and Maryanne."

"And they've brought Ruth with them."

As Fiona and Elodie let go of Olivia's arms and headed to meet their friends, Olivia scanned the crowd looking for Ebby. Nervous after hearing Elodie and Fiona's story, she wanted to lay eyes on her client, but Ebby was nowhere to be seen. Felicity came bursting around the corner, carrying a clipboard and looking harried as she walked rapidly toward the buffet table, where the chef was setting up a meat carving station. Olivia had always been impressed by Felicity and had wondered over the years why the competent, educated young woman had chosen to remain a servant. Elodie had mentioned more than once that Felicity was a talented painter, whose artwork had won awards.

"Hello, Olivia," Felicity said.

"This looks lovely, Felicity. You've outdone yourself."

"Melinda, not me," Felicity said, her eyes plastered to her clipboard.

"Come on, everyone knows you do the bulk of the work," Olivia teased.

"Right. Don't let Melinda hear you say that. Off I go. Enjoy yourself."

As Felicity hurried off, the guests continued to arrive, breaking into groups, while Elodie's gang stayed outside among the trees, laughing and talking. Olivia moved into the tent. She recognized the chef, Robin Silver, who owned the eponymous catering company that had catered her daughter Denny's wedding, and a handful of parties that Olivia had hosted when she was married and obligated to entertain her bastard ex-husband's clients. Now Robin stood before what looked like an entire cow, sharpening a knife.

"Hello, Robin," she said. "Contemplating that first cut?"

Robin looked up from the slab of meat and smiled when he saw Olivia. "Olivia. I'd hug you, but my hands are full."

"No worries. Quite a party."

"Indeed. It's good to see you. We were going to call last October, but Marcie thought you probably wanted to be left alone. Seems you're doing well?"

"I'm fine," Olivia said. Robin was referring to last October, when Olivia had been wrongly accused and arrested for the murder of her idiot ex-husband's mistress. In a twisted series of events, she had ended up diving into the freezing San Francisco Bay to save the very same police officer who had arrested her for the crime. The irony of this scenario was not lost on the half dozen bystanders who filmed the rescue and posted it on social media. Fifteen minutes after Olivia dragged the half-drowned policewoman to shore, she was an internet sensation. With her five minutes of fame came the journalists, bloggers, and television hosts from various true crime shows, who hounded her, begging for an interview, a picture, a quote. In the spirit of their long-standing friendship, Lauren Ridley, a multi-Grammy-winning, platinum-record-holding rock star, had taken Olivia under her wing and showed her how to outmaneuver the press and navigate the uncertain waters of her short-lived notoriety.

On Lauren's advice, Olivia had taken her landline off the hook and had also got a new cell phone, only giving her number to a handful of people, effectively creating a self-imposed cocoon of isolation. As the weeks went by, interest in her story faded. Now she was tentatively stepping back out into the world, eager to pick up the pieces of her life and move into the future.

"I went into seclusion," Olivia said by way of explanation. "And I have a new number. Can I give it to you?"

Robin put the knife down and plugged Olivia's number into his phone. "Got it," he said.

"I'm glad to see you, Robin. Tell Marcie to call me."

"I will. I'm glad to see you looking so well and that all that nonsense with Richard's behind you."

Robin sliced his first cut of meat, revealing its tender juicy inside.

"That looks really tasty," Olivia said.

"Thanks," Robin said, expertly cutting the meat into thin slices and arranging them on a platter. "So you're divorced now? My cousin's a lawyer. Very successful. He's divorced—"

Olivia laughed out loud. "Not ready to be set up yet. But thanks."

A girl in a chef's coat approached them. "Chef, we have a couple of issues." She cast an apologetic glance at Olivia.

"I'll let you get back to it. Take care, Robin. Good to see you." Olivia meandered through the tent, coming to rest in front of a wooden planter, which held a bushy star jasmine in full bloom. Four chairs had been arranged on either side, a clever way to provide two separate conversation areas. Two women sat on one side, their heads close as they surveyed the crowd. Olivia didn't think anything of them as she sat down on one of the chairs on the opposite side. Her feet hurt and she had a headache from the champagne and not enough food.

"Why is she here?"

"I heard Ebby hired her to find out what happened the night Cynthia was murdered."

Are they gossiping about me? Olivia moved the chair closer to the plant. Across the room, Felicity walked up to the band, waiting to speak to them. Once the music stopped, Olivia could hear the women speaking as clearly as if she were sitting with them.

"Ironic that he hired an accused murderer, right?"

"Hey, she was innocent. You saw the video, right? She saved that policewoman."

"I saw the video. Who didn't? And yeah, she's got guts. But that doesn't mean she isn't capable of murder. I think she did it. I think she got away with it."

"That's ridiculous. She didn't murder anyone. Her husband's to blame. I wonder what happened to him?"

"I heard he got some cushy job in DC, lobbying or something like that."

"Wonder why she let herself go. The gray hair makes her look so old …"

Olivia had heard this before. After she let her hair go gray, she was amazed at the number of people who thought it was their right to express their feelings about her natural hair. Most people liked it, many complimented her. Many said they thought she was courageous, which was a joke in Olivia's mind. Why did it take courage for a woman to embrace the changes in her body? Men went gray every day and no one cared. Olivia hated double standards. And then there were the women and men who thought they were obligated to remind her, as if she weren't aware, that her hair was gray. Olivia had heard it all.

She headed out of the tent but paused for a moment in front

of the two gossips and reached up to touch her hair. "Letting my hair go natural was one of the most freeing things I've ever done. Enjoy the party."

The women's eyes opened in surprise. Olivia smiled. She could feel them staring at her as she walked away.

Back outside, party guests were arriving en masse. Many walked in groups toward the tent, while the electric cart drove those who couldn't walk. The group of Elodie's friends had grown to ten people, by Olivia's count. They stood around Elodie and Fiona, carrying on in that unique way of old friends. Two of them leaned on canes, and one was in a wheelchair, specially tricked out with knobby tires like a mountain bike. Despite their age, Elodie's gang were all dressed in warm clothes and shoes that were appropriate for the outdoors. Olivia appreciated the lack of pretense. She went to join them just as Mark stepped out of the main house and onto the porch, Melinda at his side.

Although Olivia had known the Engstrom family for as long as she could remember, she had only known Melinda peripherally. Today Melinda looked the part of the elegant wife of an influential man. Mark stood next to her, dressed for a board meeting rather than an outdoor party, surveying the gathering crowd like a king amongst his courtiers. When he leaned into Melinda and whispered something in her ear, Melinda's body tensed for the briefest second, before she plastered a tight smile on her face and allowed Mark to escort her down the stairs, toward the waiting party guests. As Olivia watched, she wondered if anyone noticed Melinda's wince as Mark dug his fingers into her arm. After spending twenty-five-plus years dealing with the most brutal divorces, Olivia recognized a battered spouse when she saw one.

Olivia knew that Melinda and Mark had been high school sweethearts, but she was willing to bet that Mark Engstrom did whatever he wanted, with little regard for his wife.

The aunts had confided that Mark Engstrom was none too happy with Ebby for hiring Olivia. Would he make a scene at the party? Elodie caught her eye and gave her a thumbs-up gesture of encouragement. The gesture caught the attention of the man standing next to Olivia. He wore hearing aids, but he had the physical bearing of someone much younger. He stared at Olivia for a few seconds, a confused look on his face, as though he couldn't quite place her. Turning to Elodie, he shouted, "Who is that woman?" just as Mark and Melinda reached the group.

Olivia heard Elodie say, "That's Shirley Braithwaite's daughter, Olivia."

Mark cast a glance at Olivia. The fake smile that he had plastered into place slipped away, as he broke away from Melinda and skirted around the outside of the group. Olivia stood her ground, not backing away when Mark moved in close to her.

"Olivia, we haven't seen you in a while."

"Hello, Mark."

"Could I have a word?"

"Of course," Olivia said. She turned to Elodie. "Excuse us."

Elodie gave her a worried smile as Mark grabbed Olivia's arm and steered her away from the crowd.

"Get your hand off me, Mark. Now." Olivia wrenched herself out of Mark's grasp and turned to face him. "You have something you want to say to me? Say it."

Mark Engstrom gave her another one of his fake smiles. "Forgive me for being forward, Olivia. But my brother is not a healthy man. He is mentally unstable. Making representations you could somehow help him with a thirty-year-old crime, especially in light of his psychiatric condition, could be perceived as an ethics violation of the worst magnitude. Neither Ebby, nor my family, is in need of your legal services. Given your mother's long-standing relationship with my aunts, I'm asking nicely. Step away from Ebby. Tell him you are too busy to take his case. I'll pay you for your trouble, just name your price."

Olivia forced a convivial tone. "Come on, Mark. You and I both know there's nothing about Ebby that is remotely unstable."

Mark checked to make sure no one was listening to them. "Don't make me push, Olivia. You don't want to do battle with me. You'll never win."

"And you have absolutely no grounds or authority to interfere in my relationship with your brother. I'm going to help him. Now, if you'll excuse me." Olivia turned to step away, sensing Mark following her.

"Listen to me. If you don't back away from my brother and, through association, my family, I'll make your life hell. I'll come after you with everything I have. You're kicking outside your coverage area, Mrs. Sinclair. Step away while you can."

Olivia turned around, faced Mark Engstrom, and said in a voice loud enough for others to hear, "Are you threatening me?"

"These are my friends. You'll only embarrass yourself if you make a scene. I don't take prisoners."

"Actually, these are Elodie's friends. And neither do I. Let me be very clear. I will not abandon your brother. I will not discuss his case with you. I *will* be digging into every member of this family." Olivia enjoyed the fleeting flash of fear in Mark Engstrom's eyes and couldn't resist exploiting it. "Oh, you look like a man with a secret. Afraid of the background check? Your worry intrigues me, Mark. Makes me want to bump you to the top of the suspect pile." Mark Engstrom's face turned a mottled shade of red. Olivia gave him a sly smile, pleased that their roles had reversed, that she was the fox and Mark Engstrom was the very fat hen. "Did you know that when I practiced family law, I earned my reputation on my ability to ferret out secrets?"

Mark kept his face impassive, but there was no denying he'd heard the implied threat loud and clear. "Perhaps we could table our discussion for another time."

They were close to the edge of the tent, which was rapidly filling with people, but no one seemed to notice the unfolding scene. Either that, or the guests were too afraid of Mark Engstrom to eavesdrop. Clenching her hands into fists, Olivia stepped so close to Mark Engstrom, her face was but two inches away. "We have nothing to discuss. I'm not afraid of you."

"You should be. I've brought down more powerful women than you."

"Oh, you think you can ruin me?" Olivia laughed. "I'm already ruined. That's the difference between you and me. I don't have anything to lose."

"You're a bitch, aren't you?"

"I've been called worse. Enjoy the party." Olivia turned her back on Mark Engstrom and walked toward a waiter who carried a tray loaded with glasses of champagne.

Olivia wondered if she could simply leave, but was pleasantly surprised when she saw Brian Vickery walking up the driveway, looking handsome in a sportscoat and tie, and – blessedly – without Leanne on his arm.

Her face broke into a smile as she grabbed two flutes of champagne from a waiter and met Brian just outside the tent. "I'm so glad to see you," she said, handing him a glass.

"I'm glad to see you too," Brian said. They clinked glasses and sipped their champagne. "You look a little wound up, if you don't mind me saying so."

"Oh, I just had a bit of a run-in with Mark Engstrom. He tried to tell me to leave Ebby alone."

"And?"

"And nothing. I made my position clear. I don't kowtow to bullies. Never have. Never will." They walked back toward Fiona and Elodie who were still mingling outside the tent with their friends. "Do you want me to introduce you to everyone?"

"Not yet," Brian said. He stared at the Engstrom house. "Is that where Cynthia's murder occurred?"

"It is."

"Let's walk the perimeter. I'd like to get a feel for the place, and you can tell me what the situation was back in the day." Olivia wrapped her arm through Brian's, trying to hide the pleasure

67

she felt as they walked arm in arm. *I have missed this man,* she thought as they scooted around the crowd and walked around the back of the house. The wing where Elodie, Allegra, and Felicity had once lived and had now fallen into decrepit ruin.

"Wow," Brian said. "This is surprising. I can't believe they've let the house get like this."

"I know. It's sad. When I was a child there used to be a koi pond out here. That patch of dead grass used to be a swimming pool, and there once were clay tennis courts just beyond those shrubs," Olivia said.

The wing was a two-storied rectangle that extended from the main house. The section that faced the mountain had large windows, which were long broken and now boarded up. In places the wooden siding had come off. At the far end, the roof had caved in. Ivy climbed up the walls and into the rafters.

"It's a pity, isn't it?" Olivia said.

"So who lived in this part of the house?"

"Okay, let's see if I can get this straight. Elliot died in June of 1984. That's the year I graduated from law school. Before Elliot died, Elodie lived here, along with Felicity and her mother, Allegra. Allegra was the Engstroms' housekeeper, and she lived in."

"Do you happen to remember everyone's alibis?"

"Only what I heard from my mom," Olivia said. "Total hearsay."

"I don't care." Brian stood facing the house. "I won't hold you to it, but anything you can remember would be appreciated."

"Okay," Olivia said. She stood next to him and also beheld the old structure that used to be so beautiful, so full of life. "Let's see … Fiona wasn't here that night. The only people in the house at the time of the murder were Cynthia, who was in the study, Allegra, Elodie, and a very young Felicity. Allegra, Elodie, and Felicity were together at the time of the murder, if memory serves. And Mark was on a ski weekend in Lake Tahoe, so has a solid alibi. Ebby was at a friend's house before he came home that night."

"Got it," Brian said.

"Excuse me?"

Olivia and Brian turned as Felicity came walking around the corner, still looking harried, clipboard in hand.

"Oh, Olivia. It's you. I'm sorry. Mark said someone was trespassing around the back of house." She tucked her clipboard under her arm as she approached.

"Felicity, this is Brian Vickery," Olivia said. "He's helping with Ebby's situation."

"Oh," Felicity said. "Nice to meet you."

"Hey, Felicity, would you mind talking to us for a minute?" Brian asked.

"Sure. What do you want to know?"

"I hear you and your mother lived here at the time of Cynthia's murder? That was December 1984, right?"

"It was," Felicity said. "But we didn't live here then. We moved out the previous June after Elliot died. My mom got us an apartment. We lived there until she died. I actually inherited it from her and still live there now."

"Was your mother at the house the night Cynthia was murdered?"

Olivia could see the tension creep into Felicity's shoulders. The housekeeper looked behind her, as if to make sure no one was listening.

"We won't repeat anything you say to Mark or Melinda," Olivia said.

Felicity nodded. "Okay. My mother and I were both at the house. When we moved, my mother couldn't find care for me when I wasn't in school. So when she worked here, I would take the bus and come here after school. On holidays I would just come to work with her."

"What would you do all day?" Olivia asked.

"Read, go for walks, sometimes help my mom." Felicity smiled. "I had a good childhood, despite the fact that my mother was the hired help."

"Would you mind talking to us at the office sometime when you're not working?"

"Sure," Felicity said. "I need to get back now. Would you mind coming with me? We're sitting down to lunch soon."

Olivia and Brian followed Felicity back to the party.

Chapter 8

Olivia

Sunday, January 4

"Where's Ebby?" Brian asked as he and Olivia approached the party. Felicity had excused herself, hurrying off to help Melinda.

Olivia scanned the crowd, surprised that Ebby had yet to make an appearance. "I don't see him."

"You sound worried," Brian said.

"I am worried."

Just then, Fiona saw Olivia and Brian. She broke away from her group of friends and came walking toward them.

"You must be Brian Vickery," Fiona said, extending her hand. "Fiona Engstrom. Pleasure. Come to the tent. We've got a table reserved and a spot for the both of you." When they reached the tent, Fiona turned to Brian and said, "Do you mind if I speak to Olivia privately?"

"Of course not." Brian turned to Olivia. "How about I go through the buffet line for both of us?"

"Sounds great," Olivia said. "I'm starving."

Once Brian was gone, Fiona led Olivia away from the throngs of people. As soon as they were out of earshot, she pulled Olivia close and said, "You should have seen Mark's face after you spoke to him. What did you say? Never mind. I don't want to know. You mustn't pick a fight with him, dear. I know you're brave and you don't like being pushed around by men. But Mark's ruthless."

"I don't give in to bullies," Olivia snapped, moving away from Fiona. "I simply stood up to him."

"Mark isn't used to anyone questioning him. He's one of those men who like to be in control." Fiona cocked her head and stared into Olivia's eyes. "You're not the least bit afraid of him, are you?"

"No. Forgive me for being forward, Fiona, but your nephew's a coward. And I'd bet money that he abuses his wife."

"Always has. Poor thing covers herself up to hide the bruises." Fiona patted Olivia's arm. "You are very perceptive, my dear. But you need to be careful with Mark," Fiona added. "I know he's an egomaniacal fool, but he's a bit desperate. And you know as well as I do that desperation can make a man do strange things."

"I won't underestimate him. I have a pretty good idea what I'm dealing with here."

The tent was now full of guests. Olivia was no longer in the mood for a party, but she allowed Fiona to lead her to the table, which had been reserved for Elodie, while Brian chatted up the people in the buffet line. Once they were seated, a waiter came round with yet another glass of champagne. Olivia was glad when Brian returned. She was hungry and needed food to soak up the continual flow of champagne that had gone down so smoothly.

"This looks good," Olivia said. "I'm hungry."

"I always like a woman with a healthy appetite," Brian said.

Soon everyone was seated and the conversation turned into a subtle background murmur that Olivia found soothing.

Although Elodie had led them to believe that most of the guests were Mark's business associates, many of the people came to Elodie with hugs and birthday wishes. Olivia recognized a

72

handful of well-known artists, who knew Elodie from her involvement with the Marin Arts Council, and the tireless energy she put into raising money in support of the arts. While lunch was served, friends stopped by to chat with Elodie, as Fiona regaled Olivia and Brian with stories of the Engstrom sisters' misspent youth. She was surprised to find she was actually enjoying herself, despite Mark's earlier threats and the niggling worry about Ebby, who still hadn't made an appearance.

When lunch was finished and the plates cleared away, a huge cake was brought to the center of the room with eighty-five candles on it. After a rousing, off-key rendition of happy birthday, Elodie blew out all eighty-five candles in two breaths.

When someone yelled, "Speech!" one of the musicians handed Elodie a microphone.

Brian leaned into Olivia and said, "Should we go to Ebby's cottage and find out why he isn't here?"

"Do you think we can tactfully slip away?" Olivia whispered back.

Elodie took the proffered microphone and moved to the center of the dance floor, facing her guests. "If you insist on a speech, I'll be glad to comply."

"The speeches go on and on. Let's wait until Elodie is finished speaking. When she's finished, her friends will get up and talk about her. We can slip away then."

Brian put his arm along the back of Olivia's chair as Elodie moved to the center of the room and addressed the crowd like a pro. "First of all, I want to thank each and every one of you for being here to celebrate with me. I believe that family comes first, and although I'm meeting some new faces today, you're a delightful bunch and I'm glad to share this day with you. Earlier I was reflecting on this particular birthday, and the memories of those who aren't with me came flooding into my thoughts. I'm not going to get maudlin, but—"

Elodie stopped speaking as her eyes opened wide with shock.

Next to her, Olivia heard Brian say, "Oh, dear God." She turned around to see Ebby standing in the back opening of the tent. He wore a suit jacket and khaki trousers. The sleeve of the jacket had been ripped and it hung on his arm. The shirt under the jacket was unbuttoned and splattered with blood, likely from the open gash on his cheek. His trousers had a hole in the knee and he was missing a shoe. A sheen of perspiration glistened on his pale face, and his bloodshot eyes darted around the room.

A hush fell over the room as every single person turned to face Ebby. Olivia caught a glimpse of Mark at a table on the far side of the tent. "What the hell," he snapped, as he threw his napkin on the table and started to stand.

"I'm so sorry," Ebby cried out, and Olivia recognized a tone of desperation. "But I need to confess. I murdered my mother."

Quick as lightning, Brian was out of his chair and by Ebby's side.

Olivia said to Fiona, "Tell Elodie to keep everyone in here. We'll take care of Ebby."

Fiona grabbed Olivia's arm, "What are you going to do?"

"Get him to a hospital."

"Good," Fiona said. She hurried over to Elodie and whispered in her ear.

Out of the corner of her eye, Olivia saw Mark hurrying toward his brother. Brian had put an arm around Ebby and was leading him away from the crowd. Olivia, by virtue of her location, was able to reach Ebby's side well ahead of Mark. She also put an arm around him and together they led Ebby away.

"Olivia." Ebby's voice broke when he saw her.

"Ebby, look at me." When Ebby met Olivia's eyes, she said, "Where have you been? What happened to you?"

"When I remembered killing – killing my mother—" Ebby started to sob.

"Ebby, listen to me. You didn't kill your mother. Tell me how you cut your cheek? And what happened to your other shoe?"

74

"When I had the vision – it was so real – I ran outside. I remember running into the woods, just running and running." Ebby moaned, as he closed his eyes. "I did it, Olivia. God help me. I killed her."

"He's having a breakdown," Brian said. "He needs medical attention quick."

Felicity came around the corner of the tent holding a cigarette. When she saw Ebby, she tossed it to the ground, stamped it out, and came running.

"He needs an ambulance," Olivia said.

"I'll call for one. Let's take him to the front of the house." Felicity reached in her pocket for her cell phone and dialed 9-1-1 with shaking hands.

Olivia nodded.

Behind them, Olivia could hear Elodie speaking to the crowd, her voice surprisingly calm and measured. "My nephew has been having some difficulty. If you could honor my wishes and stay seated, I'll get the waiters to top off your champagne. Let me tend to my family, and I'll be right back with my speech. Where's my nephew? Mark? Mark, come up here and entertain these people. Tell them jokes or something. I'll be right back."

Elodie hurried to Olivia and Ebby, a worried look on her face.

"Felicity's calling an ambulance," Olivia said. Ebby was mumbling incoherently as they eased him onto one of the chairs on the front porch.

"Can you go with him to the hospital, Olivia? I'll see that the champagne flows so everyone will get good and snockered. Then I'll slip away and meet you."

"Ambulance is on its way," Felicity said.

Tears welled in Elodie's eyes. She grabbed Felicity's arm, as if she were going to faint.

"Catch her," Brian said.

"Elodie?" Felicity cried out, grabbing Elodie just as she was about to topple.

75

"I'll be fine," Elodie said, leaning on Felicity. "Just give me a second."

They heard Mark's voice over the PA system followed by laughter. Ebby started to quietly sob, his shoulders heaving, as Felicity supported Elodie, who looked like she was about to have a heart attack. Brian kept a hand on Ebby's shoulder, his touch steady and sure. When Olivia caught his eye, he said, "It'll be all right." Olivia wasn't sure if he was talking to her or to Ebby.

Elodie took a deep breath, then another. The color slowly returned to her cheeks. She pushed away from Felicity. "That's enough nonsense. You two take Ebby to meet the ambulance. I'll be with you shortly."

"Elodie, you should be checked out by the ambulance," Felicity said. "You look a little weak, dear."

"No ambulance. I am about thirty minutes from completely losing my composure. I need to use that precious time to extricate myself from this party. I will see you at the hospital. If I need medical attention, I will get it then." With that, she turned and walked back to the tent.

No one said a word as they waited for the ambulance. The fifteen minutes it took to get there seemed like hours. By the time Ebby was loaded up, he had stopped crying. "I killed her. My God. I'm a murderer. I can't hold it in anymore. I'm a murderer. I killed my mother."

"Only one of you can ride in the ambulance," the paramedic said.

"I want Olivia," Ebby mumbled.

"Should I wait for Elodie?" Felicity asked.

"I think that's a good idea," Olivia said. "Can you drive her? She's had quite a bit to drink."

"Yes," Felicity said. "You'll stay with him and make sure he's okay?"

"I will."

"Okay. See you soon, Ebs." Felicity squeezed his arm and hurried off.

"I'll follow," Brian said.

"Thanks," Olivia said. She climbed into the ambulance and reached for Ebby's hand.

"Olivia?" Ebby cried out.

"I'm here," Olivia said.

As the paramedic took his vitals, he said to Olivia, "Is he on anything?"

"No, I don't think so, but I have no way of knowing for sure," Olivia said.

The paramedic looked at Olivia. "Given the murder confession, I'm obligated to call the police."

"I understand," Olivia said.

As they drove away from the house, sirens blaring, Olivia had a premonition that things were about to get bad for Ebby Engstrom. Very bad indeed.

Chapter 9

Olivia

When the ambulance pulled up to the emergency entrance at Marin General Hospital, the police were waiting for them. Ebby clung to Olivia's hand so hard, the paramedics and the nurses agreed it would be best if she were allowed to remain by his side until he was seen by the doctor. Olivia followed along, aware of the two uniformed officers traveling in their wake. Ebby continued to cling to Olivia's hand as they wheeled him into a curtained bay in the ER. At one point, he sat up, looked at the two policemen and said, "I killed her. I murdered my mother. Are you going to take me to jail?" Then, turning to Olivia, he said, "I'm going to prison for the rest of my life," before he collapsed in tears.

He remained hysterical as the paramedics moved him from the gurney to the bed, tossing his head from side to side, his face damp with sweat. Every few minutes he would gasp and become frighteningly still, his panic-stricken eyes darting around the room. Outside the curtained-off area, one of the policemen peered through a gap in the curtain trying to get a look at Ebby.

A nurse approached the policeman who was trying to look in. "Excuse me. You need to go wait over there. Don't make me tell you again." She stepped into the room and moved over to Ebby. Olivia waited while she took his pulse.

"Are you his next of kin?" the nurse asked.

"No, just a friend."

"Name?"

"Olivia Sinclair." The nurse's eyes shot up in recognition when Olivia said her name.

"Olivia needs to stay here," Ebby said through dried lips. "Please. I'm giving you permission to speak with her about my condition. I killed my mother. My God. I killed my mother. I need Olivia. Lawyer. Olivia …"

"Okay, Mr. Engstrom. Don't worry. She'll stay right here." The nurse bent over Ebby and put a reassuring hand on his arm. "What did you take?"

"I didn't take anything," he said.

"Does he have a history of drug use?"

"No," Olivia said.

The nurse noted the chart. Outside the cordoned-off area, Olivia saw a portly man with red hair and thick glasses in conversation with the paramedics and the police officers. Soon the curtain swooshed open and the red-headed doctor came in.

"I'm Dr. Lister." He stepped close to Ebby and spoke to him in a voice that was kind and unthreatening. "Ebby, can you hear me?"

"Yes," Ebby croaked.

"I'm just going to examine you, okay? My stethoscope is going to feel cold on your chest." Dr. Listen spoke softly as he listened to Ebby's heart. "Do you mind if I flash a light in your eyes for a minute?"

"No," Ebby said.

The nurse handed him the chart she had been scribbling in. Olivia watched as Dr. Lister read the nursing notes, jotted something down, and handed it back to the nurse. "Start him with that to keep him calm. And I think he's rather dehydrated, so let's get a drip going and monitor him closely.

"Ebby?" Dr. Lister stood over Ebby's bed. "This is what I'd like to do, if it's okay. I'm going to give you a sedative to keep you calm. I think you're dehydrated, so I'm going to start an IV. In a few hours, you'll wake up and feel much better. At that time, we can talk about your mother, okay?"

"Okay. Thank you," Ebby said through cracked lips.

Dr. Lister stepped away from the bed. "We've a private waiting room for family. Let's go speak there."

"I'm not going to leave him with those policemen out there."

Dr. Lister peered at Olivia over his glasses, before he nodded at her. "Understood. Give me a minute." Olivia waited while the doctor stepped outside the curtain and spoke to the police. "This patient is not able to see or speak to anyone tonight. I'm going to need you gentlemen to leave."

When they were gone, Olivia moved over to Ebby's bed and said, "I'm going to speak with the doctor, okay?"

Ebby mumbled something incoherent, but he let go of Olivia's hand, opting instead to clutch the bedrail as though hanging on for his life.

"This way," Dr. Lister said as he led Olivia into a room furnished with two overstuffed comfortable-looking couches and a mismatched assortment of chairs arranged around a large coffee table.

"Have a seat, Mrs. Sinclair," Dr. Lister said. "What can you tell me about Mr. Engstrom? What's brought this on? Does Mr. Engstrom suffer from paranoid delusions?"

"Dr. Lister, I'm an attorney who Ebby hired to help him navigate a tricky legal situation with his family. I don't mean to sound uncooperative, but I don't feel comfortable telling you

Ebby's story. His aunt should be here any minute. I'd feel more comfortable if she were the one to speak to you."

Olivia was interrupted by two sharp raps on the door. It opened and the nurse stuck her head in. "Mr. Engstrom's family is here."

"Thank God," Olivia said.

Elodie pushed past the nurse, Felicity and Brian tagging behind her. "I'm sorry it took us so long to get here. I was in the middle of my birthday party when Ebby – never mind that." She held out her hand. "I'm Elodie Engstrom, Ebby's aunt. I raised him after his mother died. Please, tell me he's going to be okay?" Her voice cracked with emotion as tears welled in her eyes.

Dr. Lister, who had stood when Elodie and Felicity came into the room, gestured to the chairs. "He's going to be fine, Mrs. Engstrom. I'm Dr. Lister. Please, ladies, let's all have a seat." Once everyone was seated, Dr. Lister remained standing. Olivia noticed the surreptitious glance at his watch. "I can't spend a lot of time right now, so let me tell you what I know. I believe Ebby is suffering from some sort of a breakdown. Additionally, he is dehydrated and exhausted. I'm hoping you can enlighten me as to his repeated claims that he murdered his mother."

Elodie took a deep breath. "I'll give you the short version, Doctor. Thirty years ago, Ebby witnessed his mother's murder. Ever since then, he's suffered from dissociative amnesia. He was under the care of a psychiatrist and had been managing rather well until about four months ago. He quit therapy and weaned himself off his various medications." Elodie took a handkerchief out of her purse and wiped her eyes. "Since that time, he's been having vivid flashbacks of the night his mother died. He thinks he's remembering it."

"He is remembering it," Felicity interjected. "He's determined to remember what he witnessed that night. He wants to find out what he saw. And – I'm sorry, Elodie, but this needs to be told – he thinks he's the one who murdered his mom. But he didn't do it. I was at the house that night. I know he didn't do it. And I'll tell the police that if they ask me."

Although Olivia was impressed by Felicity's loyalty to Ebby, she was surprised at how certain she was of Ebby's innocence. Then she remembered that the two were childhood friends and were probably as close as siblings.

"Okay," Dr. Lister said. "The police were here. We're obligated to report these things. But I've sent them away and I'm going to keep Ebby overnight for observation. He really does need to resume therapy, even if he doesn't take medication. If he's remembering the events that caused the dissociative amnesia, he needs medical care during the process. I'm going to suggest that."

"I'll stay with him," Elodie said. "He'll be glad of a familiar face when he wakes up."

"No, I'll stay," Felicity said. "You need to get back to the house, Elodie. I can stay here."

"Dr. Lister," Olivia said. "I'm concerned that the police will try to speak to Ebby while he is in the hospital."

"That won't happen, Mrs. Sinclair. Not under my watch."

A nurse peeked into the room. "Excuse me, Doctor, but they need you on the floor."

"Of course," Dr. Lister said. "If you'll excuse me."

Once Dr. Lister left them, Olivia turned to Elodie. "I don't want Ebby speaking to the police. He could very well wake up tomorrow and not remember anything that happened today."

"But surely he should cooperate with the police?" Elodie said. "He hasn't done anything wrong. Isn't it best if he's honest and forthright?"

Brian, who had tucked himself into the corner of the room, spoke for the first time. "They don't operate that way, I'm sorry to say. They'd trick him, try to get him to admit to something or get permission to go snooping in his house. Olivia's right. We don't want Ebby speaking to the police."

"Oh, I don't know," Elodie said.

"Elodie, I don't have time to mince words right now, so I'm going to be direct with you. The police won't just ignore Ebby's confession. They have to look into it. They'd be remiss if they didn't."

"What do we do?"

"I'll stay with him," Felicity said. "Let's get permission for me to spend the night in his room. Don't they have fold-out beds? If the police come, I'll call Olivia."

Elodie's voice softened as she patted Felicity's arm. "You're a good girl, Felicity."

"He'd do the same for me," Felicity said.

"I think it would be prudent for you to get him a good criminal lawyer. I'll make some phone calls for you, if you'd like," Olivia said. She was tired all of a sudden, emotionally drained. She wanted to go home, take a hot bath, and put on her pajamas.

"No calls. You'll be his lawyer." Elodie spoke in that stubborn tone of hers that Olivia had come to know over the years.

"It's unethical to represent a friend. I can't."

"Olivia Braithwaite Sinclair. You have to represent Ebby. You're the only lawyer with a personal connection to him."

"Exactly! Given my history with your family, given our friendship, honestly, Elodie, it's not a good idea. You need a neutral attorney, someone who doesn't know you. My emotional connection to you and to Ebby could be a hindrance."

"I want you, Olivia. Please don't make me beg."

Olivia sensed Brian watching her. When she met his gaze, he gave her a look so full of compassion and understanding that she capitulated to Elodie. Just knowing that Brian was in her corner gave her courage.

"Okay," Olivia said.

"Great. Now that we've got that settled, let's find the doctor and convince him to let me stay tonight." Felicity took Elodie's hand and led her out of the room.

Once they were gone and Olivia and Brian were alone, Brian

said, "I was about to ask if I could buy you a drink, but you look knackered, if you don't mind me saying so."

Olivia wished Brian would take her home and crawl into bed with her. But as her mother used to say, "If wishes were horses …"

He put his arm around her. The feel of him sent a jolt to her heart. "Come on, I'll drive you home. We can get your car tomorrow."

As they walked out into the cold January night, Olivia said, "We should prepare for a search warrant, don't you think?"

"Probably. I doubt they'll let it go," Brian said. They got into the car, and once Brian had started the engine and cranked the heater, he turned to her. "I think Ebby's having a type of PTSD reaction. Olivia, I know what you're going to say to this, but you should be prepared to face the idea that Ebby might well have killed his mother. He's a good guy – I get it. But he was thirteen at the time, and you have to admit, it sounds as though his life was hell."

"He didn't kill anyone," Olivia said. "I need you on board with this one."

"I'm on board, Liv. I'll help you in any way I can. You know that."

"I know," Olivia said. She closed her eyes and leaned her head back, wishing that things were different between the two of them.

Chapter 10

Brian

Sunday, January 4

Stomach rumbling and desperate for two fingers of Scotch in one of his Waterford tumblers, Brian pulled into the parking space at his apartment complex. As he walked toward his front door, he thought of the frozen pizza he'd make for his dinner and had a moment of longing for his dead wife. He used to come home at ungodly hours when he was a homicide cop. Maureen would always be waiting for him, a smile on her face, a drink at the ready. "Miss you, babe," he said out loud as he put his key in the lock.

He let the wave of nostalgia wash over him, savoring the memories of Maureen and all the times he had walked in the door, as eager to see the woman he loved now as he had been the day he married her. The memory was short-lived. Brian was no longer at his old house. He was in a small apartment by himself. When he stepped inside, the smell of roasting chicken and garlic met him. His stomach rumbled in response.

"Brian?" Leanne stepped into the hallway. She wore an apron

decorated with martini glasses and had a smile on her face. "I thought I'd surprise you. I hope that's okay? I went to the farmer's market today and bought a huge chicken and a bunch of vegetables. Please tell me I didn't overstep? You've got that look on your face."

A week ago, Brian had let Leanne do laundry at his house when her washing machine had gone on the fritz. At that time, he'd given her a key and had forgotten to get it back. For a minute, Brian felt irritated at Leanne for presuming to commandeer his time, for coming into this apartment and acting like she lived there. Then he thought of the frozen pizza that awaited him. Why was he so hard on Leanne? She was just being nice. And she knew Brian's position. His stomach rumbled.

"I've had a long day, and I'm starved. Roast chicken sounds wonderful."

Leanne sighed. "Oh, thank goodness."

Brian followed Leanne to the kitchen and poured himself a glass of wine as she took a perfectly roasted, golden-brown chicken out of the oven and set it on the cutting board. As she strained the drippings from the pan to make gravy, Brian refilled her wine glass.

She held her glass up in a salute. They took their time over dinner, languishing over the meal until they finished the bottle of wine. Although Leanne wanted to watch a movie, Brian was too tired. He thought about begging off and calling it an early night.

"Brian, I want to talk to you about something."

Here we go. Brian hoped Leanne wasn't going to revisit the relationship conversation.

"It's not about us, don't worry." She gave him a sheepish smile. "I was just wondering how well you know Olivia."

"Why do you ask?"

"At first, I figured you had known her for years, but then you told me you had only met her last October. I know that she was accused of murdering her husband's mistress. Now that I know

86

you, I see the expertise you bring to your business relationship, all the clients and work that you have. At dinner the other night you let it slip that Olivia is struggling to find her way professionally, and I can't help but wonder what she brings to the table." Leanne stared at her wine glass, as if giving Brian room to think. "We haven't known each other very long, but I consider you a friend. If our roles were reversed, I'd want you to tell me—"

"Tell you what?" Brian asked.

"Tell me if you thought someone was playing me," Leanne said. "I'm not asking for you to discuss your relationship with Olivia if you don't want to. That's none of my business. I just want you to be careful, that's all. There's something about her that I don't like. She's manipulative."

"Has something specific happened to make you say that?"

"No," Leanne said. "I guess it's just women's intuition, if you believe in that. The way she looks at me, like she thinks I'm after you. Have you two ever been intimate?" Leanne held up her hands. "I'm sorry. I didn't to mean to pry, and I don't expect an answer. But I swear, she has feelings for you. And if that's the case, she's probably jealous of me."

"Olivia isn't the jealous type," Brian said.

"You're probably right," Leanne said. "Olivia and I just need to spend some time together, so we can get to know each other."

"Agreed. Maybe we could all have lunch together?"

"Perfect. I want us to be friends."

"You will be," Brian said.

"Good." Leanne pushed away from the table. "Now how about some of that apple pie?"

Leanne's comment had surprised Brian. He'd never thought of Olivia as anything other than a decent person who had been blindsided by her cheating ex-husband. Since October, he and Olivia had spent quite a bit of time together. He had found Olivia to be an intelligent woman, with a unique world view. He remembered those two weeks they had lived together and shared a bed. Those magical, earth-shattering, life-changing two weeks. Brian had fallen in love with Olivia Sinclair. The feelings, so intense, had completely unhinged him. And Olivia, in her knowing way, had worried they had moved too fast, given his feelings for Maureen. Which to Brian's mind was ridiculous because he didn't regret a thing. All the things he wanted to say but couldn't, stayed unresolved between them.

Brian hadn't regretted falling in love with Olivia. He didn't regret still loving her. He didn't know what had caused both of them to step away from each other, their hands metaphorically held up in surrender. Even though they never spoke of that time, it hung between them, the elephant in the room. For the first time, Brian wondered, *had* Olivia been playing him? If so, to what advantage?

At moments like this, Brian missed his marriage, missed his dead wife, who had understood him and who was so very easy to be around. Last October, Brian had thought he might have a future with Olivia. If he was brutally honest with himself, he had halfway hoped she would have offered up an explanation by now as to why she had pulled away. Women were so much better at communication and talking about their emotions than men were. If Olivia brought the subject up, no matter how uncomfortable, Brian would have discussed it with her. Maybe she wanted to give him room to finish grieving for Maureen.

God, he was confused. He hadn't planned on being single at this age. He certainly hadn't planned on falling in love with Olivia. With a sigh, he picked up the empty wine bottle and followed Leanne into the kitchen.

Leanne had sliced two generous pieces of apple pie and set them on plates. "I brought ice cream, so we could have our apple pie à la mode."

"Sounds good," Brian said. As he rinsed the dinner dishes, he realized how much he liked sharing the simple day-to-day things with another soul. Yes, he missed Maureen. And yes, he had unfinished business with Olivia Sinclair. But Olivia wasn't here right now, was she?

Leanne hummed under her breath as she put the lid back on the ice cream and put it back in the freezer. Brian admired her trim waist and her comely ankles. Her auburn hair, thick and vibrant as a woman half her age, cascaded down her back. She turned to face him. When she smiled, her eyes crinkled at the corners. "Why are you looking at me like that?"

In a move that was totally out of character, Brian took a step in Leanne's direction and pulled her toward him. Surprised, she grabbed the back of his neck and stood on her tiptoes. Their lips touched. Against his better judgment, Brian let himself go.

Chapter 11

Ebby

Monday, January 5

Ebby woke up with a start, realizing that he wasn't home. He lay on an unfamiliar bed, looking up at the sterile white ceiling, wondering where he was and how he had come to be here. He blinked his eyes a couple of times, checking to make sure he wasn't having a strange dream, before he turned on his side and saw Felicity, tucked into the chair in the corner of the room, her head at an uncomfortable angle. He was in a hospital. He remembered going for a hike. He vaguely recalled walking in the woods toward Elodie's party and the sound of the music and the murmur of voices in the tent. Everything after that was a blur.

Felicity stirred, opened her eyes, and slowly sat up, rubbing her neck.

"Good morning," Ebby said, his voice scratchy. His tongue felt thick and his lips were dry and cracked.

"Good morning," Felicity said. She stood, stretched, and opened the curtains of his private room.

"Have I been here all night?" he asked.

"You were admitted yesterday afternoon. Elodie, Olivia, and I agreed it would be best if you weren't left alone, so I volunteered to stay." She poured him a glass of water from the pitcher by the side of his bed and waited while he drank thirstily. Then she refilled it and sat down on the bed. "How do you feel?"

"Hungry, thirsty, and a bit confused. What happened? Why am I here?"

"You don't remember?"

"Not a thing," Ebby said.

Felicity let out a long, slow breath. "Oh, Ebby. It's a mess. You confessed to killing your mom. You were having one of your episodes. You stood at the tent, in front of God and all Elodie's guests and confessed to the murder."

"I don't remember any of that. Elodie must be beside herself."

"She's more than a little worried." Three nurses walked by Ebby's door, chatting among themselves.

Felicity looked tired and disheveled, and Ebby felt a pang of guilt at what he'd put his family and friends through. His eyes lit on one of the visitor's chairs, which held his backpack. "What's that?"

"Elodie packed you some clean clothes."

"Great." Ebby swung his legs over the side of the bed and tried to stand up. When the floor undulated beneath him, he sat back down.

"That's the sedative that's making you dizzy." Felicity started to come over to help, but Ebby pushed her away.

Ebby met Felicity's eyes. "Was I that bad?"

Felicity hesitated. "You were that bad. You showed up at the tent right in the middle of Elodie's speech. You looked like you'd been in a fight. You had that nasty cut on your cheek, you were missing a shoe, the front of your shirt was stained with blood, and your eyes were wild."

"Oh, no."

"You confessed to a murder in front of over a hundred witnesses," Felicity went on. "Thank God Olivia was there. She called an ambulance, and, with Brian Vickery and Elodie's help, managed to keep Mark out of the fray. You scared the hell out of me."

"Would you mind getting me coffee? A large one. And if they have anything decent to eat, I wouldn't complain. What time is it?"

Felicity pulled her phone out of her pocket. "It's 7:45 a.m. Back in a tick."

Just after Felicity left, a nurse came in. She took his blood pressure, asked him a few questions, and made notes in his chart.

"When can I go home?" Ebby asked.

"After the doctor clears you. He's right behind me. I'll disconnect you from the IV for now. I can't take the needle out until Dr. Lister clears you to leave."

"Thank you," Ebby said.

"Be careful when you get out of bed, okay? They gave you a sedative, and we don't know if all the drugs have cleared your system yet. Do you need anything? The breakfast tray will be coming soon."

"No. My friend just went to get me coffee and breakfast."

"Okay. Just push the button if you need anything."

After the nurse left, Ebby put on the pair of sweatpants that were in his backpack. He splashed cold water on his face and brushed his teeth, finally feeling halfway normal, despite the memories of yesterday, which were slowly coming into focus.

"Ebby? Can I come in?" The doctor, a portly man with a thatch of red hair and the thickest glasses Ebby had ever seen, stood outside his room.

"Of course," Ebby said.

"I'm Dr. Lister. You may not remember, but we met yesterday. You're looking much better this morning. How are feeling?"

"Feeling fine. Worried about how I came to be here."

"Can't say I blame you," Dr. Lister said. He picked up the chart and skimmed through it. "I'm not a psychiatrist, but I know what happened – I know about the dissociative amnesia."

"My aunt told you?"

"She did. And she told me that you've recently stopped therapy and medication."

"I have. I want to remember what happened that night. The medication keeps me lethargic. When I'm medicated, the memories stop. The psychiatrist I was seeing didn't seem to be interested in helping me. Every time I asked to wean off my medication, he ignored me and prescribed more pills." Ebby prepared himself for the certain lecture and was surprised when Dr. Lister nodded in agreement.

"I'm sorry about that. If I were in your shoes, I'd want to find out what happened to my mother too.

"I think you're being remiss if you proceed along this route – which could be dangerous – without the care of a doctor. Find a psychiatrist you like, just to be safe. You could ask your doctor to put you on meds temporarily, or at least work on a therapeutic regimen that meets with your approval. You're an adult. You should absolutely have a say in your course of treatment. There are plenty of good doctors in the area, and I'd be happy to recommend a few."

"I'll keep that in mind," Ebby said.

Dr. Lister smiled and stood. "And that's my unsolicited two cents. Also, you were really dehydrated and exhausted when you came in yesterday. I'm releasing you, but you must avoid stress at all costs. I think it would be prudent to stay with someone for a while, just for a few days."

"He can stay with me," Felicity said. She came in carrying a tray with two coffees and what looked like bagels and cream cheese. "And forgive me for eavesdropping, but I heard what the doc said about seeing a psychiatrist. I'm going to bug you about that."

"Fine," Ebby said.

"Good. I'll leave you in this young lady's capable hands." Dr.

Lister stood and shook Ebby's hand. "The nurse will be back with the discharge papers."

Half an hour later, Felicity and Ebby left the hospital, Ebby reluctantly agreeing to exit the building in a wheelchair, pushed by an orderly. "I'll be right back with the car, Ebby."

Felicity started toward the lower parking lot where she'd parked yesterday, just as an unmarked Ford Crown Vic with a government license plate rolled to a stop in front of Ebby. In a flash, Felicity was back, firmly planted between Ebby's wheelchair and the police car.

"What are you doing?" Ebby asked.

Felicity commandeered Ebby's wheelchair. "I'll just push him to my car and we'll bring the wheelchair back."

"That's not allowed," the orderly said. "I'm to make sure he is safely placed in the vehicle that will transport him."

"We're changing the rules today," Felicity said to the orderly, who responded with a confused expression.

"What's wrong with you? Why are you in such a hurry?" Ebby asked.

Felicity bent down and whispered into Ebby's ear, "Those cops. I think they're here for you."

There were two of them, a man, who had the body of a fighter, striking blue eyes, and a woman, taller than average, a no-nonsense look on her face. The man walked behind the woman. "Mr. Engstrom?"

"Yes," Ebby said.

"Edward Engstrom?" the woman said.

"Yes." Ebby felt his heart drop into his stomach. *They've come to arrest me.*

"We need you to come with us," the woman said.

"But he's just been discharged from the hospital," Felicity said, as she pulled out her cell phone and dialed Olivia's phone number.

"And you are?" the man asked Felicity.

"I'm the woman who's calling Mr. Engstrom's lawyer," Felicity hissed.

As Felicity frantically tried to reach Olivia, the woman said the words Ebby had heard so many times on television, "Mr. Engstrom, we have a warrant for your arrest for the murder of Cynthia Engstrom. You have the right to remain silent …"

Ebby went numb as they carefully loaded him into the back of the car, making sure he didn't hit his head as he transferred from the wheelchair to the caged back seat that smelled of vomit. He leaned back and closed his eyes, knowing that he should be worried, scared even. But he wasn't. In some fashion, this arrest was a gift. If it took him getting arrested to get the police to reinvestigate his mother's murder, then so be it.

Chapter 12

Olivia

Since October, Olivia had taken to calling her life before her arrest for the murder of her husband's mistress – and the startling climax that had exonerated her – *the before times.*

On this particular morning, she awoke with a bad feeling deep in her gut. That familiar intuition that had lain dormant since she quit practicing law had niggled its way into her psyche, leaving her worried about Ebby. She'd never witnessed anyone suffering as Ebby had yesterday, and the image of him standing at the tent, completely destroyed, haunted her.

As she dressed in wool trousers and a button-up silk blouse, Olivia wondered if any of those guests, like the two women who had been gossiping about her in the tent, had whipped out their cell phone and filmed Ebby's confession. There was nothing to be done about that.

She had just poured her coffee when her cell phone rang. Felicity.

"Good morning, Felicity. How's Ebby?"

"We have a problem."

* * *

Thirty minutes later, Olivia and Brian were headed south on Highway 101 toward the Marin Civic Center. Once there, they were ushered into a windowless room, made dingy by the lack of windows, and the grayish linoleum floor. There was one table and two rickety chairs. Olivia sat in one of them, while Brian remained standing. Based on his state of mind at Elodie's party, Olivia expected Ebby to be panic-stricken after being arrested immediately on his release from the hospital. Instead, he was calm and stoic as a sheriff led him into the room.

Once they were alone, Ebby said, "I don't remember confessing to killing her. I don't remember a thing."

"The first thing I want to focus on is getting you out of here. Once we do that, we'll make a plan," Olivia said.

"At least I got what I wanted," Ebby said.

"What do you mean?" Olivia asked.

"They're going to reinvestigate my mom's murder," he said.

Olivia nodded at Brian. "It doesn't work like that, Ebby."

"What do you mean?" Ebby asked, a bewildered look on his face.

Olivia let Brian answer.

"They're going to look for evidence that implicates you, Ebby. Their focus isn't on the truth now, it's on you."

"You'll find out what really happened," Ebby said. "You and Brian. We'll get to the bottom of this."

"Do you remember anything that happened yesterday? What about the events leading up to you being taken to hospital?" Olivia asked.

"I don't remember confessing to killing my mother or being taken to the hospital."

97

A sheriff's deputy came in. "I need to take him, ma'am. The nurse needs to evaluate him, so we can finish processing him."

"Don't talk to anyone, Ebby. I'll see you tomorrow morning."

Ebby stood waiting for the sheriff's deputy to lead him back to his cell. "I trust you, Olivia. I know you'll make this right."

After Ebby was led away, and Olivia and Brian were alone in the tiny room, Olivia said, "He doesn't seem the least bit worried."

"Wait until he spends the night in jail. That'll get his attention."

As they walked toward Brian's car, Olivia said, "We should have an investigation plan. Thoughts on where to start?"

"From the beginning. We should talk to Ebby's family members, not only to see what they remember of the night Cynthia died, but to get a list of other people who might know something. Cynthia Engstrom had enemies. Who were they? And where were they on December 28th, 1984?"

"I'll draft a discovery request and a motion to suppress Ebby's confession. That way I can file it tomorrow after his bail hearing. Once we get discovery from the DA, we can make a cohesive plan."

"Agreed," Brian said.

"Don't you think it was a bit rash to arrest Ebby just based on a crazed confession? I can understand why that would raise a red flag and cause the police to investigate, but the arrest seems a bit overzealous."

"My thoughts exactly."

"Something's not right about this," Olivia said.

They rode the rest of the way home in silence. Just as Brian was about to drop Olivia off, he said, "I'd like for you to have lunch with Leanne and me tomorrow after Ebby's bail hearing. At The Left Bank. I know you're going to be busy and your head's going to be wrapped up in Ebby's case, but you need to eat, right?"

Olivia hesitated. Ever since she started practicing law, Olivia had made it a point – weather and schedule permitting – to take a walk after a court appearance. Sometimes she'd sneak her walk in on the lunch recess, changing into sneakers and a sweatshirt in her car. She used the time to clear her head and step away from the inevitable conflict inherent in all litigation. One of the benefits of being a solo practitioner was the freedom to carve the time to take her walks, and over the years, the post-court stroll had become an important thing to her.

"For me," Brian said.

Deciding she could take her walk after lunch, she smiled at Brian, wishing she could kiss him. "For you? Of course."

Chapter 13

Olivia

Given the full arraignment docket, Olivia wasn't able to see Ebby on Tuesday morning prior to his case being called. While she waited in the spectator seating, along with a handful of other lawyers – recognizable by the papers they studied and their nonchalant attitude about the proceedings – Olivia paid attention to the cases that were arraigned before her, trying to gauge the judge's temperament. It was always good to know if she should come on like gangbusters or play it cool.

When Ebby was finally led into the courtroom, wearing the standard-issue orange jumpsuit and a look of total bewilderment, Olivia pushed her initial worries about her client's welfare away and moved to the front of the courtroom.

When Ebby's case was called, the two of them moved to the defendant's table. Olivia cast a sidelong glance at the assistant DA assigned to the case. He looked like he'd just graduated from high school – but everyone looked young to Olivia these days. When she met his eyes, he surveyed her from head to toe, not bothering to hide his sarcastic smirk. Ebby stood by her side, anxiety coming off him in waves as the clerk called the case and the judge summarized the charges. "Let's enter appearances and the plea for the record."

"Seth Woodson for the People."

"Olivia Sinclair, for the defendant, Your Honor." She braced herself for the inevitable flash of recognition at her name following the events of the previous October. However, the judge didn't react, rather he stared at the file before him. Finally, he looked up. "Your plea, Mr. Engstrom?"

Ebby cleared his throat. "Most definitely not guilty," he said.

"Let's hear from the People on bail."

The ADA rose and buttoned his jacket before he addressed the court. "We request remand, Your Honor. The defendant confessed to murdering his mother in front of nearly one hundred witnesses."

"Mrs. Sinclair?"

"The murder at issue took place over thirty years ago when the defendant was only a child. Mr. Engstrom has never been in trouble with the law. Mr. Engstrom was thirteen years old when he witnessed his mother's murder. Since that time he's had dissociative amnesia. His memories are starting to come back and they are affecting him. Mr. Engstrom doesn't even remember confessing. He collapsed and was rushed to the hospital, after which he was treated for exhaustion and dehydration. The DA was overzealous in his enthusiasm—"

"Let's save all that for trial, Mrs. Sinclair. Bail is set at $500,000. The defendant is to surrender his passport. The case will be referred to the criminal calendar for assignment of a judge and a scheduling conference."

"Thank you, Your Honor," Olivia said. With a nod, Seth Woodson grabbed his briefcase and walked out of the courtroom. The entire proceeding had taken less than two minutes, leaving Olivia feeling like she had just stepped off a rapidly spinning merry-go-round.

"Do I come with you now?" Ebby asked.

"You'll go with the deputy and be processed out. Elodie's here to take care of that. I have to go to the clerk's office. I'll talk to you outside, okay?"

Ebby nodded and allowed himself to be led away.

* * *

After Olivia filed her motion to suppress Ebby's confession and her request for discovery, she stepped into the hallway of the civic center, her mind occupied with the things she needed to do to prepare Ebby's defense, including finding a forensic psychologist who was conversant in dissociative amnesia, when she walked right into Seth Woodson.

"Mr. Woodson. Can I talk to you privately?"

Seth Woodson once again gave Olivia the once-over. He actually started at her feet and worked his way up her body, judging her like a piece of meat. She nearly recoiled, but didn't want to alienate him so early in the case. "What about?"

"The case," Olivia said, biting back her irritation.

"Follow me," he said. Olivia trailed behind Mr. Woodson as he hurried her along to the wing that housed the District Attorney's office. They walked past a row of secretarial desks, until they wound up in a conference room, with banker's boxes stacked against one wall and papers scattered all over the table. Once they were inside, Seth closed the door. He didn't sit down, nor did he invite Olivia to sit. "What do you want?"

"Have you done any investigation into the circumstances of this case? The arrest seems a bit hasty from where I'm sitting."

"Your case is a dog, Mrs. Sinclair. Your client's guilty."

"Aren't you interested in the truth? Someone got away with murder thirty years ago. I thought you'd want to put the right person behind bars."

"I'm interested in taking you to school, Mrs. Sinclair. You're a murderer. You killed a young girl out of jealousy. You should have been disbarred." He smiled and gazed at Olivia with cold empty eyes. "I'm looking forward to kicking your ass in trial."

"Do you make it a practice to try and intimidate opposing counsel? Or do you just save that for the female lawyers?"

Olivia knew the Marin County District Attorney, Gwen Kyleson, had zero patience for sexism. She was gratified to see Seth wince at her words. But he recovered in a heartbeat.

"From where I'm sitting, you've got a guilty client who's gullible enough to hire an inexperienced second-rate divorce lawyer. Do your client a favor and let him get someone with experience."

Olivia gave Seth a smile so open and genuine and full of goodwill that Seth actually took a step away from her. "Here's my motion to suppress. Have a nice day."

* * *

Olivia headed out into the January chill, surprised to see Elodie and Ebby braving the weather as they waited by her car. Ebby looked like something the cat had dragged in, and even though Elodie was dressed appropriately for court in a black dress and sensible shoes, there was no denying the worry lines etched around her eyes.

"I hope you haven't been waiting long?" Olivia said.

"No," Ebby said. "I needed to be in the fresh air."

Olivia understood. She remembered her night in jail not so long ago. "Are you okay, Ebby? You look like you could do with a good nap."

"I'll be fine." Not missing a beat, he added, "What are we going to do, Olivia? How are we going to investigate?"

"*We* aren't doing anything. There's no we. Do you understand? Here's what I propose. Ebby, I think you need to eat a good meal and catch up on your sleep. I'm betting you haven't closed your eyes, have you?"

"No," Ebby admitted. "It's noisy in there."

"Let's meet first thing tomorrow morning, okay? At that time, I'll answer your questions, tell you what I know, and discuss trial strategy. I have a plan. Right now, you need to rest and get healthy so you can help me defend you."

"That sounds like a good idea," Elodie said.

"Okay," Ebby agreed. "I'm going to Felicity's. You have my cell."

"Good idea. We'll discuss everything tomorrow. My office, nine o'clock, okay?"

They nodded, then headed to their car. Olivia sat in her car, her stomach in knots as she watched Ebby and Elodie drive away through the rearview mirror. The divorce cases she had handled in the past often boiled down to a battle of expert witnesses, accountants who dealt with finances, and psychologists who dealt with child custody and visitation rights. The entire process, of course, was laced with legal maneuverings and manipulations. That was the nature of the business. And although the stakes were high in divorce cases, especially when children were involved, criminal law was a completely different beast. Criminal law, it seemed, was going to be a dog fight.

Olivia punched in Brian's number. He answered on the first ring. "Ebby's out of jail."

"That's good," Brian said. "How is he?"

"Tired. He's coming to the office tomorrow morning. I told him to go home and get some sleep now."

"Sound advice. See you at The Left Bank?"

"I'll be there," Olivia said.

They hung up and Olivia headed south on 101 toward Larkspur, to the dreaded lunch with Brian and his new girlfriend.

Chapter 14

Olivia

Tuesday, January 6

The last thing Olivia wanted to do was eat lunch with Brian and Leanne. For the briefest moment, she thought about begging off, claiming a headache and promising to have lunch another time. That way she could go for a walk and turn her attention to Ebby's case. But she'd made a commitment to Brian. She needed to show up, have lunch, and put this attempt at polite society – insofar as Leanne was concerned – behind her.

Situated on Magnolia Avenue, down the street from Olivia's office, The Left Bank was her go-to restaurant. Given the restaurant's excellent food, and its proximity to her house and office, Olivia had ordered takeout so often lately she was on a first-name basis with the staff. The hostess smiled when she saw Olivia and greeted her by name. "I'd offer to take your coat, but your party is eating outside."

Given Brian's penchant for sitting outdoors when it was cold, Olivia wasn't surprised. The day was a perfect combination of bright sunshine and winter chill. Brian and Leanne sat with their heads together in conversation. Brian smiled, as though he and Leanne had shared a secret, and suddenly Olivia felt like an interloper. Leanne was bundled up in a coat and hat and had even had the foresight to wear fingerless gloves. From a distance, they looked like any other happy couple, chatting easily and drinking coffee out of steaming mugs. Plastering a fake smile on her face, Olivia took a courageous step toward them.

"Sorry I'm late," she said. "Long line at the clerk's office."

"No problem," Brian said.

"Brian told me you got your client out of jail," Leanne said. "Congratulations."

Ever the gentleman, Brian stood and came around to pull Olivia's chair out for her. "How's Ebby holding up?"

"He looks a little rough, but a good night's sleep will put him right," Olivia said. She picked up her menu and pretended to read, even though she already knew every item on it by heart.

"I'm glad you made it today, Olivia," Leanne said. "I know you must be really busy right now. How does it feel to be back to work?"

Olivia smiled. "Not sure. I feel like I dove into the deep end today."

They were interrupted when the waitress came and took Olivia's order – salad niçoise and a cup of chamomile tea – and the conversation flowed. After asking Olivia a handful of questions about her career as a lawyer, Leanne recited her entire history without any prompting, not noticing that she was doing most of the talking. By the time dessert came, Olivia knew that Leanne grew up in San Francisco, went to Galileo High School, and moved to Los Angeles to attend nursing school, where she lived with an aunt.

She had married and lived most of her life in Minnesota, but moved back to California when her husband died. She now worked as a travel nurse, and, much to her delight, she would be working at Marin General Hospital for the foreseeable future. "And I've just rented a condo right across from the hospital on the water. The view is stunning. I'd love to have you both over for dinner one night."

"That sounds great," Olivia said.

Leanne picked up her glass of water. "To new friends. I'm so glad to know you, Olivia."

Something was different about Brian and Leanne today. Olivia noticed the way their hands brushed, the way Brian put his arm around the back of Leanne's chair, a gesture of casual intimacy that spoke volumes. *They've slept together.* Olivia reeled at the realization and felt her stomach turn as a vision of Brian and Leanne writhing in passion ran across her mind's eye.

"Liv, are you okay?" Brian interrupted Leanne mid-sentence.

"I'm fine," Olivia lied. "Just thinking about the case." She picked at her salad, no longer hungry.

* * *

Glad to get away from Leanne and Brian, Olivia hurried home, changed into her walking clothes, and headed back into the congested midday traffic on Magnolia Avenue, Larkspur's version of Main Street. The sidewalk tables outside the local patisserie were filled with people dressed for the cold. Some read the newspaper, some wrote in journals. A group of young women sat around a table, each of them holding a small dog in their lap. Although Olivia preferred walking on the Tiburon bike path, with its spectacular view of the Golden Gate, today she opted for the path near Marin General Hospital. It didn't have a view of the bay, but it was closer to home, and the view of Mt. Tam would do just fine.

Olivia sat in the line of cars at a stop light, thinking that after her walk she would spend the afternoon reading the medical examiner's report from Cynthia's murder, and finding a forensic psychologist, when she noticed Brian's car ahead of her. When the light turned green, Brian turned toward the hospital. Olivia realized he must be on his way to drop Leanne off at work. Olivia, who often parked in the lower lot at the hospital when she went walking, followed Brian, careful to keep her distance so as not to be seen. When Brian pulled into the road that led to the upper parking lot and the hospital's main entrance, Olivia pulled into the lower lot and parked in her usual place. From her vantage point, she saw Leanne lean over and kiss Brian's cheek before she got out of his car and headed into the hospital for her shift. Olivia ducked when Brian drove past her car.

She took her time putting on her coat and checking that her keys were zipped in her wallet. She was just about to get out of the car, when she caught sight of Leanne in her rearview mirror, coming down the stairs toward the lower parking lot. Not wanting to attract attention, Olivia sat still as Leanne got into a shabby Honda Accord and drove away.

* * *

Olivia's living room was at its best in the afternoon, when the bright light flooded the huge picture windows that overlooked Mt. Tamalpais. Her walk hadn't been as relaxing as she had hoped. Her mind strayed to Leanne and the way she'd sped out of the hospital parking lot in the car that Olivia believed was in the shop. She dropped her hat and gloves on the hall table, put the kettle on, and lit the gas log fireplace. Once she was situated on the sofa, she tried to focus on making a to-do list for Ebby's case, but gave up after about ten minutes.

Sipping her tea, Olivia booted up her computer and went to the website for the California nursing board. Clicking through to the consumer section, she followed the drop-down menu that said *verify a license* and entered Leanne Stoddard. Three names popped up: a Leanne Stoddard who was deceased as of January

18, 2012, a Louise Engle-Stoddard, whose license was inactive, and finally there was a Nina Marie Stoddart, who resided in Colorado. There were no other Stoddards listed.

Olivia tried to come up with a legitimate reason as to why Leanne Stoddard wouldn't be listed on the nursing board's website, but couldn't think of any. If she was a nurse in California, she would need a license. If she had a license, it would be listed on the website. Wouldn't it? Was Olivia just being petty and jealous because of her feelings for Brian? Maybe Leanne was using her married name for her nursing license.

"Stop it, Olivia! You're acting like a fool!"

Her phone rang. *Unknown number* flashed across the screen.

"Olivia Sinclair," she said.

"Olivia? This is Fiona Engstrom. Is it convenient for us to meet? I'd very much like to speak to you. Are you at your office? I'll come to you, if you'd like."

"Sure. I can meet you at my office in about ten minutes, if that's convenient for you?"

"Not a problem," Fiona said. "See you then."

* * *

Olivia recalled her mother, God rest her soul, used to say that there were times when Fiona Engstrom looked exactly like Queen Elizabeth. Although Olivia hadn't thought that at the party, today was a different story. Fiona stood near the office door, dressed in a wool coat, scarf, and brooch, with wisps of gray hair curled around her face. The resemblance to the queen was uncanny.

"Olivia. Thank you for all you've done for us, especially for Ebby. My sister's beside herself with worry, but I know she'd be even worse if it weren't for you. You've been a comfort to her and Ebby, and I appreciate it."

As Olivia went to unlock the door, she noticed the box on the ground. Despite her age, Fiona picked it up easily, hoisted it onto her hip, and followed Olivia into the office.

"Would you like me to carry that?" Olivia offered.

"No, thank you."

"Come on back," Olivia said. "I can make you tea?"

"Oh, no. Not necessary. I've a couple things to say, a couple things to give you, and then I'll be on my way."

Olivia turned on the lights as she walked down the hall to her office. "I'm in here." She flipped the thermostat, took a seat at her desk, and waited while Fiona Engstrom put the box on one of the two guest chairs and sat down on the other."

"Despite what my nephew thinks he remembers, he most certainly did not murder his mother."

"I agree," Olivia said. "I think we can all agree that he's not a killer."

"Now that he's been arrested, you'll need proof of his innocence. I have it in this box." She patted the lid of the banker's box. "If you look at the medical examiner's report from the original investigation, you will see that Ebby couldn't have physically committed this crime. I'll let you read the report on your own. When you read it, you'll see that Ebby wasn't tall enough to have stabbed his mother in the chest and throat. At the time of the murder, he was only 5'2" tall."

Fiona lifted the banker's box from the chair onto Olivia's desk. She lifted the top and started stacking file after file.

"What's this?" Olivia asked.

"This, my dear, is the original investigation file from Cynthia's murder. A friend at the sheriff's office gave me copies in 1999, when I hired a private investigator after the case went cold."

"You hired an investigator?"

"What else could I do? The police thought someone in my family murdered Cynthia. When the case went cold, I hired a private investigator to see if he could come up with something the police missed, maybe something to at least exonerate my family. My belief is that the murder had something to do with those coins. I've also given you every newspaper clipping related to the case. I thought the historical and social context might be helpful. I think it would be prudent for your investigator to start fresh, investigate each one of us. My nephew Mark, although the favored child, was driving Cynthia to the brink of madness."

"Do you think he could have killed his mother?"

"I don't know. But we'd be remiss not to suspect him, wouldn't we? In fact, of all the family members, I would say he has the best motive."

"What motive?" Olivia asked.

"Money, of course. Cynthia had grown tired of bailing Mark out financially and she made noises about changing her will. But I'm not going to influence you, Olivia. You need to conduct your investigation the way you see fit." She pointed to the tall stack of files. "In those files, you will find everything the police did in the original investigation."

Olivia took a file off the top of the stack and thumbed through its contents. There were police reports, witness statements, an autopsy report, and a myriad of photographs. She had picked up her pen earlier to take notes during the meeting, and now she wrote furiously. "Do you remember off the top of your head who the medical examiner was? I'd like to try to talk to him."

"It's on the report. I remember he was very young at the time. My recollection is that he was quite shaken by the violence."

Olivia eyed the box. She wanted Fiona to leave, so she could go through its contents by herself, without Fiona hovering and giving advice.

"Do you mind if I ask you a couple of questions?"

"Not at all. But I want to tell you three things first. Number one, I know the police think a family member murdered Cynthia. I don't agree, as we discussed. What I would like to add is that the coins – the British sovereigns that my brother collected – were valuable. There were a dozen or so extremely rare coins in the collection. And my brother was proud of them. So people were aware of them.

"Number two, I had an alibi that night, just in case you were going to ask." Fiona stared at her lap for a moment, as if gathering her thoughts. "Did you know I had a lover?"

The revelation startled Olivia.

"I didn't think so. His name was Herbert Hemmings. Bertie. The love of my life. He was married. It was the perfect situation for me. No strings, no man telling me what to do. Just friendship, sex, companionship, and then I was left to my own devices. We were together the night Cynthia was murdered. We had dinner at The Hilltop in Novato and then we went back to the beach."

Fiona paused, giving Olivia time to catch up with her note taking.

"That night, Herbert insisted on driving home, over the hill to his house in Mill Valley. They think he fell asleep at the wheel …"

Olivia stopped writing and looked up at Fiona. Tears welled up in her eyes. She took a handkerchief out of her purse and dabbed her tears. "I don't mean to get maudlin. That was thirty years ago. I've learned to live with my loss, but it stings sometimes." Fiona gave Olivia a sheepish smile.

"I'm so sorry," Olivia said.

"Thank you, Olivia. You always were a kind soul."

Fiona stood. "I'm hoping that no one in my family is a murderer, Olivia. You and I both know Edward – Ebby – is innocent. You must discover who did this, so Ebby can be free."

"What do you think happened to the sovereigns?" she asked.

"Sold. Probably to some private collector." Fiona met her eyes. There was no mistaking the steely determination there.

I pity anyone who gets on this woman's bad side. Olivia waited, knowing Fiona had something else to say.

"And thirdly, there's something else, something I don't like to speak about. But I'm going to tell you in the spirit of full disclosure. It probably has nothing to do with Ebby's situation, but one never knows. And you may well find this out on your own, and I won't be accused of keeping things back. Cynthia Engstrom and I were very close childhood friends." Fiona stood. "Thank you for meeting me, Olivia. I am glad we have you helping Ebby."

The two women shook hands, and Olivia walked Fiona to the door. After she left, Olivia sat at her desk contemplating what kind of woman Cynthia Engstrom really was.

Chapter 15

Ebby

Ebby and Elodie were silent in the car on the way home from jail. Last night had been the worst experience Ebby had ever gone through, and if he closed his eyes, he could smell the tiny cell he had stayed in, a nauseating combination of urine, fried food, and disinfectant. There was no sleeping. Inmates were calling out to each other, not caring that they kept others awake. Now all he wanted to do was sleep.

Elodie kept casting glances at him. She hadn't wanted him to go to Felicity's and had tried to convince him to stay with her. Even though he loved her more than anyone else, her smothering concern was too much for him to deal with, as he navigated this fresh set of circumstances. He had to make plans. On his own. Last night had been a sobering wake-up call. At first, he was willing to accept that he might have murdered his mother – why else had he confessed? He was willing to accept the consequences, believing the truth about her murder would set him free.

114

He wondered if he'd made a mistake going off his medication and turning his back on the psychiatric help that he probably needed. He needed sleep and then he needed answers.

"Oh, no," Elodie said. "That didn't take long."

The journos were already encamped by the gates at the main driveway. Ebby ducked, just in case, as Elodie drove by the main entrance and turned down the dirt road that led to their respective houses. So far the reporters hadn't discovered this part of the property, but it would only be a matter of time.

"You can park at yours and I'll walk the trail. If they've discovered my cottage, I'll just come back to you and wait for Felicity there," Ebby said.

"Be careful," Elodie said. She pulled her car up next to the trailer and turned off the engine.

"I want to thank you, Elodie, for everything you've done for me. Thank you for suggesting I hire Olivia, for arranging bail, for everything." Ebby was dismayed to see a lone tear roll down Elodie's wrinkled cheek.

"Why won't you stay with me? I can care for you as well as Felicity can."

Ebby met Elodie's gaze and held it. "I don't need caring for. Not anymore. I need to find out what happened to my mother, and then I need to think about my life."

Elodie took a wrinkled tissue from her coat pocket and dabbed at her tears. "I understand."

Ebby took his car key off his key ring. "Can you just move the car to your trailer within the next couple of days? I'll come and get it as soon as I can."

Once he was at his cottage, Ebby sent a quick text to Felicity, saying he would be ready to be picked up in fifteen minutes. He took a moment and stood in the living room, saying goodbye to the place he had called home for so many years. Funny how the cottage that he had built with his own sweat no longer felt like a sanctuary. Now all he wanted to do was pack his meager belongings – Ebby had never been an accumulator of stuff – and get away.

Using a footstool, he opened the closet near the front door and pulled down his big suitcase from the top shelf. He was just about to haul it into his bedroom, when the front door opened and Melinda stood on the threshold.

"Ebby?"

He nearly gasped when he saw her eye was bruised and swollen shut. "Melinda? You startled me." Melinda had once again taken a beating from her husband and Ebby had a good idea why.

"Sorry. I saw Elodie's car drive by the house. You saw the reporters there?" Melinda shivered and drew her jacket tighter around her. "I wanted to make sure you were okay."

"Why did Mark hit you?"

"He was pretty angry with you, Ebs. You confessed to murder in front of all of our guests."

"Your guests? It was Elodie's party."

"You know what I mean."

"I don't understand why Mark hit you after I confessed. What have you got to do with it? Why do you stay with him?"

"Why did you confess to murdering your mother?" Melinda countered. "Have you remembered something from that night?"

As a young boy, Ebby had always thought Melinda was pretty, with her heart-shaped face and bright blue eyes. Now her hair had grown lank, her skin sallow. She ate a like a bird, so her cheekbones were too prominent, giving her eyes a fevered, haunted look. Ebby felt sorry for Melinda. Life with Mark had taken its toll.

Melinda followed Ebby into the bedroom and watched as he folded his clothes and put them in his suitcase. "Where are you going?" Melinda asked.

Ebby ignored her. He didn't have many clothes, and packing didn't take long. He made his way into the living room and pulled his favorite books off the shelves: *Hike Your Own Hike*, *A Confederacy of Dunces*, and six leather-bound journals, old and weathered from the many times Ebby had read them, filled with his father's essays and sketches.

"Ebby? Where are you going?" Melinda asked again.

"I'm not going to tell you," Ebby said.

"Why?" Melinda insisted. "We love you. Mark and I both care about you."

Ebby laughed.

Melinda wrung her hands. "I know that Mark loves you and only wants what's best for you."

"You actually believe that?"

"You're being a little harsh, don't you think? We should all sit down and talk. This hasn't been easy on Mark and me. Yesterday the police came to the house and searched the attic. They were there for hours."

Suspicious now, and certain that Melinda had an agenda, he turned to her. "Talk about what? You're obviously here because Mark wants me to do something. Tell me what."

Melinda swallowed, her eyes darting side to side. "Ebby, if you murdered your mother, you did so as a minor. Mark thinks – and I agree – that you should plead guilty and let Olivia get you a short sentence. I bet she could make this go away. I mean, look at you. You're a successful man, you contribute to society. I'm sure this can all be resolved without much fuss and embarrassment to the family. You could serve your sentence and we could all move on."

"I was unwell when I confessed, Melinda, and have yet to see any evidence of my guilt. But just so I'm clear, you basically want me to plead guilty to a crime I may not have committed so you and Mark won't be too inconvenienced?" Ebby kept his voice impassive and maintained his control when Melinda let out a long sigh of relief.

"Yes. Doesn't that make the most sense? We can slip under the radar and save face. Olivia's a good lawyer. I bet you wouldn't even have to go to jail. Maybe you could be on – what do they call it? – house arrest, or something like that."

"I'd like you to leave," Ebby said. When Melinda didn't budge, he said, "Now! Please." Once she was out of his house, he called after her, "You can tell Mark that I'm going to find out who killed our mother, whether he likes it or not."

He shut the door and locked it.

Ebby and Mark's relationship had always been strained. From the Olympian vantage point of adulthood, Ebby realized his aunts had protected him from Mark's bullying, conspiring to make sure he wasn't left alone with his mean-spirited brother. Despite their valiant efforts, Mark always managed to get his jabs in. He was the type of brother who looted Ebby's piggy bank and stole his Willie Mays baseball card. Ebby knew this because he found the card in Mark's desk drawer. At the time, he had reclaimed the card and hidden it in his room so Mark couldn't steal it again.

As adults, Ebby and Mark's relationship had only deteriorated further, perhaps due to sibling rivalry. But Ebby didn't see Mark as a rival. At one time, he had even looked up to his older brother, had tried to gain Mark's approval. It hadn't worked. Every time he trusted Mark with a secret or a dream, Mark would betray him or embarrass him, and take a sick pleasure in the process. By the time he was ten years old, Ebby knew the best course of action was to stay clear of his older brother.

The two brothers couldn't have been more different. Mark wore Italian suits to work and promised to turn his friends into millionaires. Ebby earned his living cooking for people, working shoulder to shoulder with employees he loved like family, and spent his spare time surfing and riding his mountain bike in the Marin County hills. In the spirit of family, Ebby had tried to extend the olive branch to Mark on more than one occasion, but every attempt at friendship had been rebuffed. Mark had never eaten at The No Name Diner, and, as far as Ebby could remember, hadn't uttered a kind word in ages. Despite Ebby's success, Mark still treated Ebby as though he were damaged, incapable of managing his own affairs.

118

And now Mark wanted Ebby to take the blame for a murder he didn't commit, so Mark could *save face*. Disgusted, Ebby grabbed his suitcase and hurried out the front door, eager to be away from his family once and for all.

Chapter 16

Olivia

After the bail hearing, lunch with Brian and Leanne, and a text from Ebby saying he was at Felicity's and was looking forward to seeing her in the morning, Olivia couldn't wait to cocoon herself at home. The sun was just going down as she sat before the fire, a mug of tea in hand, and the files from Fiona arranged on the coffee table in front of her. Starting with the newspaper articles, Olivia read the carefully cut out sheets of yellowed paper, worn thin with age. Many were faded and barely legible, but once Olivia started reading about the murder and the valuable coins that were taken that night, she was hooked. She blitzed through all the articles, making notes of important people who might be relevant to Ebby's case, before she turned her attention to the police files. Although the information contained in the investigation notes wasn't as entertaining – or sensational – as the newspaper articles, Olivia felt as though she had hit the mother lode.

Picking up the photos of the crime scene, Olivia cast her

mind to what she knew about the actual murder. She had read somewhere that stabbing in the face and throat spoke to the killer's rage. Based on this theory, Olivia discounted the idea that Cynthia Engstrom's murder was the result of a robbery gone awry. The murder had been too violent, too personal. The question remained: who hated Cynthia Engstrom enough to murder her?

They'd have to start at the beginning – at the foundation, as Brian liked to call it. Olivia knew that in the spirit of leaving no stone left unturned, Brian would investigate every single family member. He wouldn't be satisfied until he cleared them himself. He'd start with Ebby, of course, and methodically work his way through all the family members. Olivia thought of Mark's aggression at the party. Mark had always been a bully. Like all bullies, he was a coward underneath. Did he have the nerve to murder his mother and steal the gold coins? Could he have driven home, committed the crime, and driven back to Lake Tahoe? Olivia shook her head. These tangents weren't helpful. And as much as Olivia didn't like Mark, she couldn't see him doing the killing. To her mind, it didn't fit.

Fiona, Elodie, and Mark had all given statements that a sterling silver ornamental dagger with semiprecious stones bezel set into the hilt had gone missing after the murder. The police had speculated, and the ME confirmed in his findings, that this dagger was likely used to murder Cynthia Engstrom.

Olivia put all the files back in order, her Post-it Notes flagging important documents.

The speculation about the coins captivated her, much as they had captivated the public at the time of the murder. On a whim, Olivia picked up her cell phone and called her friend Vonnie Wilson. Vonnie had spent the bulk of her adult life working for the jewelry department at Sotheby's in London, and she traveled between Geneva and Hong Kong to facilitate the auctions of some of the finest jewelry in the world. Now she worked privately, finding gems and treasures for a handful of clients who preferred to keep their collections private and their purchases of art and jewelry a secret. Vonnie had her finger on the pulse of private collectors, and with any luck, would be able to help Olivia.

"Olivia?" Vonnie answered after the first ring. "How have you been? It's so nice to hear from you. I've been out of the country since the end of November, and I'm just now catching up on returning phone calls. I was going to call you and see if you wanted to go to the ballet. It's *Peter and the Wolf*, a matinee, but the seats are good. My tickets are for the 15th of February."

"I'd love to go to the ballet, and I'm doing well," Olivia said. "I know you're busy, but I'm actually calling for some information and maybe a favor. Do you remember the Cynthia Engstrom murder in 1984?"

"Of course I do. Wasn't there a treasure, a cache of gold or something? Wait. I remember now. The elusive duffel bag full of gold coins. Nineteenth-century sovereigns, if I remember correctly."

"I was wondering if you know how I could find out if any of the stolen coins have been purchased by a private collector? I know it's a long shot, but any help would be appreciated."

Olivia heard papers being rustled and voices in the background.

"Definitely a long shot, but let me ask around, okay? There's a cadre of fellows who collect rare sovereigns. I'm leaving for Hong Kong Monday. I'll poke around and email you if I hear anything. Mark your calendar for Sunday the 15th of February for the ballet. I'll drive and take you someplace swanky for lunch. I need to run."

"Thanks, Vonnie," Olivia said.

She knew there was little chance of Vonnie finding out anything helpful, but there was always some hope, and to top it off, Olivia had got an invitation to the ballet. Win-win as far as she was concerned.

An email from Brian popped into Olivia's inbox. *Confirming receipt of email. Can we get together at your house before your meeting with Ebby? I have something I need to discuss with you.*

Something about the tone of the email gave Olivia pause. The missive lacked the usual informal bonhomie that she and Brian shared. She wrote back quickly. *Of course. See you at eight?*

Seconds later Brian wrote back: *Okay.*

She shook her head and chastised herself for trying to interpret the tone of an electronic communication, but Brian had never been so abrupt with her. Something was wrong. She could feel it. Sometimes she missed the old days when people would actually talk to each other.

* * *

Wednesday, January 7

Olivia woke up to gentle rain on her roof that had turned into a full deluge by the time she showered and poured coffee. The damp gray weather suited her mood. At exactly eight o'clock, Brian pulled up in front of the house. Olivia watched from the kitchen window as Brian got out of the car and walked toward the front door, his mouth pursed into a tight thin line. He didn't use an umbrella and the rain clung to his too-long hair, causing it to curl at the neck.

"Come in. Coffee?"

"No, thanks." He followed her into the living room.

"Have a seat." Olivia sat back down on the couch and curled her legs underneath her.

Brian remained standing. "What's up with Leanne?"

Olivia felt her cheeks go hot. "What do you mean?"

"Come on, Liv. I know you. You were polite at lunch – you're always polite – but I could tell something was up. Why don't you like her?" He stood with his back to her, staring out her window at the gray rain mingled with the green of King Mountain.

"Brian, I need to tell you—"

"I don't regret that night, Olivia," Brian said at the same time. When he turned to face her, Olivia saw his anguish and knew how difficult this conversation was for him. "I don't regret those few weeks you let me stay here after my house burned down. You're so easy to be with. I thought of a future with you, still do, if I'm honest. But you had just been betrayed in a horrible way by a man you trusted for three decades."

Olivia felt the hot tears well in her eyes.

Brian ran his hands through his hair. "It would have been really easy for us to fall into a relationship, but when you stepped away, I didn't know what to do, didn't know how to say how I felt. I wanted to tell you – I've wanted to say that I wanted to pursue this feeling between us." Brian shook his head. "I can't do casual, Olivia. Not with you. And I thought we both needed time. I didn't want to be – what do they call it? – the rebound person. And God knows I have my own issues with Maureen. I'm not ready to let myself go with someone."

"Are you falling in love with Leanne?"

Brian's face softened. "No. And she's not falling in love with me. We've discussed it, and she knows my position. We're friends. Our relationship is casual. If I'm honest with myself – and with you – I got involved with her because I thought she would be leaving after her contract at Marin General was up. Believe me, I was more than a little surprised to discover she'd extended it. She's assured me she's not looking for anything serious."

Olivia rose from the couch and walked over to Brian. She stood next to him, looking out at the green hills, made more lush by the rain. "I realize what it took for you to come over here and talk to me."

He gave her a sweet smile. "Tell me why you don't like her."

"Okay. Come and sit down," Olivia said. Brian sat on the couch, while Olivia sat on the chair opposite him. "Can I ask you something?"

124

"Of course. Anything."

"What do you know about Leanne's background?"

Brian shrugged. "Let's see. Other than what she told us at lunch, she grew up in the city and married her husband while working as a nurse at Kaiser in San Francisco. He was a private pilot who broke his leg in a car accident. They fell in love, got married, and moved to Minnesota. Minneapolis, I think. Then he died of a heart attack, so Leanne moved back to the Bay Area to be near her family. She works as a travel nurse. And that's it. Why?"

"You're not going to like this," Olivia said.

Brian's brow furrowed. "Go on."

"I don't trust her, Brian. Never have. And I'm aware that those feelings could be a result of jealousy. But that's not it. There's something about her that doesn't quite seem right. Last Monday I caught Leanne snooping in your office. I swear she was going through your desk. She had one of your desk drawers open and was taking photos of paperwork with her cell phone. When she saw me, she closed the drawer and started looking through your calendar, said she was going to surprise you with a weekend away." She waited, giving Brian time to digest what she had discovered. "There's more. After lunch yesterday, I was behind you at the light when you turned to drop her off at the hospital. She said her car was in the shop, right?"

"Yes. The repair was delayed because they couldn't find the part."

"I was going to take a walk on the bike path by the hospital. You know I park in the lower lot, right? I saw Leanne get into a beat-up Honda Accord right after you dropped her off, and drive away. I would have followed her, but I was afraid she would have seen me."

Brian didn't say anything. He stared down at his feet, his body still. When he looked up at her, his eyes were incredulous.

Eager for him to believe her, Olivia continued. "I know, that's not much. After that, I couldn't let it go. I went to the California nursing board website. There is no one named Leanne Stoddard with a California nursing license."

Brian let out a long sigh. Still Olivia waited, knowing she'd just done the emotional equivalent of dropping a bomb on his personal life.

"I can show you. You can look on your phone."

"I believe you. Do you know how tempted I was to investigate Leanne's background before we went on our first date? But I told myself that was ridiculous and that I needed to learn to be more trusting. It's not like I'm going to marry her."

"After what I've been through, I think if I were going to let someone into my house, I'd run a background check on them. Maybe it's just a sign of the times or a result of Richard's betrayal, but I don't trust people anymore."

"Do you trust me?"

"Implicitly," Olivia said. "And I admit that what I just told you could easily be explained away. Maybe her nursing license is under her maiden name, maybe she had an emergency and had to leave the hospital."

"I don't think she had an emergency," Brian said.

"Well, let's give her the benefit of the doubt, okay? For now."

Brian leaned his head back on the couch and closed his eyes. Olivia noticed the underside of his strong jaw, the patch of gray stubble he'd missed when he shaved that morning. God help her, she wanted to kiss him.

"What are you going to do?" she asked.

Brian stood. "I'm going to find out what she's up to. If she has a criminal history, I'll find it." Brian looked at his watch. "We should get to the office. Ebby will be there soon." They stood and walked to the front door together. The air felt lighter between them.

"Thanks for being so open-minded," Olivia said. "I was afraid you'd not thank me for meddling."

"Ah, Liv, the trust goes both ways. I'll always consider your words." When Brian put his arm around Olivia, she leaned into him.

"She had a key to the office," Olivia realized out of the blue.

"What?"

"She said you gave it to her because your laptop was running slow and she was going to fix it for you."

"But I don't keep a laptop at the office," Brian said.

"She must have brought one with her," Olivia said. "Because she picked up the case and put it on her shoulder. I remember that."

"Quite the clever little planner, isn't she?" Brian's words mirrored Olivia's thoughts. "And as for the key, she didn't get it from me, and I haven't noticed mine missing. Unless she took it and had a key made without me knowing? I guess that's a possibility, especially because I wasn't the least bit suspicious of her. I keep my office keys in the console of my car. You gave me a key a few weeks ago, long before I needed it. I suppose she could have taken it and had a copy made. For all we know, that's not the first time she's gone snooping," Brian said. "I'll get the locks changed today. What do you think about a security camera?"

"Good idea," Olivia said.

"I'll do a little digging of my own. If she's up to something, we'll figure it out. And onto a different topic, I was going to follow Mark Engstrom this morning, unless you need me at the meeting with Ebby? I was thinking about the sovereigns and who in the Engstrom family would have the guts to steal them."

"That would be Mark."

"It's probably a dead end. If he sold the coins, then in all likelihood they are long gone. But I'm interested in how he earns his money and how he spends his days. Have you seen his website? He acts like a bigshot."

"Yet his house is falling down around him and he's desperate to sell it. Good. You go ahead. I need to talk Ebby into seeing a psychiatrist. Probably best if I do that alone." Olivia pointed at the box of documents Fiona had delivered yesterday. "You'll want to go through those as well. Once we get discovery from the DA, we can regroup."

"Are those the documents from Fiona? Great. And I have a call with my connection at the bank. I won't be able to get detailed info about Mark's banking history, but I'm hoping for some insight on his business practices."

Olivia told him about her call to Vonnie Wilson.

"That's a long shot," Brian said.

"I do like a long shot." Olivia smiled.

* * *

Ebby was waiting for Olivia at the office, looking well rested and considerably less stressed. He carried a tray that held two large paper cups.

"Good morning." She unlocked the office. Once Ebby was in, she locked the door behind them. "Let's go to my office. All the way back and to the right."

"I've brought you coffee," he said.

"You're alone today?" Olivia asked as she booted up her computer.

"Elodie wanted to come, but I need to do this on my own. I feel like I need to distance myself from my family right now." Ebby gave Olivia a sober look. "I need to know whether or not I did this, Olivia."

"Have you remembered anything else?"

Ebby shook his head. "I honestly don't think I killed my mother, but I'm fairly certain I saw who did. I just can't remember. It's so frustrating."

"Let's talk about your case." She handed Ebby a fresh pad of legal paper and a pen. "Just in case you want to take notes. The first thing I'm focused on is a motion I filed to suppress your confession. I haven't received a hearing date for that. If I can get the judge to toss your confession, the DA will have to dismiss the case."

"That's good right?"

"Yes, but I'm going to move forward as if we are going to trial," Olivia said. "I always assume the worst, that way I can be pleasantly surprised. Did you know that Fiona hired a private investigator in 1999? At that time, she somehow managed to get a copy of original investigation files from the police."

"Fiona? I had no idea. I'm assuming her investigator didn't discover anything new."

"That appears to be the case. Brian and I are going to start studying those files. We'll report to you anything that's helpful."

"Okay. What should I do?"

Olivia set her coffee down and leaned back in her chair. "With regard to your murder case, nothing for now. However, there's something I think you should do. You're not going to like this."

"You think I should see a psychiatrist," Ebby said. "I'm going to. Felicity's insisting. In fact, the only way she agreed to let me stay with her is if I went back to the doctor."

"Why did you stop going?"

"Too many prescription meds and not enough discussion about why I need them. I always left my appointments feeling like I didn't matter, like I hadn't been listened to. None of the doctors listened to me. They were more interested in the clinical issues surrounding my amnesia. Some of them were flat-out rude."

"Why don't you let me put a list together of a few doctors that I think you'll like working with? Then you can interview them," Olivia said.

"Interview them?"

"Why not? You're paying them. You're the patient."

Ebby smiled. "I never thought of it that way."

Olivia wrote the names of five psychologists and three psychiatrists on a sheet of paper, tore it off and handed it to Ebby. "These are who I would see if I needed help. The last three are medical doctors, so they can help with medication. The first five are psychologists. You need fresh eyes and fresh ears, Ebs. Call them. Find one you like."

"Okay," Ebby said. "Should we meet again in a few days?"

"Let me go through Fiona's files and get discovery from the DA. Once I have that, I'll call."

"You'll find out the truth, won't you? If I killed my mother, you'll tell me? Promise."

"I promise, Ebby."

"If I did it, I'll plead guilty."

"Let's not get ahead of ourselves," Olivia said.

Chapter 17

Brian

Wednesday, January 7

Despite being glamorized on television, surveillance work in reality involved hours of sitting, doing nothing, and – at least to Brian's way of thinking – drinking endless cups of coffee. He sat outside Mark Engstrom's office in the high-rent district in Mill Valley, lucky enough to grab a parking place that allowed him to see Mark's office and brand-new BMW. All that was left to do was watch. And wait.

With time on his hands, Brian thought about Olivia's snooping into Leanne's background. For the briefest moment he'd been irritated that she'd gone behind his back. He let his anger go when he realized that if the tables were turned, he would have done exactly the same thing. As he waited, Brian used his cell phone to search the California nursing board's website. Olivia was right. There was no evidence that Leanne had a nursing license in California.

Pushing those thoughts away for now, he turned his focus to

the case at hand and continued reading the newspaper articles he had copied from Fiona's file. The story of Cynthia Engstrom's murder read like a 1950s film noir. According to one reporter, the crime had been a brutal bloodbath that spoke of an eruption of stifled rage, while another, entitled BLOODY GOLD, speculated the crime had been all about the massive quantities of gold sovereigns that were stolen and never recovered.

Suspicious of any facts gleaned from this sensational nonsense, Brian stuffed the newspapers aside. As he turned his attention to the actual investigation reports, he realized information about the likely murder weapon – a jeweled dagger that had been used as a letter opener – had been kept from the press on purpose.

Brian's stomach had started to rumble when Mark Engstrom strolled out of his office at 11:35 and drove to Il Fornaio, one of Brian's favorite haunts. The restaurant was housed in a busy shopping center, so Brian was able to follow Mark into the restaurant and take his usual seat at the bar without being seen. The bartender knew Brian by sight and had a glass of his favorite Pinot Noir waiting for him when he sat down. Brian had no intention of drinking the wine, but he thanked the bartender anyway.

"The usual, Mr. Vickery?"

"Please," Brian said. He ate his Caesar salad and capellini al pomodoro – angel hair pasta with an exquisite tomato sauce – all the while keeping his eyes on Mark Engstrom and the long-legged brunette who had been waiting for him at his table. Three waiters hovered around Mark's table, giving him the full VIP treatment. One of them opened a bottle of Dom Perignon with a flourish. After pouring two glasses, he left so another waiter could swoop in with fresh bread and the exquisite olive oil the restaurant used in lieu of butter. After that waiter scurried away, a third stepped up to the table to take their lunch order.

Once he was gone, Mark lifted his glass to the brunette and uttered a toast. They clinked glasses. Mark drank greedily and finished his champagne in one swallow, while the woman across from him touched the glass to her lips, barely taking a sip. Soon the waiter brought out their antipasto. He refilled Mark's glass. The brunette covered her glass with her hand and shook her head to signal no when the waiter offered her more champagne.

Mark tucked his tie over his shoulder and dug into the antipasto like a greedy child. The brunette barely touched the food and Brian couldn't help but wonder if she was put off by her fellow diner's atrocious table manners. Every few minutes some random person would stop at Mark's table to chat for a few minutes. From Brian's perspective, Mark sat at his table like a king presiding over his courtiers. By the time the waiter brought out their main courses – a giant plate of pasta for Mark and a salad for the brunette – Mark Engstrom was done with social niceties. He put both of his elbows on the table while he leaned toward the brunette, talking to her while he ate, his body language enough to discourage any passerby who wanted to stop and chat. The conversation between Mark and his lunch companion seemed to be one-sided. The only time the brunette opened her mouth to speak, Mark shushed her with a scathing look and kept talking, running his mouth even though it was full of food.

After inhaling the food on his plate, Mark leaned back, picking at his teeth with his fingernail. Brian signaled his waiter and asked for his check.

By the time Mark and the brunette came out of the restaurant, Brian was tucked into his car, his binoculars at the ready, should he need them. Out of habit, he scanned the parking lot of the restaurant and noticed a gray Taurus parked out of the way, its driver watching Mark with a camera and telephone lens. Hadn't he seen a car like that near Mark's office? Focusing on the car, he saw two men. The man behind the steering wheel was holding a set of binoculars, while the man in the passenger seat held a camera with a long lens pointed at Mark Engstrom and the brunette.

When the couple approached Mark's car, the brunette waited while Mark got in and rolled down the window. After reaching across the passenger seat, Mark handed the brunette what looked like a legal-sized envelope. In the spirit of being thorough, Brian used the camera on his cell phone to take pictures of Mark and the brunette. While he was at it, he snapped a few pictures of the men in the silver Taurus. Soon Mark drove away, leaving the brunette on her own in the parking lot. To Brian's surprise, the girl walked over to the silver Taurus and handed the envelope to the man with the camera. Then she got into an old but well cared for Toyota Camry and drove away. The Taurus followed her out of the parking lot, turning toward the onramp to Highway 101.

After Brian wrote down the license numbers of the Taurus and the brunette's Camry, he sat for a few minutes, digesting all he had seen. He'd bet money the Ford Taurus was a government-issued car. Securities and Exchange Commission? FBI? He wondered if their surveillance of Mark Engstrom had anything to do with Cynthia's murder so long ago. In any event, he and Olivia would have to be careful. It seemed that bigger things were in play.

Brian cursed himself for being careless when his passenger door opened and one of the suits from the Taurus slid into the car next to him. Unbeknownst to Brian, the Taurus had doubled back and now blocked him in. The man was young; Brian guessed him to be in his early thirties. He tried to grab for Brian's phone, but Brian was quicker and grabbed his arm, twisting it to an uncomfortable angle while he tucked his phone deep into his suit pocket. "Keep your hands to yourself."

Brian let the agent wrench free of his grip – he didn't want to take away the kid's confidence – and said, "What do you want?"

"I saw you watching Mr. Engstrom. I'm telling you to back off."

"Which agency are you with? SEC? FBI? What's he done, money laundering?"

"I appreciate your curiosity, Mr. Vickery, but our interest in Mr. Engstrom need not concern you. You need to cease your investigation immediately."

Brian believed whole-heartedly in cooperating. He also had

plenty of respect for law enforcement, especially an agency designed to track down white-collar criminals, men who stole the life savings from unsuspecting hardworking people. But something about this agent's tactics, his lack of respect and need to dominate, pushed Brian's buttons and made him not want to capitulate so easily.

"I can't promise that. I'm not interested in Mr. Engstrom's financial dealings. So I'll stay out of your way. That's the best I can offer."

The agent met Brian's gaze, his baby-faced cheeks flushed.

"Sorry if I hurt your arm," Brian said. "But you did ask for it when you got in my car without permission."

"This is an informal request for you to back away from Mark Engstrom. Next time I won't play nice." The agent got out of the car, fussed with his coat, and sauntered back to the Ford Taurus. As the car pulled out of the parking lot, the agent stared at Brian, trying without success to look intimidating.

Chapter 18

Mark

Mark Engstrom returned to his office after his lunch date with the lovely and ever so corrupt Brenda Eldridge, certain he was being followed. In fact, he wouldn't have been surprised had someone been watching him while he ate his lunch. Not that he cared. After barking out an order for a single espresso to the bimbo who answered his phone and served as general dogsbody, he scurried back to his office and shut the door. Once there, he'd peered through the blinds at the street below. Sure enough, there was the same gray Taurus that he had seen in the parking lot at the restaurant. Well, he wasn't sure it was the same car, but how many Fords were there in Mill Valley, the land of Mercedes and BMWs?

Ever calculating, his thoughts strayed to his bookkeeper, Brenda, the only person who was privy to his financial shenanigans. Would she turn on him? If she had been approached by the SEC with a promise of immunity in exchange for her cooperation, would she betray him? *If I go down, she goes with me.*

Grabbing the Zeiss binoculars his father had given him for high school graduation so many years ago, Mark peered through the lenses to the car across the street and nearly toppled backwards when he saw a man using binoculars watching him. Gasping in surprise, Mark closed his blinds all the way before he repositioned the binoculars and continued to watch until another man in a cheap suit got in the passenger side and the car sped away.

A sheen of sweat had formed on Mark's face. He swiped his forehead with his shirt sleeve and cursed out loud.

"Here's your coffee. And Mr. Seymour's here."

"Mr. Seymour?"

"Your 2:30? New client? Wants to open a trust fund for his grandson?"

"Thank you. I'll let you know when I'm ready."

She didn't say anything as she closed the door and left him on his own. He was tired of the women in his life. Melinda, the bimbo, and Brenda the bookkeeper with her doom-and-gloom financial reports. Yes, he was in trouble. But he'd been in trouble before and had somehow managed to sort it all out. Reaching for a fresh button-up shirt and undershirt, he stripped naked from the waist up, went into his private washroom and splashed cold water on his face.

As he dressed, he thought of the soft-spoken man he'd met at the last fundraiser he and Melinda had attended. After doing a little digging, he'd discovered Mr. Cyril Seymour had inherited an exorbitant amount of money from a long-lost uncle. Mark smiled at himself in the mirror. With any luck, he'd get the sweet old guy to write a check for a couple of million. Everyone wanted a piece of his business. His strategy had been brilliant, keeping it exclusive, making investment opportunities by invitation only. He'd used the funds from the initial round of investors – those who never dipped into capital – to pay out exorbitant interest rates to newcomers. And, with Brenda's help, had been sending out statements every month with grossly inflated returns. Money begets money, and Mark's investors spoke of his genius to their friends. Soon he had more money than he had expected, some of which went for his management fees, some of which was simply syphoned off the top and transferred into his account in Zurich, with his clients none the wiser.

Mr. Seymour would invest. Everything would work out. If it didn't, there was always his *go strategy.* As in, use the fake passport he had hidden away at home, loot his company and go, leaving everyone else to clean up the mess.

Maybe he was being followed, but he still had the upper hand. All he had to do was walk away from it all. Back in his office, he used the intercom on his phone to buzz the bimbo. "I'm ready for Mr. Seymour."

When the bimbo disconnected without saying a word, Mark thought about how much he would enjoy firing her.

Cyril Seymour gave off the impression of physical frailty, yet his brown eyes were direct and spoke of a certain quiet intelligence that signaled Mark to pay attention and maneuver carefully. "Come in, sir," Mark said, ushering Mr. Seymour into one of his comfortable office chairs. "It's good to see you again."

"Thank you," Mr. Seymour said. Once Mark was seated, Mr. Seymour gave a gentle cough. "I felt I should come and speak to you directly, rather than leave a message. I know when we met I all but committed to investing with your firm. But I had my people do a little digging, and I'm afraid I won't be able to invest while your company is being investigated by the SEC."

Son of a bitch. "Mr. Seymour, I don't know where you got your information, but that is a misstatement. Now, if you'll let me show you—"

"I'm not wrong," Mr. Seymour stood. "And I can tell by the look in your eyes that you know it. I don't think we have anything else to discuss. As I said, I simply came here to tell you man to man why I wouldn't keep my promise."

Mark turned and stared out the window as the anger started to boil deep in his belly. It took every ounce of discipline he had not to let loose on Mr. Seymour and tell the supercilious bastard just what he could do with his man-to-man dignity. Instead he said in a calm voice, "The investigation is routine, Mr. Seymour ..." He turned around to discover Mr. Seymour had left.

Using his cell phone, he quickly accessed his Swiss bank accounts. Seconds later he received the message: *This account has been frozen. Please contact our help desk at the following link.*

As the reality of Mark's situation sunk in, he was overcome by a feeling of calm. He'd prepared for this eventuality. He knew what to do. Pulling his checkbook out of his suit jacket, he scribbled a final check to the bimbo – it would probably bounce, but he didn't care – Mark approached her desk, only to find her speaking on the phone.

"It's your wife," she whispered.

"Here's your final paycheck. You're fired. Lock the door on your way out."

Chapter 19

Olivia

After her meeting with Ebby, Olivia spent the morning doing legal research, boning up on the case law needed to get Ebby's confession – and his entire case – dismissed. She knew the chance of the confession getting tossed was slim, but she had to make the argument, if for no other reason than to see and evaluate her opposing counsel. Seth Woodson was an unknown quantity. Was he a good lawyer? Olivia couldn't say. Not yet. But she put herself in his position. What would she do against a lawyer who was trying to keep a bogus confession out of evidence?

At one o'clock she walked the three blocks to Ebby's restaurant, which was situated in an old house among a grove of redwood trees right off Magnolia Avenue. As she sat at the counter waiting for her food to come, she noticed how smoothly the restaurant operated and how well the staff got along, even though Ebby wasn't there, a sure testament to his management skills and the loyalty of his employees. Once her classic Reuben with fries arrived, she took her time with her food, reading the last of the newspaper articles about Cynthia Engstrom's murder.

Six beat reporters covered the murder, but Olivia quickly homed in on one in particular, Gordon LaPorter, whose articles seemed to be intelligent, balanced, and based largely on empirical data rather than speculation and opinion. Thinking that Mr. LaPorter might have insight if he were still alive, Olivia used her phone to search his name, only to turn up an obituary. Mr. LaPorter had died five years ago.

Back at the office, Olivia found Brian focused on his computer, tapping away with two fingers.

"Hey," she said. "How's it going?"

He looked up, startled.

"What did you find?" Olivia stepped into the office.

"What makes you think I've found something?"

"You get this look in your eyes. It's your tell," Olivia said.

He smiled at her and pointed at the tasking chair tucked into the corner of his office. "Come sit."

Olivia pulled the chair close enough to Brian's desk so she could see his computer. "Is this about Mark Engstrom?"

"It is. I followed him to Il Fornaio, where he met an attractive brunette for what I thought was a lunchtime tryst. The man has an ego, on full display at the restaurant. I don't like him."

"Me neither. Was the brunette his mistress, do you think?"

Brian shook his head. "Based on body language, she didn't much care for Mr. Engstrom's company. But the interesting part happened after the meal. When Mark finished eating, I paid my check and hurried to my car. Soon Mark and the brunette came out of the restaurant. That's when I noticed the tail."

"Tail?" Olivia repeated.

"Yeah. A gray Ford Taurus, government issue. FBI or SEC, I'm guessing. They were following Mark. Anyway, Mark handed the

141

brunette an envelope. The brunette got into her car, and once Mark drove away, she passed the envelope to one of the men in the Taurus." Mark sighed. "I had a buddy check the license plate. The brunette is one Brenda Eldridge. She has a freelance bookkeeping service. Works out of her house. I'm betting she's cooperating with whichever government agency is investigating Mr. Engstrom."

"So what do we do now?"

"We go out of our way to keep a distance from the agency running this investigation. Something tells me that what I saw today has nothing to do with the murder or the theft of the coins. My gut is saying we should leave it alone. Unless you think otherwise?"

"No, let's keep our distance for now," Olivia said.

"And I found out who the medical examiner was in 1984 – a guy by the name of Duncan Wymark. He lives in San Anselmo. I thought we could call him. He might remember the murder. Worth a shot?"

"Definitely worth a shot," Olivia said. "We should move forward under the assumption that I can't get Ebby's confession thrown out."

"I'll call him. Who knows, he might be able to help."

"Well, don't you two look cozy?" Leanne stood in the doorway to Brian's office. At her sudden appearance, Olivia stood up and moved away from Brian, as if she were guilty of something inappropriate.

"Hey, Leanne. We were just going over some work. If you'll excuse me." She started for the door, not trusting herself to hide her suspicions.

"Wait, Olivia. You don't have to go. I didn't mean to interrupt. I just had some business in town and I stopped by to see if I could take the two of you out to dinner. What do you say? My treat."

"That sounds really nice. But can I take a rain check? I didn't sleep very well last night." Olivia rubbed her neck. "I'm knackered."

"You do look tired." She turned to Brian. "How about you, Brian? Want to grab a quick bite?"

Olivia didn't wait to hear what Brian said. She went into her office and shut the door. By the time she was ready to call it a day, Brian and Leanne were long gone.

Chapter 20

Brian

Brian didn't appreciate being played for a fool and had every intention of finding out exactly what Leanne was playing at. Last night, he had gone into professional mode, using the same tricks he used when he worked undercover. He'd even managed a passionate kiss goodnight by pretending he was kissing Olivia.

"Wow," Leanne had purred when Brian finally pulled away. "Where did that come from?"

Brian had just smiled, given Leanne a wave, and walked away.

Tossing and turning in his bed, Brian didn't stand a chance of getting any sleep. As he reviewed his relationship with Leanne, he realized she'd been acting suspiciously since the day he met her. She'd told Brian her husband was a pilot, but also said on another occasion that he was a lawyer. When he'd asked her about it, she said he must have misheard because her husband was most definitely a pilot. In hindsight, Brian realized that the dates of her husband's death didn't jibe. In one instance, she'd said her husband had died two years ago, another time he'd been dead for five years. There were a handful of other incidents like that, but Brian didn't pay them much attention at the time. As he lay awake, questions wound round and round his head. What was Leanne up to? Why had she involved him? How could he stop her?

When the sun crept up the next morning, his eyelids were gritty from lack of sleep, but Brian knew what he had to do. After a morning run around Phoenix Lake, a long shower, and a hot breakfast, Brian felt halfway normal. He was still thinking about all his past encounters with Leanne, recalling every word and gesture and comment about her family and friends through a lens of suspicion. As he thought about their relationship, he realized she had grilled him, well and truly grilled him, about his life and his marriage, making it seem as though she was genuinely interested, when really, all she wanted was information. And he had played right into her hands, like a gullible idiot. No more.

At eight o'clock on the dot, he dialed Leanne's number and gave the performance of his life, telling her he missed her, that he was going to be busy until Ebby's trial, but that he wanted to steal a few minutes with her today. The flattery worked.

"I have to be at work at 10:30. Would you like to have dinner tonight?"

"Can't," he said. "Working. Why don't I come and get you and we can have coffee this morning?"

She readily agreed to meet at him at Peet's in Bon Air Shopping Center in an hour.

Brian now assumed that everything Leanne said to him was a lie. "Are you sure you don't want me to pick you up at your new condo? I am looking forward to seeing it. It's supposed to rain, and I know you don't have a car …"

"Oh, that's okay. I have a couple of errands to run. I'll meet you at Peet's."

"Why won't you let me come and get you?"

145

When Leanne didn't answer right away, Brian worried he had pushed too hard and aroused her suspicion.

"Are you okay, Brian? You sound different."

"I'm fine. Just really want to see you. I'll run a couple errands myself and see you at Peet's, okay?"

"Perfect." He heard the relief in her voice.

Lately, the bulk of Brian's business centered around background checks for his corporate clients. And although desk work was not exactly his favorite thing, he had ponied up the money for the software that allowed him to conduct detailed searches on anyone, anywhere. With the click of his mouse he could uncover associations between businesses, assets, and people, via access to public records, criminal records, and credit reports. Glad to have this resource at his disposal, he opened the program and entered Leanne Stoddard's name into the database. There was a Leanne Stoddard in Dayton, Ohio, who had a record for welfare fraud, but she had died a month ago. Another Leanne Gretna Stoddard was wanted for bank robbery but was doing time in upstate New York. He searched for criminal records only and about two dozen names came up, along with corresponding photos. None of them matched his Leanne Stoddard. Certain now that Leanne Stoddard was an alias, Brian realized there was nothing to be done until he discovered her real name.

It started to rain just as Brian arrived at Bon Air Shopping Center, thirty minutes before he was scheduled to meet Leanne. He drove around the lot until he scored a parking place that allowed him to see the front door of the coffee shop and the approaching walkway from each direction. Through the glass window that faced the street, Brian could see Peet's was jammed today, a good indicator that Brian and Leanne wouldn't get a table. No worries. He wasn't really interested in sitting down and talking to Leanne. No, he was more interested in dropping her off at the hospital and seeing what she did after he left.

Soon Leanne came walking down the sidewalk carrying a large

canvas shopping bag. Brian locked his car and hurried through the rain to meet her. As he ran, he reminded himself to act natural and let her do the talking.

"Hello," Brian said.

"Well hello there." She stood close to him and pecked him on the cheek. "I'm so looking forward to our trip to Mendocino. I don't even care if it rains. Our room has a fireplace and I have about ten novels that I've been wanting to read. I'm just looking forward to getting away."

"Me too," Brian lied. There would be no trip to Mendocino, of that Brian was certain. He'd rather chew off his own arm than go away for a romantic weekend with Leanne – or whoever she was. They stepped into the coffee shop. As expected, a long line had formed and there wasn't a table to be had.

"I don't have a whole lot of time, I'm sorry to say. Do you mind if we get coffees to go?"

"Not at all," Brian said.

"I have to go into work early. Someone called in sick and we're short-staffed."

Fifteen minutes later, they headed out into the rain, coffees in hand. "Let me get the car. You wait here and stay dry."

They didn't speak on the ride to the hospital. When Leanne reached over and took Brian's hand, he squeezed back and forced himself to smile.

"Is something wrong, Brian? You seem preoccupied."

"Just work. I become boorish when I'm working on a case. Used to drive my wife nuts," Brian said. By the time he pulled up in front of the hospital, he was ready for Leanne to be out of his vehicle.

"See you soon, Brian."

He waited until she'd walked into the main entrance of the hospital before he backed into one of a dozen doctors' parking places near the front door and settled down to wait. Sure enough, not five minutes later, Leanne came back outside. She didn't

147

notice him as she hurried in the rain to the lower parking area and got into a black Honda Accord. He followed her at a distance as she drove west on Sir Francis Drake Boulevard to the small town of Fairfax.

Ultimately, she wound up at a nondescript gray apartment complex on Sir Francis Drake Boulevard. By Brian's count, the building held approximately twenty units, providing enough cars and parking to allow Brian to stay hidden. Not that he need have bothered. Leanne had no idea he had followed her. He double parked in front of a pickup truck, safely out of Leanne's line of sight, as she walked to an end unit and let herself in with a key.

Brian then pulled into an empty parking space in Leanne's complex, far enough away so Leanne wouldn't notice him but close enough to allow him to see her apartment. He waited, his eyes glued to her front door, patient as a saint. Soon the rain stopped, and the sun came out. After about an hour, Leanne came out of her apartment, this time dressed in jeans and a warm jacket. She got back in the Honda and drove away. Brian thought about following her, but then a better plan popped into his head.

Careful not to be seen, Brian walked to Leanne's apartment and knocked softly on the door. After double-checking to make sure no one was watching him, he used his library card to jimmy the cheap lock and was inside the apartment in no time. He walked through the living room to a sliding glass door that led to a private patio with a tall privacy fence. Calculating that he could easily jump over the fence in a pinch, Brian covered his hand with his shirtsleeve, so as not to leave fingerprints, and opened the sliding glass door a crack. If Leanne came back and surprised him, he could slip out the back and be over the fence in a heartbeat.

Once his escape route was in place, he stood in the middle of Leanne's apartment. A lone couch and a coffee table were the only furniture in this room. No pictures hung on the walls, no personal items were scattered about. The space was barren and completely without soul. He moved into the kitchen. A patina of dust and grime covered the counters and the stove. The refrigerator was empty. As in not one lick of food. So were the cabinets. He remembered Leanne's promise to make Olivia and him a nice dinner at her condo near the hospital. He wondered what she would have done if they had taken her up on her offer.

Unlike the rest of the house, the bedroom showed evidence of occupancy. A full-sized bed sat in the middle of the small room, unmade and messy. Several dresses and two purses were tossed in the middle of the bunched-up covers, as though Leanne had tried on various outfits and couldn't be bothered to put away the discards. A three-legged dining chair served as a nightstand, holding a wind-up clock and a small dish that held a pair of cheap costume earrings. The dresser was the only nice piece of furniture in the house. It looked like an antique, probably made of mahogany. Lipsticks, a broken mirror, and a pile of unopened mail sat on top of it.

Brian picked up the letters and thumbed through them. It took a couple of seconds for his brain to register the name on the envelopes. Taking the stack of mail over to the window, Brian studied the envelopes in the light. He went back through the rest of the pile: an offer for a VISA card from Bank of the North, an interest-free credit card, a new Macy's card, a bank statement, an electric bill, and a phone bill, all addressed to Maureen Vickery, Brian's deceased wife, at this apartment's address. Now he knew what Olivia had stumbled on when she found Leanne in the office.

White-hot anger bloomed deep in Brian's psyche. How dare this woman use Maureen's good name for her scheme? God help him, he could kill her and not feel a drop of remorse. Heart pounding, Brian took out his cell phone and took photos of each and every envelope. He had half a mind to steal the lot of them, but knew that wasn't a good idea. The last thing he needed was Leanne to become suspicious.

When he was finished, he emailed the photos to himself, just in case something happened to his phone before he got back to the office. He'd have to involve the police, no doubt about that. But the dynamic had changed now. Careful to make sure no one saw him as he slipped out of the apartment, Brian headed to the safety of his car. The tables had turned. Brian, who had been Leanne Stoddard's prey, was now the predator.

Chapter 21

Ebby

Thursday, January 8

Ebby stared at the flames from the gas logs in Felicity's fireplace. They weren't the same as a real fire, with the sound of crackling wood and the familiar smell that triggered memories of a happier time, but the evening was chilly, and the warmth felt good. On its surface, the scene seemed peaceful. Felicity sat on the couch, her laptop resting on her legs, beavering away on Ebby's written notes. A half-empty bottle of wine and a pizza box took up most of the space on the coffee table. Just underneath this tableau of domestic bliss were the worries about his current situation, namely his arrest for a murder he didn't remember.

She looked up and they both stared at the licking tendrils of fire, momentarily mesmerized.

"What is it about the sound of crackling wood that is so relaxing?"

Ebby refilled Felicity's wine glass.

"Thanks," Felicity said. "Ebs, don't worry, okay? I know how hard this is. But you didn't kill your mother. Olivia will be able to prove that."

"I certainly haven't made it easy for her, have I? Confessing at the party, confessing to the police." He stared at the fire while Felicity turned her focus back to Ebby's notes.

She read one of the pages, comparing it to the computer screen. Satisfied, she set the page aside and picked up her wine glass. "This cookbook is really good, Ebs. The instructions are easy to follow, and the recipes are similar to the ones you serve at the restaurant. Tell me again what your agent said."

Ebby smiled at Felicity's attempt to change the subject. "She loved it, but maybe isn't quite as enthusiastic as you are."

As Felicity went back to the computer, Ebby pulled out the notebook he'd been using to write down what he remembered about his mother's murder, along with any information that might be useful to Olivia. The writing had been cathartic, and since he'd been documenting his memories, his vivid dreams and flashbacks had stopped.

Ebby's memories of that time of his life were disjointed and vague. Although he and Felicity were close in age, they didn't really spend a lot of time together as children. Lately Ebby had been wondering why that was. Did his mother – always the domineering engineer of her children's social lives – deliberately keep Ebby and Felicity apart?

"How come we never played together when we were kids?" Ebby asked Felicity. "We were close enough in age, and we lived in the same house."

Felicity kept typing, her fingers flying over the keys. "Your mother hated my mother. And she hated me."

"Hate's a rather strong word."

"No, it's the truth. We were beneath you." Felicity spoke without emotion as she flipped the page she was typing from over. "Don't worry. My feelings weren't hurt. Your mother – God rest her soul

– was a horrible snob. It wouldn't do for you to play with the help. She probably thought I'd be a bad influence."

"I'm sorry, Felicity. My family has not treated you well." He wanted to ask, for the hundredth time, why Felicity stayed on as an employee after all these years.

"No need to apologize." Felicity turned her attention once again to her laptop, while Ebby cleared away the pizza box and dirty dishes and carried them into the kitchen.

When he came back into the living room, he found Felicity gazing at the fire, her wine glass in hand. "Do you remember when Mark was a senior in high school, and he conned all of his friends into investing in some imaginary scheme?"

"No," Ebby said. "What happened?"

"Well, Mark wound up with a chunk of change. I can't remember how much. He got his friends to invest, promising that he would double their money. Eventually their parents found out and they came to Cynthia." Felicity sipped her wine. "This was just before your dad died, if my memory serves. Oh, your parents were furious with Mark. He had spent the money, blown it on God knows what. I thought your mother was going to kill him. Your father wanted to see Mark prosecuted for fraud, but your mother wouldn't allow it. She covered Mark's debt and paid all the parents back. But she told him in no uncertain terms that he had abused all her grace, and she had half a mind to disinherit him."

"How do you know this?"

Felicity smirked. "How do you think? I overheard it. I was the daughter of a servant. I was invisible."

"Why do you keep working for them? Come to work at the restaurant. I'll give you a raise. And treat you with the respect you deserve."

She didn't look at him. "I need to stay where I am, Ebby. At least for now."

"Let me know when you're ready," Ebby said.

* * *

153

For the first time in months, Ebby slept through the night. If he had any dreams, he didn't remember them when he awoke the next morning. When he rose from the couch, groggy-eyed and disoriented, he realized Felicity must have left for work a while ago. Alone in the house, he stepped into Felicity's bedroom and studied the surroundings. Until Felicity had graciously taken Ebby into her home, he'd never spent much time here. They usually spent time together at his house or out with his friends, when he could cajole her to join them for a meal or a hike. He had come to believe she lived a humble life and didn't want him to see her apartment. But he'd been wrong. Her apartment was a spacious one-bedroom, with big windows and lots of light.

Her decorating style was an unusual combination of austerity and classic. The queen-sized bed sat on a floating platform that made it look like it was hanging suspended in midair. A pristine white duvet, countless comfortable-looking pillows, and a silk tapestry in muted shades of blues gave the room a warm, inviting feel.

Moving into the living room, Ebby studied the original painting that hung over the sofa, an abstract of a rainy street. The monochromatic vibe was broken up by colorful pillows and the vibrant pottery she had scattered around the apartment. The room was tasteful, artistic, and reflected Felicity through and through. As he popped two pieces of fresh sourdough bread into the toaster and poured himself coffee, Ebby once again wondered at the current situation. Although he had faith in the justice system, he'd watched enough television to know that juries could be fickle. What if his case went to trial and the jury didn't like him? What if the evidence Olivia presented didn't convince a jury of his innocence? The idea of spending the rest of his life in prison filled Ebby with a sense of terror. Why in the world had he confessed?

The toaster dinged and his sourdough bread popped up. He didn't want it anymore, the hunger in his belly replaced by a knot of worry. As he turned to walk into the kitchen, he inadvertently tripped on the rug, sending his coffee flying. Most of it landed on the wood floor, but some of it splattered onto the white Flokati rug.

"Crap," Ebby said out loud. Grabbing his phone, he did an internet search for "how do you clean coffee out of a flokati rug?" The instructions were very straightforward. After mixing a solution of warm water, white vinegar, and liquid dish soap, Ebby grabbed a towel and went to work. The potion worked like a charm and soon Ebby had the rug spotless. After moving the couch, he pulled the rug over to the large window, positioning it so the wet spot was in the direct sunlight. He'd leave it there for an hour or two. With any luck, by the time Felicity got home the rug would be dry and she'd be none the wiser.

Just as he was pushing himself to his feet, Ebby felt one of floorboards underneath his knee wiggle. Curious, he crouched down and ran his fingers over it, surprised when it easily lifted away to reveal a small cubbyhole. A legal envelope had been folded in half and crammed into the small space. Without thinking of the consequences – Felicity, who kept her secrets close, would be furious if she knew Ebby was going through her personal papers – Ebby lifted the envelope out of its hiding place, unclasped it, and carefully drew out a folder. Inside the folder was an envelope with the words LAST WILL AND TESTAMENT OF ELLIOT MARCUS ENGSTROM in bold calligraphy, with a plain letter-sized envelope.

Why would Felicity have a copy of his father's will? When Elliot had died, Ebby had been too young to be involved in the probate of his father's estate. Upon his mother's death, Elodie had become his guardian. She had seen to his financial wellbeing, so there had never been any reason for him to see a copy of his father's will. Figuring that his father had left a sum of money to Allegra for her years of service, Ebby opened the envelope, unfolded the thick legal document, and started to read. His father's bequests were rather straightforward. The bulk of his assets were to be transferred to Cynthia in the form of a life estate, meaning she had access to his money and property until she passed, at which time, said assets would be held in trust for his children, namely "Mark, Edward (AKA Ebby), and Felicity Matthews". Felicity Matthews? Ebby reread the sentence, once, twice, three times.

He crumpled onto the couch and buried his head in his hands, trying to wrap his mind around the idea of Allegra, the kind-hearted housekeeper who Ebby loved like family, and his father, not only having a child, but acknowledging the child. What had his mother thought when she discovered Elliot had provided for Felicity in his will? Had his mother known about the affair? Did this mean that Felicity was his half-sister? Ebby thought back to his family dynamic when he was young. He recalled his mother not being overly fond of Allegra. Try as he might, Ebby didn't have many memories of his mother and father demonstrably showing their love for each other.

Over the years, as Ebby processed the grief he felt at his father' death, he realized that Elliot and Cynthia were very different people. In fact, Ebby had often wondered what they had seen in each other. Elliot was unassuming and outdoorsy, while Cynthia was ambitious and socially conscious. As much as he hated to admit it, he could see his father falling for Allegra. Cynthia Engstrom had been a strong-willed woman, who liked to have unfettered control over her family. Ebby believed Mark inherited this characteristic from her. His father, on the other hand, had been a quiet gentle soul. He had heard his mother and his aunts say on more than one occasion that Ebby took after his father. But somehow – at least according to Ebby's recollections – his father had always managed to maintain his quiet authority.

Could Allegra have murdered Cynthia? Could the two women have quarreled over the love of a man? Over money? Over Felicity's inheritance? If only he could remember what he had witnessed the night of his mother's murder, but the more he tried, the harder his subconscious mind clamped down on the memory.

* * *

Thirty minutes later, Ebby was driving too fast on the twisty road to his family home, finally coming to a screeching stop near the trailer, sending gravel flying. Elodie, probably disturbed by the racket, came flying out of the house, brandishing a rolling pin like a weapon.

When she realized the aggressive intruder was Ebby, she shouted at him. "What the devil is the matter with you?" She stepped off her porch and hurried toward his car, her anger morphing into worry. "What's happened? Have you remembered?"

"This isn't about what I witnessed, not about the fact that I'm in all likelihood going to go on trial for my mother's murder. This is about Felicity. I know about Felicity, that she's my half-sister. Have you known all along?"

Elodie's face registered shock, followed by dismay. "Oh, Ebby, honey," Elodie said. "Come in. I'll make you a cup of coffee."

"You have known. I can tell by the look in your eyes," Ebby said. "This can't be cured with a cup of coffee, Elodie. Are there any other secrets being kept from me? Any other half-siblings tucked away in apartments? I am so tired of the way everyone in this family treats me. I am realizing that I can't force you to respect me. How you feel about me, or how you think about me is your problem, not mine. But I'm so tired of being treated like I am unable to cope. You had no right to keep that from me, Elodie."

"Felicity's parentage and her position in her family are not for me to discuss. You've every right to be angry, but you've no business directing your anger at me. I was your guardian. In the process of executing those duties, I discovered the truth about Felicity. And I would thank you not to accuse me of treating you with disrespect." Her voice broke with emotion. "I love you more than anything and would defend you with my last breath."

Ebby shrunk with guilt. God, she was right.

"Come in," Elodie said. "Let's talk. I'll tell you what I can. You look like you could use some comfort food. When did you last eat? If you don't mind me saying so, you look a little peaked."

Ten minutes later, Ebby was digging into a grilled cheese sandwich, his childhood comfort food.

"The police came and searched the main house yesterday. They were there all day. Mark was none too pleased," Elodie said as she buzzed around the kitchen, salting the iron skillet that she used to make the sandwich and wiping it clean with a paper towel. The minute Ebby finished eating, Elodie cleared away his dishes and washed them. He knew she was buying time. When she finally sat down across from him, she looked at him with worried eyes and said, "I won't tell you Felicity's story, but I will tell you about your father."

"I can't believe he cheated on Mom," Ebby said. "And I can't believe my mother didn't raise holy hell when she found out. And Allegra – it's all too much to take in."

"Don't judge too harshly, Ebby. It wasn't like that. Relationships can be complicated. Your father and Cynthia fell out of love. It happens sometimes."

"Why did they stay together? If my dad loved Allegra so much, why didn't he marry her?"

"Because he was devoted to his family, to you kids, and in some ways, he was devoted to Cynthia as well. Cynthia had a lover, too, just so you know. And she did know about Elliot and Allegra's relationship. She wasn't happy when Felicity came along, but they managed to work things out so they could peacefully co-exist. They were careful to keep their complicated triangle away from you kids."

"Very forward-thinking of them." Despite Elodie's explanation, Ebby couldn't fathom his seemingly staunch parents in a love triangle with Allegra. He thought back to his childhood, surprised that he couldn't remember his parents ever fighting. Not once. As far as he could tell, they had a happy marriage and were devoted to each other. And Allegra had loved Ebby and Mark, of that he was certain. Casting his mind back, he tried to remember his father with Felicity, tried to remember if he had ever witnessed the paternal tenderness of a father and daughter.

"Will you be okay, Ebby?"

The concern in his aunt's eyes nearly broke Ebby's heart. He reached out and grabbed her wrinkled hand. "There's really nothing to be done about it, is there? I'll be fine. Thank you for being honest with me."

"I'll always be honest with you, Ebby. You can be sure of that."

He stood. "I need to go talk to Felicity."

"Can't you wait and talk to her tonight? When she's not at work? This is going to be a huge conversation, Ebby. You need to not get angry with Felicity."

"I know. I guess I should be happy," Ebby said. "I now have one sibling who I actually get along with."

Elodie swatted him with a kitchen towel.

"I should go," Ebby said. "Thanks for lunch."

"Come back and see me soon?" Elodie said with a smile.

"I will," he said, zipping his coat as he stepped into the frigid January day.

Chapter 22

Brian

Brian and Olivia had decided the best way forward was to go over the original investigation and re-interview any witnesses that could be tracked down. To that end, Brian finished his morning to-go cup of coffee just as he pulled to a stop in front of the large house high atop one of the many hills in Tiburon, knowing full well the interview he was about to have was probably a colossal waste of time.

During his tenure as a police officer, Brian had seen some horrific things. He'd quickly learned to compartmentalize, stuffing away the ugliness he saw at work so he could live a normal life at home and in his marriage. But the situation with Leanne unnerved him. He'd been played and now he was struggling mightily to stuff his fury into that metaphorical box.

He reminded himself that he was a professional. He had a job to do, working a tragic case resulting from a bogus arrest. He'd asked around about Seth Woodson and had discovered the ADA was an ambitious young man, who was making enemies in the DA's office quicker than he was making friends. Brian didn't need a law degree to know that there was no probable cause to arrest Ebby Engstrom, and he couldn't help but think that Olivia had stepped right into a witch hunt.

Brian got out of the car and took a moment to take in the spectacular view of Richardson Bay and the Golden Gate Bridge, as wisps of morning fog hung snaked over the water, propelled by the coastal breeze. The January sun would burn away the fog by noon. He stopped for a moment and sucked in a huge lungful of fresh air.

Brian's background check had revealed that at the time of Cynthia Engstrom's murder, Eleanor Benedict had been the girl-friend of David Wiseman, a long-time friend of Mark Engstrom's. She and David had married, but had divorced in 1999, at which time Eleanor had received a generous property settlement, including this spectacular house. Since that time, Mrs. Wiseman hadn't remarried and seemed to have led a quiet and uneventful life. The interview would be a quick one. Once Brian verified that Mark Engstrom had indeed been at the cabin in the mountains at the time of the murder, he could get back to the office and continue reviewing the piles of documents Fiona Engstrom had given them.

Brian was just about to knock on the front door, when it was opened by a physically fit fifty-something woman with shoulder-length gray hair. "Mr. Vickery?"

"Yes, ma'am," Brian said.

She smiled at him. "Do come in."

Brian followed Mrs. Wiseman into a sweeping flagstone entry hall, which ran parallel to a large living room. The wall facing the bay was all glass from floor to ceiling. This, plus the thick white carpet, gave the room an inviting spaciousness. Two large fireplaces graced each side of the room; both had comfortable overstuffed couches arranged before them. One of the fireplaces was lit.

"Stunning view," Brian said.

"Isn't it just? I've lived in this house for decades and I'm still not tired of it." She led him over to the fireplace at the far end of the room. "We'll sit here. I've got tea for you and apple pie fresh out of the oven."

Under normal circumstances Brian wouldn't dream of taking food from a potential witness, but his stomach rumbled at the mention of apple pie. Hunger forced him to capitulate.

"I read in the paper that they arrested Ebby for the murder. That's ridiculous. Ebby was, what, thirteen years old at the time? I probably don't have anything new to tell you, Mr. Vickery."

"That's okay. Would you mind just telling me what you remember about the Engstroms during that period of time? Anything you want to share."

After she gave him tea in a china cup and a huge slice of apple pie, Eleanor Wiseman made herself comfortable and started talking.

"In the summer of 1984, my then boyfriend, now ex-husband, David, myself, Mark Engstrom, his wife Melinda, and four other friends were a pretty tight group. Two of the friends died, the other two moved away. Mark, Melinda, David and I are the only ones still around. Earlier that year Mark Engstrom talked all of us into looting our college savings accounts and investing it with him. He told us that he got a hot tip from his father and that he could triple our money, guaranteed. He suggested we could pocket the profits and put the funds back in our college accounts with our parents none the wiser. Of course, being the gullible kids we were, we believed him and gladly turned over our money. You can imagine what happened. Mark claimed the market took an unexpected dip. He said he was sorry, but the money was gone. Personally, I think he put it in his pocket. He was always a greedy, spoiled little bastard. Pardon me for being crass, but he really was.

"All of our parents were furious. I was grounded for months

and my parents took my car away. Mr. and Mrs. Engstrom paid all of us back. Elliot, Mark's father, died that summer. It was a terrible year. Anyway, after the money was lost, our group of friends disbanded. We were all in such trouble. My parents were glad that I wasn't hanging around Mark Engstrom anymore. Then out of the blue, Mark approached us with the offer of a ski weekend over the Christmas break. He offered the trip as an apology, footed the bill, rented us a house, ordered in catered dinners, the whole works. Probably paid for it using the money we gave him. That's where we were when we got the news of Cynthia's murder." Eleanor stared off into the distance. "Mark was pretty devastated."

Brian set his plate down and picked up his tea.

"What about Melinda? Wasn't she there?" Brian racked his brains. He knew that Mark Engstrom and Melinda were high school sweethearts. Did he read something in the police report about Melinda not being on the ski trip?

"Melinda couldn't come. She had to work. I don't how to say this without sounding snobby, but Melinda's family wasn't like our families. Her father was a welder, and her mother was a homemaker. They were nice enough people, but they lived a completely different lifestyle than we did."

"I'm surprised Mark Engstrom would date someone like Melinda."

"We were surprised too. I'm sure you've figured out that Mark's a first-rate jerk, but he and Melinda loved each other. They always have. There's something else. I don't like to speak ill of the dead, but Cynthia Engstrom was not a nice woman. She was ruthless. My parents didn't like her. My mother called her a tough broad. She came from humble circumstances, too. Not that there's anything wrong with that. My mother used to say that Cynthia North Engstrom did a brilliant job of remaking herself. My parents both respected her business acumen, but they had reservations about her personally." Mrs. Wiseman stared out the window. Her voice became wistful. "Mr. Engstrom, Elliot, was a dear man. Always had a kind word, always had time for us kids. Our ideas and attitudes were so different back then. Mr. Engstrom wanted to know what our lives were like, if that makes sense."

"You didn't like Melinda?"

"No, I did not."

"Any particular reason?"

"Because Melinda and my husband were screwing each other like rabbits every chance they got. I caught them red-handed. David was embarrassed, but Melinda was furious at me. Can you imagine that? She was furious at me because she got caught with my boyfriend? We never really liked each other, but that little scenario ended whatever semblance of polite friendship existed between us." Mrs. Wiseman stopped speaking. "You know, I just remembered something, which may nor may not be relevant. Cynthia was so tired of Mark's behavior that she was threatening to rewrite the terms of the Engstrom Trust in such a way that Mark wouldn't have such unfettered access to his inheritance from his father. He was telling us about it that weekend in Tahoe. I remember him saying, 'This may be our last hurrah.'"

"Did Mark ever find out about Melinda's relationship with David?"

"I don't think so," said Mrs. Wiseman. "And between you and me, I don't think David was the only one. My belief is that Melinda was an opportunist. She was looking to marry money. She loved Mark, don't get me wrong, but I always had a sense that Melinda would hitch her wagon to the first available wealthy man who asked for her hand."

Brian finished his tea and set the cup and saucer down on the table before he stood. Mrs. Wiseman walked him to the door. Before he stepped outside, he turned back to Mrs. Wiseman. "Do you think Mark Engstrom killed his mother?"

Mrs. Wiseman shook her head. "Mark Engstrom always struck me as a coward. And there's no way he could have snuck home from our weekend. We would have noticed. I'm sorry I can't be of more help."

Chapter 23

Olivia

Olivia had never met, nor had she appeared before, the judge who had been assigned Ebby's case. Judge Renaldo Gaston had a reputation as a stickler for procedure. He never allowed cameras in his courtroom and was very quick to sequester a jury. Judge Gaston rarely heard motions on Fridays but had made an exception in this instance because he had a trial starting the following week and didn't want his docket to get backlogged.

As Olivia parked her car and headed up to the courthouse, she was glad that she could get this obstacle out of the way before the weekend. Once she knew where she stood with her evidence, she could move forward with a trial strategy.

Seth was already at the defense table when Olivia stepped into the courtroom. He nodded at the bailiff who went to get the judge.

"All rise."

Olivia and Seth stood as Judge Gaston came into the courtroom. "Be seated. Good morning, everyone," the judge said.

"Let's go on the record. Case 15-00654, the People versus Edward Engstrom. We're here this morning on the defendant's motion to suppress the confession of murder by the defendant."

"Mrs. Sinclair?"

Olivia stood. "This is a very simple issue, Your Honor. My client was never Mirandized when he confessed to murdering his mother. More importantly, at the time he was arrested, Mr. Engstrom was *non compos mentis* in that he was extremely dehydrated and delusional, to such an extent that he was immediately transported to the hospital. There is no way Mr. Engstrom could have knowingly and intelligently conversed with any policeman whatsoever during his time in the hospital. During this time, the police heard a bogus confession to a murder that took place over thirty years ago, when my client was thirteen years old."

"When Mr. Engstrom confessed, did the officers know he was *non compos mentis?*"

When Seth Woodson opened his mouth to speak, Olivia interrupted. "They spoke to him while he was in the emergency room for symptoms of dehydration and exhaustion."

Seth shot Olivia a look before he spoke. "My officers responded to the report of a confession to murder. They arrived at the hospital after Mr. Engstrom had been unloaded from the ambulance. Mr. Engstrom's confession was given voluntarily, in front of a party of one hundred people, then again in the ambulance, and again in the emergency room. Over and over. At the time, Mr. Engstrom was not in physical custody by the police. The defendant was never in police custody when the confession was made. In fact, at the time he made the confession, he could have left the hospital at any time."

"Mr. Engstrom doesn't even remember confessing," Olivia said. "Moreover, I must reiterate, he's confessing to a murder that was investigated over thirty years ago, when he was thirteen years old."

"It's the People's position the confession should stay in, Your Honor, and that the veracity of the statement and Mr. Engstrom's state of mind when he confessed – voluntarily and many times – to murdering his mother, should be decided by a jury."

"I've heard enough. I'm siding with the People on this issue. The confession is in. Counsel will reach out to my clerk to discuss scheduling. We're off the record."

Seth Woodson jammed his paperwork in his briefcase and hurried out of chambers, Olivia hot on his heels.

"Seth, wait," she called.

He stopped and slowly turned to face her. "I never invited you to call me by my first name. It's Mr. Woodson to you."

"Very well, Mr. Woodson. When can I expect discovery? I want the old investigation file."

"It's being delivered to your office as we speak." He turned to walk away.

"Wait a second. I'd like to speak to you about the case, off the record. You're making a mistake by prosecuting Edward. He didn't do it. You know he didn't do it."

Seth looked around to make sure no one was listening. "I don't meet with people off the record, especially old bitches like you with an axe to grind. I know you're on some feminazi crusade. I couldn't care less. You should be ashamed of what you did to your husband. Women like you have no place in the legal field." Seth stepped close to Olivia, in an aggressive violation of her space. "I'm coming for you, Mrs. Sinclair. I don't give a shit whether or not your client is innocent."

Seth Woodson turned and walked away.

* * *

Once she was in her car, Olivia pressed her forehead to the steering wheel, wondering what she'd done to make Seth Woodson hate her so, and – even more importantly – what she could do to fix the situation. Seth Woodson wasn't the first arrogant attorney she'd come across, but his personal vendetta gave Olivia pause and made her nervous. There was something suspicious about his attitude toward her and the case against Ebby. Olivia had never lodged a complaint against another lawyer in her life. Lawyers were by nature egotistical and loved to hear the sound of their own voice. But Seth had threatened her, said he was coming for her. What had he meant?

Although she was shaken from her interaction with Seth Woodson, Olivia had to stay focused on the task at hand. Brian had been able to track down the original medical examiner, one Duncan Wymark, who not only remembered the Cynthia Engstrom murder, but who had agreed to meet with Olivia to discuss the case. Brian had arranged a meeting, and – in the spirit of going the extra mile – had done a background check on Duncan to make sure Olivia wasn't walking into an unsafe situation. Olivia thought the background check was overkill, but reckoned Brian was sensitive, given the situation with Leanne.

Olivia sent Brian a quick text: *Confession stays in. Off to talk to Duncan Wymark. See you at the office?*

Brian texted back: *As expected, nothing new from Eleanor Wiseman. We got discovery. See you back here. I'll get lunch.*

* * *

Duncan Wymark lived in a Craftsman-style bungalow on a tree-lined street in San Anselmo. The house was painted bright yellow, with white trim, surrounded by a white picket fence. A rose garden had been planted in the front yard, now trimmed to stubs and mulched. Olivia thought wistfully of her own garden as she navigated the brick walkway to the porch.

The front door was opened by a man close to Olivia in age. He wore baggy jeans and a well-worn fisherman's sweater. Birkenstocks and argyle socks completed his ensemble. He wore his salt and pepper hair in a short ponytail at the nape of his neck. "Olivia Sinclair?"

"Mr. Wymark. Thanks for agreeing to see me on such short notice."

"Come on in."

Olivia followed Mr. Wymark into a sunny front room that faced the street. The original built-in cabinetry with beveled glass doors had been refinished and left their natural color. Clean white walls covered with a myriad of gorgeous black and white photographs, two leather couches, and an original Aubusson rug finished off the room in fine style. Mr. Wymark, it seemed, was a man of taste.

"Did you do the remodel on this house?"

"I did most of the work by myself, with the exception of electrical and plumbing, and extra labor where needed. It was a mess when we bought it, but my wife is actually a very accomplished builder. She showed me the way. Now, I found a copy of my report with regard to Cynthia's Engstrom's murder. It's on the table there. Why don't I leave you to read it while I get us some coffee?"

"You have the report? Isn't that—"

"Mrs. Sinclair – may I call you Olivia?"

"Of course," Olivia said.

"The Cynthia Engstrom case was my first murder. It was gory and horrible. I'll never forget it. I've never spoken about this to anyone, but that case gave me nightmares. In school, we're trained to examine from a detached, clinical perspective. But it's hard to do the work of an ME and not feel the personal aspect of each situation. If I'm honest with myself – and with you – Cynthia Engstrom's murder made me realize that I wasn't cut out for life as a medical examiner. I stuck with it for five years and left."

"But why did you hang on to the report?"

Duncan laughed. "You can imagine what my family thought after I quit my job to pursue a career in photography. My father was furious with me. Threatened to disinherit me, pushed me for years to take another job. I never gave in. Every time I thought about capitulating to his demands, I'd pull out that report and read it. It served as a stark reminder of why I made the decision to change careers."

Duncan left, and soon Olivia heard him opening cupboard doors. She picked up the report and started to read. When he came back into the room carrying a coffee tray, she was only two pages in.

"I was thinking it might be better if I just discussed my findings." Duncan poured coffee for them. Olivia waved off the cream and sugar. "I read they had arrested Edward, Cynthia's youngest?"

"Correct. Ebby. He was thirteen at the time of the murder."

Duncan shook his head. "The child did not kill his mother. My report proves that without a doubt."

"That's good news." Olivia smiled. "So my question for you is this: would you go through your report and explain your findings to me in lay terms, and, secondly, would you mind testifying at Ebby's trial? The ADA is a little overzealous. Honestly, I'm surprised he even charged Ebby."

"I'd be happy to. Let me just start by saying again that there's no way that child – your client – murdered his mother. Not only was there no sign of blood on him, but it would also have been physically impossible for him to commit the crime based on the evidence." Duncan turned to the pages of the report that depicted an anatomical drawing of a human body. He pointed to the straight lines emanating from the stab wounds, and the accompanying measurements noted in tiny precise handwriting. "My measurements, which I double-checked and had a colleague check once again, indicated the height of the person who inflicted these stab wounds was between 5'7" and 5'8". Your client, the child, was only 5'2" tall at the time of the murder. There's no way he could have committed this crime. Stabbing is a messy business. If that boy murdered his mother, there would have been blood all over him. And, finally, the wounds were in the chest and throat. Whoever stabbed Mrs. Engstrom was rather strong. In fact, one wound into the sternum – the breastbone – was remarkably deep.

I've delineated all of this in great detail in that report. I'm happy to testify. I can't help but wonder if the prosecutor even looked at this report. Did he review the old case before he made an arrest?"

"Apparently not," Olivia said. "Can I have this?"

"Yes. That copy is for you. I don't miss that part of the job."

"What part?"

Duncan gave her a wry smile. "The politics, especially among the lawyers. Don't get me wrong, many of them are good, hard-working civil servants, passionate about law and order and justice. But – as I'm sure you know – there's always one in the bunch who's out for himself. Wants to get his litigation experience in, so he can switch sides and work the big cases, make the money, and get famous. Sort of like your ex-husband." He gave her a sheepish smile. "In any event, I'll make myself available. Whatever you need."

"Thank you, Mr. Wymark." Olivia set her coffee cup down. "I'll be in touch."

Duncan Wymark walked her to the door. "Sure. Just let me know when you need me."

Chapter 24

Olivia

Friday, January 9

Olivia was a mess by the time she returned to the office. Her encounter with Seth Woodson had upset her more than she realized. As she let herself into the office, she hoped Brian's morning had been as fruitful as hers. She found him hunched over his computer, tapping away with two fingers.

"I see you there, Liv," Brian said. He took off his reading glasses and rubbed his eyes. "I was just going to order – what's wrong?"

She walked into his office, kicked off her shoes, and sat down in the chair across his desk. "Seth Woodson is what's wrong. I have a problem with him. Or I should say, he has a problem with me."

"What happened?"

"I asked him if we could meet off the record to discuss the case." Olivia felt a headache coming on. She took a deep breath and bit back the tears. "He said, and I'm quoting now, 'I don't meet with people off the record, especially old bitches like you with an axe to grind. I know you're on some feminazi crusade. I couldn't care less. I'm coming for you, Mrs. Sinclair. I don't give a shit whether or not your client is innocent.'

"I swear, I could have throttled him. I'm beginning to regret taking on this case. I'm wondering if I have the stomach for criminal law."

"What are you going to do about it?" Brian asked. "Ethics complaint?"

"I could. God knows I'm mad enough, and his conduct warrants investigating, at the very least."

"Or?" Brian asked.

"Or I could exploit Seth's bad behavior to my client's advantage."

"How do you propose to do that?" Brian asked.

"Not sure yet. I do have some good news. Duncan Wymark remembers the Engstrom murder. Not only did he have a copy of his report, which exonerates Ebby, he also agreed to testify. His position is that there's no way Ebby could have stabbed his mother. He wasn't tall enough or strong enough."

"That's great. That's definite forensic evidence," Brian said.

"I know. I'm going to do my best to get his case dismissed at the prelim. In fact, I'm thinking that I'll call another expert to verify Duncan Wymark's findings. We'll see what Seth Woodson does with that. Is that the discovery from the original investigation?" Olivia pointed to the singular banker's box sitting on the floor in Brian's office.

"Yep. Delivered this morning," Brian said.

Olivia went to the box and lifted the lid, surprised to see one lone file inside. She picked it up and thumbed through it. "There are photographs and police reports missing. And there's no report from Duncan Wymark. Seth Woodson didn't give us everything."

"What are you going to do?"

"I'm going to do a comparative inventory with what I got from Fiona. If Mr. Woodson is engaging in discovery shenanigans, I'm going to enjoy giving him a hard time about it."

"Do you need my help?"

"No. That's okay."

Brian stood. "I've got a handful of errands to run. Do you want lunch?"

"Sure. Thanks. I'll have whatever you're having." Olivia took all the documents received from Seth out of the file, pleased to see they were in chronological order. With Seth's documents next to Fiona's, she set about comparing the two, making note of the documents Seth failed to provide. Surprisingly, the process went a lot quicker than she thought it would. Olivia felt a plan start to form in the back of her mind. She smiled to herself and focused on the task at hand.

* * *

They ate their burgers off paper plates in Brian's office, sharing an order of fries heavily doused with ketchup.

"Thanks for lunch," Olivia said, wiping her fingers.

"No problem," Brian said. "I stopped by a friend's office when I was out. Got a little intel on our buddy Seth Woodson. It seems young Seth has a history of filing criminal complaints without sufficient probable cause. You may know the DA, Gwen Kyleson, has been out on medical leave?"

"Yes," Olivia said. "Breast cancer, right?"

"Correct. She's recovered and will be returning to work any day now. While she was gone, Seth Woodson has had two cases dismissed at the preliminary hearing for lack of probable cause. As you know, that rarely happens. When I was a cop, I testified at my fair share of probable cause hearings. From what I understand, dismissals at that stage are rare. And his colleagues don't trust him. Seth plays dirty and has been known to tamper with exonerating discovery."

"I don't know Gwen personally, but I've met her at Bar Association functions. I know she's ethical. In fact, that's her schtick. She doesn't put up with any shenanigans from her ADAs. At all," Olivia said. "I have an idea."

"Go on," Brian said.

"What if I had a meeting with her to discuss Seth's behavior, tell her I'm going to file an ethics complaint, but wanted to give her a heads-up beforehand. Then I draw her attention to the evidence in the case, which wasn't turned over to me *and* proves Ebby couldn't have committed the murder, to make my point. There's no refuting the evidence. That coupled with the likelihood of a dismissal at the prelim could work in our favor." Warming to the idea, Olivia picked up a pen and started scribbling notes on the legal pad near her elbow.

"You'll go over Seth's head?"

"Why not? He's already on a mission to 'come after me'. What's the worst thing that could happen?"

"You'd blow your strategy and give Seth an opportunity to prepare an argument as to how Ebby could have committed the crime, despite his height."

"There's no argument, Brian. Ebby could not have killed his mother. That impossibility is substantiated by evidence. The ME's report speaks for itself, and Mr. Wymark said he'd testify. I'll go to Gwen, tell her I'm there as a professional courtesy prior to an ethics complaint."

"And if she doesn't bite?"

"Then I present evidence to the judge. If he doesn't dismiss the case, I'll take it to a jury."

"It's risky," Brian said.

"I know it's tricky going over opposing counsel's head. I'm willing to take that risk. Gwen Kyleson is a reasonable woman. I think I can appeal to her common sense," Olivia said.

Olivia made a few more notes on her legal pad, set her pen down, and leaned back in her chair.

"You know what I was thinking," Brian said. "Now that we have evidence exonerating Ebby, it occurs to me that someone in the Engstrom family committed a perfect murder."

"It seems that way, doesn't it?" Olivia said.

"And whoever killed Cynthia Engstrom was furious. This case was personal. Stabbing someone in the face and throat is an act of rage."

"And let's not forget the sovereigns. I wonder where they are?"

"We may never find out," Brian said.

"I guess at the end of the day that doesn't much matter. My concern is Ebby. And now, thank goodness, I can call him and tell him that he definitely didn't murder his mother. He's going to push about continuing to investigate, but I can't worry about that right now. I need to stay focused on Ebby's case. I'll leave the finding out who really killed Cynthia up to you."

"Got it," Brian said.

"Changing the subject now. Tell me what you found out about Leanne."

"You were right. I drove her to work and waited to see if she would leave. She did, and I followed her to an apartment complex in Fairfax. I waited until she left and then I broke in and found credit cards, bank statements, and loan applications – a pile of mail – addressed to Maureen Vickery."

"Maureen? Are you telling me—"

"—that Leanne is using my wife's identity to get credit cards and take out loans? Yes, I am. And I'm furious at her and at myself."

"Oh, Brian. I'm so sorry."

"How could I have been so stupid?"

"You got conned. It can happen to anyone. You have to report this to the police."

"Sure. And tell them that I followed the woman I'm dating to her secret apartment, broke in when she left, and discovered she's taking out credit cards and opening bank accounts in my dead wife's name?"

"Absolutely. And give yourself a break, Brian. You're not perfect. Everyone makes mistakes."

"Everyone isn't a retired cop who should know better."

"Excuse me, but you're talking to the woman who was rather

excellent at recognizing adultery in other people's husbands. Imagine the grief I would have been spared if I could have recognized it in my own."

"Olivia—"

"We're debating semantics. Forgive me for being pushy. You know you need to report this. Tell the cops you suspect Leanne. You don't have to tell them why."

"Agreed."

"Eventually, social security will catch up to her. You say she's opened a bank account? I wonder how she got away with that," Olivia said.

"I'd like to find out her real name," Brian said.

"Don't con artists, grifters, whatever, use a semblance of truth in their stories?"

"Yes, I would say that's accurate," Brian said.

"Are you sure Leanne is from Minneapolis, or do you think she was lying about that?"

"No, I believe that part. We met a couple one night when we were out to dinner who came from St. Paul. They talked about the city, restaurants, things like that. Leanne – or whatever her name is – knew what she was talking about. Why? What are you thinking?"

"Doesn't the Department of Corrections in each state post mug shots of wanted people? If Leanne has a criminal past, she might have a record. She might be wanted for something. Can I sit at your computer?"

Brian stood up. "This is a total long shot."

"I know," Olivia said. "Good thing I'm the queen of long shots, isn't it?"

It didn't take Olivia long to find the Minnesota Department of Corrections list of wanted fugitives. Most of the mugshots were of men, and they had flipped through pages upon pages of thumbnail photos when Olivia spotted Leanne.

"There she is," Olivia said. Brian, who was standing behind

her as she navigated the website, leaned close. The woman in the photo was named Andrea Seaton. Andrea had blond hair that was worn in a pixie cut, and although she was a few pounds heavier than Leanne Stoddard, there was no doubt the two women were one and the same. "It's her. Picture her ten pounds lighter, with auburn hair."

"Wow," Brian said. "You've got a good eye, Liv."

Olivia clicked on Leanne's picture and was given the court case number, the county in which the criminal action was pending, and the agent in charge of the case. The charges pending against Leanne were listed as theft by swindle, insurance fraud and homicide. When Olivia clicked on the court case, they received a notice that the file was sealed and that they should contact the agent. Olivia moved her mouse over the agent's email address. "Should we?"

"Absolutely."

Brian pulled a chair next to Olivia and together they drafted an email to the agent handling Andrea Seaton's case. When Brian was happy with the email, Olivia said, "Ready for me to hit send?"

"Hit it," Brian said.

Olivia did.

Chapter 25

Ebby

Ebby hung up the phone after speaking with Olivia, relieved to know she had found evidence that exonerated him of his mother's murder and pleased with her plan to meet with the DA, despite the risks. When Ebby had reminded Olivia that he wasn't going to walk away until he discovered who killed his mother and remembered what he had seen that night so long ago, she had assured him that Brian Vickery would help with that, after Ebby's case was finished. "But we have no new leads, nothing to go on. You may have to let it go," Olivia had said.

"Not going to happen, Olivia," Ebby had responded. "What about the sovereigns?"

"I have someone looking into that," Olivia had said. "If that lead doesn't bear fruit, that's something we can talk about. But my focus right now is on your case. I'll be able to turn my attention to finding out who murdered your mom once your case is resolved. I'm just being honest, Ebby. When I'm finished with your case, I'll work with Brian, okay?"

"Okay," Ebby had said.

All that was left was for him to talk to Felicity about their relationship. He'd been putting it off, not quite sure how to broach the subject.

The muted winter sun shone through Felicity's living room windows as Ebby changed into comfortable clothes and made himself lunch. He'd called Felicity twice, but she didn't take his call. He'd also sent her texts, but she had yet to respond to those. Booting up his laptop, Ebby spent the afternoon answering emails.

At 7:30, Felicity texted him. *Sorry didn't respond sooner. Dinner and drinks with friends. Don't wait up. F.*

At eleven o'clock, Ebby took his pile of folded blankets and made up his bed on the couch. The lights from the street below cast their shadows along the darkened corners of the apartment. By midnight, Ebby's eyelids felt heavy. Try as he might, he couldn't fight off sleep. He was dozing peacefully when Felicity opened the door and quietly tiptoed into the living room. Through half-opened eyes, he watched as she tried to creep past the couch and not wake him up.

"I'm awake."

She jumped and yelped, clutching her chest with her hand. "You scared me," she snapped.

Ebby sat up and turned on the small lamp on the table next to the couch. "Sorry. Didn't mean to, but I want to talk to you."

"Ebs, I'm tired. Can we talk tomorrow?"

"No. I'd like to talk now. Please. It's important." Ebby studied her face and could tell by the tight lines around her mouth and the way she wouldn't meet his eyes that she knew he had snooped, knew what he had discovered. No wonder she'd been avoiding him. "I found the papers you had stashed under the floorboards. Were you ever going to tell me that you're my half-sister?"

Ebby watched the myriad of emotions play across her face:

indignation, shock, and, finally, anger. "How could you? I bring you into my home, let you stay here, and how do you repay me? By snooping?"

Ebby ignored her and plowed on. "I didn't go snooping, it was an accident – never mind. Talk to me. Felicity, please."

She sighed, and with drooping shoulders, shuffled into the kitchen and came back with two beers. She handed one to Ebby, kicked off her shoes, and sat down next to him on the couch.

"My mother and your father were very much in love." Felicity sipped her beer and waited, as if giving him some semblance of privacy while he coped with his complex feelings. "I've wanted to talk to you about this for so long. Now I don't know where to start."

"Start at the beginning," Ebby said.

Felicity took another sip of beer. "Okay. Here goes. As a young girl, I always thought your father was just one of those exceptionally kind men. No matter what he was doing, no matter how busy he was, he always had time for me. I remember him coming to my childhood events, his face in the background at my piano recitals and school plays. Sometimes he would come and tuck me into bed, holding me on his lap while he told me a bedtime story. I remember going into the study to see him. He was always interested in what I had to say. As I grew up, I just thought he was a kind soul who cared about people.

"When my mother and I moved into this apartment, I was surprised that she could afford it. Then, when I graduated from high school and found out there was money for college, I was once again surprised and impressed that my mom could save so much money on her wages. I just assumed – well, I didn't find out Elliot was my father until my mother was dying. She told me everything, explained how they were in love, and how I was a much-loved daughter." Felicity dabbed her eyes with the backs of her hands. "My mom explained her relationship with Elliot like it was a beautiful love story. And so many things clicked into place! Like why we moved after he died, and why my mother was more heartbroken than she should have been."

"Is that why you've stayed in your job? You could have gone anywhere."

"I wanted to be near you and the aunts. You're the only real family I have. That's important to me. You were orphaned at a young age, Ebby. Surely you can understand that. I also felt like I needed to stick around for you, especially after that night."

It took a second for Ebby to process the implication of Felicity's words. "Did you see something that night, Felicity? The night my mother died? Because you were at the house, weren't you? It was Christmas, and you always came to work with your mom during summer and holidays."

"Ebby—"

"Please, Felicity. I can tell you saw something just by looking at you. What did you see?"

Felicity set her empty beer bottle on the coffee table, leaned back, and crossed her arms over her chest. "Okay. I'll tell you, but you can't tell anyone."

"But I might have to tell Olivia." Ebby felt a frisson of guilt. He wouldn't need to tell Olivia anything, at least not based on the evidence she had uncovered that exonerated him. But he didn't want to be backed into a corner, not now. Heart thumping, Ebby had a feeling that Felicity knew something about his mother's murder. He wasn't going to let up until he found out what that something was.

"After your mother's murder, my mother made me promise on her life that I would never tell anyone what I saw that night. You should have seen the fear in her eyes, Ebby. I'll never forget it. And I promised I wouldn't say anything." Felicity got up and paced across the living room twice before she grabbed two more beers and sat down again. "When I was twenty-three, fresh out of college, and my mother was dying of cancer, she once again made me promise not to tell anyone. And she was still afraid.

So now, you're asking me to break the most solemn oath I've ever made."

"Okay. I get it." Ebby couldn't ask Felicity to break the oath she'd made to her dead mother, at least not now. If Olivia hadn't found evidence to prove his innocence, he would have continued to push. Luckily he didn't have to do that.

"No, I'm going to tell you," Felicity said. "You've suffered enough. You need to know. Maybe if I tell what I saw, you might start to remember."

Nervous now at the idea of remembering what happened, Ebby said, "Wait. You don't have to tell me because of my arrest. Olivia found forensic evidence that proves I didn't kill my mom. So if you're only telling me because of my legal case, you don't have to. I don't want to be the reason you betray your word."

Felicity wiped her tears with the back of her hand. "I've been carrying this for so long. I think my mother will forgive me." She tipped her head back and closed her eyes for a minute. When she met Ebby's gaze, her expression was wistful. "My mom was in the attic ironing the Christmas linens, so she could pack them away until next year. I was in Elodie's rooms watching television, when we heard you screaming bloody murder. My mother ran down the stairs to see what had happened, and I took off after her. We found you in the study, holding your mother, screaming. You were covered in her blood and scared to death.

"My mother turned to me and told me to go back upstairs and stay there. I'll never forget the way she spoke to me. She was terrified. I passed Elodie coming down toward the screaming. I can see it so clearly. She'd been in the tub and came down in her bathrobe. I headed upstairs, but couldn't pull myself away, so I watched through the banisters. I saw Elodie go to you, strip you naked, and carry you upstairs to the bathroom. How that woman managed to carry you without any help amazed me. You were in a frenzy, hysterical. You scared us all to death. Elodie was beside herself with worry. I eavesdropped as best I could. Elodie called

184

the doctor, who gave you a sedative. My mother made it very clear that she didn't want me speaking to the police. She brought me hot chocolate and made me a nest on Elodie's couch. I couldn't sleep, as you can imagine. Later that night, after your mother's body was removed and the police had gone, I saw lights in the woods. It was a fire. I realized later that she was burning your bloody clothes. I pretended I was asleep and overheard Elodie and my mom come up with the lie about you being found soaked outside the window – so they could explain why they'd had to undress you and get you into a fresh set of clothes."

As the impact of Felicity's words sunk in, Ebby's emotions whirled between anger and fury at Elodie for keeping the truth away from him. "My God. Do you realize that these lies may have contributed to my lifetime of psychiatric issues?"

Tears welled in Felicity's eyes and ran down her cheeks. "I do. And I understand if you can't forgive me. I think Elodie suffers too. But she was trying to protect you, Ebby. I swear. And so was my mother. The last thing Elodie wanted was your name in the headlines. She couldn't have kept you out of it. And she was scared for you. You were covered in blood. Elodie was afraid the police would think you were involved. She acted rashly, but it was out of concern for you. No one knew you were going to wake up the next morning with amnesia. In hindsight, I see all the flaws in Elodie's logic. She would have told the truth, but she was scared."

"Do you think Elodie knows who killed my mother?"

"No. I – I don't know."

Ebby knew Felicity was right. Everything Elodie had done ever since Cynthia's death had been in Ebby's best interests. Reminding himself, not for the first time, that he loved his aunt even more than he had loved his mother, Ebby found he didn't have the strength to conjure up any more animosity. All he wanted now was the truth. "Do you have any idea who murdered my mother?"

"No," Felicity said. "And neither does Elodie, of that I'm certain. She's watched you grapple with amnesia all these years. She would have done anything to help you find the truth. Once the case went cold, there was just nothing to be done, except to provide you with emotional support."

"Who do you think did it, Felicity?"

"Honestly, I was always suspicious of your Uncle Gary. He was a bad guy. Went to prison for bank robbery and rape, I think. Cynthia adored him. She thought he was innocent, framed for a crime he didn't commit, and was on a mission to get him out of prison. Do you remember that?"

"Yeah, I do, actually."

Ebby hadn't thought of his mother's brother, Gary North, in ages.

"But it wasn't him. He was in the jail at the time, and he adored his sister."

"So we're back where we started," Ebby said.

"Except you have a sister," Felicity said, giving him a sheepish smile.

Ebby moved to the couch, sat next to Felicity, and put his arm around her. "That makes me happy."

"Me too, Ebs." Felicity finished her beer. "I feel like a huge weight has been lifted. And guess what? I'm quitting my job. I'll call Melinda and tell her personally. I'm tired of acting like everything is just fine. It's not. Hasn't been since Cynthia's murder. It's time for me to move. I should have quit long ago.

"I'm off to bed." Felicity stood and stretched, before she gathered up the empty beer bottles and carried them into the kitchen. "Goodnight, Ebs." Before she closed her bedroom door, she said, "I'm glad we talked. No more secrets?"

"No more secrets," Ebby said.

After Felicity closed her door, Ebby sat on the couch for a long time. There was something niggling in the back of his mind, something about the night his mother died, elusive and slippery. He let it go and got ready for bed. But sleep wouldn't come, and Ebby couldn't shake the feeling that things were going to get worse before they got better.

Chapter 26

Brian

Monday, January 12

Olivia and Brian had sent their email to the agent in Minnesota on Friday. Now, three days later, two detectives from Minnesota, along with two local detectives were waiting for Brian at the Central Marin Policing Authority as the uniformed officer showed him into a spacious conference room with a large window overlooking Mt. Tam. Brian had met Detective Rathman several times while working as a San Francisco homicide detective. Jeanette Finley, who looked surprisingly young to Brian, seemed on first glance to be all business. Brian was glad he wore a dark shirt and a blazer, for he could feel the sweat as it formed between his shoulder blades and went trickling down his back. He'd spent his entire working life hunting criminals, tracking them into dark alleys and booby-trapped buildings. He had been beaten, stabbed – twice – and shot in the leg. Never once had he balked at danger. Now he looked at the three men and one woman sitting around the table and saw himself as he used to be, the hunter, the predator, relishing the chase in the pursuit of justice.

As he made eye contact with the officers who would take down Leanne Stoddard AKA Andrea Seaton, he recognized the anticipation of the chase and wondered where that part of his personality had gone. Once upon a time, the chase had excited him, pulsed through his veins and made him feel alive. Now he was finding out the hard way that he no longer had the stomach for it.

A tall, cadaverously thin man with a thatch of gray hair and piercing brown eyes stood up and extended his hand. "Brian Vickery? I'm Detective Summerfield, the agent in charge of Andrea Seaton's case. This is my colleague, Detective Daniels." Summerfield nodded at a young man who also stood. On quick glance, the kid looked to be in his early thirties and had the build of a high-school football star.

"Pleased to meet you, sir," Detective Daniels said.

"Let's have a seat and we can talk about Andrea Seaton," Detective Summerfield said.

Detectives Finley and Rathman were seated at the end of the table. Brian took a seat across from Detective Summerfield.

"If it's okay with you, I'll brief you on what we know, tell you what I'd like to do, and then you can ask questions. Okay?"

Brian nodded, knowing full well he didn't have a choice in the matter.

Detective Summerfield pushed a pad and pen over to Brian. "If you have any questions as we go along, just write them down. When I've finished briefing, I'll clarify and answer any questions. Fair enough?"

"Okay," Brian said, surprised at Detective Summerfield's candid way of speaking.

"In 2010, Andrea Seaton was hired as a low-level claims processor at Minnesota Life and Casualty, which is where you had your insurance when your house burned down, correct?"

"Yes," Brian said.

"Thought so. We'll come back to that. In any event, as soon as she was hired, she and her husband took out life insurance policies on each other, sizeable ones. About eight months after they bought insurance, Andrea's husband started having stomach problems. They would come and go, and at times would be bad enough for him to land in the hospital. Andrea was all concern, especially since her husband, Theodore Seaton – Teddy to his friends – was under a good deal of stress. He was a prosecutor for the Minneapolis District Attorney's office. As you know from your time on the police force, that sort of job carries its fair share of intensity. Anyway, a couple of years go by, and Mr. Seaton slowly gets better. Then, out of the blue, his stomach troubles come back with a vengeance, he is admitted to the hospital, but dies within twenty-four hours.

"Andrea played the grieving widow. She sobbed and cried and acted like her entire world had crashed around her. The autopsy revealed that Teddy Seaton had been slowly poisoned with antifreeze. He suffered a horrible death. Of course, the wife is always a suspect. When we interviewed witnesses, Dora, Teddy's nineteen-year-old daughter, didn't hesitate to point the finger at her stepmother.

"We brought Andrea in to answer some questions. When we told her Teddy had been murdered, she acted shocked and eager to cooperate. She seemed genuinely heartbroken and readily agreed to take a polygraph, just so she could be eliminated and we could focus on finding the real killer."

"And that's where we made our first mistake," Daniels interjected. "While we questioned her, she had been sobbing and crying and asked if she could take the polygraph the next morning. We agreed, like idiots. She promised to show up at 8:30 the following morning, so we let her go home. She never showed. Went on the run and we haven't seen her since."

"What did she do for money?" Brian asked.

Detective Summerville said, "She cleaned out her husband's accounts before she left. Our investigation revealed she'd been writing herself checks and signing his name for months. We think her husband may have discovered the forgery, threatened to turn her over to the authorities, and that's why she killed him."

"What do you want from me?"

"I'll let Detective Rathman explain the plan. It was his idea. To be quite honest, I know you're a retired cop, but I'm not completely comfortable with having a civilian participating in—"

"The truth of the matter is that she did a good job covering her tracks," Detective Rathman interrupted. "Of course, we could just arrest her, but we'd be doing Detective Summerfield and the Minneapolis PD a huge favor if we could get Andrea to admit she murdered her husband on tape. To that end, we need you to wear a wire. This is what we're thinking." The plan was a straightforward one, and after Rathman explained the logistics, along with several contingency plans should things go wrong, Brian's confidence returned.

"Are you up to this, Brian? Because if it's too much, we can make other arrangements," Rathman asked.

"I'll be fine. I just can't believe I didn't see it."

"She fooled us too," Detective Summerfield said.

Rathman said, "It'll be easier to convince you that you aren't a fool after she's arrested. You should assume she's watching you. She's clever. We don't want to arouse her suspicions. So be careful and act natural."

"What made you suspicious about her in the first place?" Detective Daniels asked.

Brian shook his head. "Nothing. I didn't suspect a thing. My business partner had a gut feeling and did some digging on her own. If it weren't for Olivia …" Brian couldn't bring himself to give voice to the significance of this particular *what if.*

"Look, Brian," Detective Rathman said, "Don't feel bad that you got conned. I can see you're full of doubt and maybe even a little fear. That's understandable. This woman is a consummate professional. She could have gotten to any one of us."

"I admit to feeling more than a little foolish," Brian confessed. "A year ago, I would never have fallen for her. Why did she pick me?"

"We think she got a look at your file when she worked at Minnesota Life and Casualty. Our investigation revealed that she regularly inquired into male beneficiaries who received large payouts, something she wouldn't have done in the course and scope of her regular duties. She saw that you had been paid out on your wife's death and on your home, when it burned," Detective Summerfield said. "Maybe she just liked the look of you. Who knows?"

"So she was using the insurance database to troll for victims? That's just great. Are you sure you want to wait until Saturday night?" Brian asked. "I'd like to get this over with."

"We're tracking her communication with her next victim," Detective Summerfield said.

"Next victim?" Brian asked, incredulous. "Aren't you afraid she'll run?"

"She can run all she wants, and we'll be right behind her," Detective Summerfield said. "We've rented the apartment next door to her in Fairfax. We're tracking her internet use, and we've got a GPS tracking device on her car, so we know her movements at all times. And just for your information, we're not doing anything about the bank accounts and credit cards she's taken out in your wife's name, not yet anyway. We want her to think that she is skating under the radar. Once we arrest her, we'll sort all that out for you."

"Okay. What's next?"

"Can you call her and set up the dinner date?" Detective Rathman asked.

"Now?" Brian asked.

"Now," Rathman said.

"No," Brian insisted. "Tell me where and when you want us to be and I'll get her there. I'm not going to set up the meet with everyone listening in. She'll sense something's up."

"He has a point," Detective Rathman said.

"Okay," Detective Summerfield agreed. "Let us know the logistics, and we'll make arrangements to get you wired up beforehand."

"Are you okay with all of this?" Detective Finley spoke for the first time. Brian could see the worry in her eyes. He didn't blame her. Had he been in her position, he would have been worried too.

"I'm fine. I'll just be glad when this is behind me."

"Me too," Detective Finley gave him a shy smile.

Brian stood, shook hands with everyone and hurried out into the cold January air.

Part of him wanted to go to Olivia, but he didn't. Instead he went home to make his phone call. Leanne answered on the first ring.

"Hello, Brian. I thought you'd forgotten about me."

Brian closed his eyes and conjured up Olivia's face as he spun his lie. "How could I forget about you? I've been busy with work, but wanted to see if you were available Saturday night for dinner?"

"Saturday sounds perfect. Any chance we could get away this weekend?"

How easily you lie.

"Can't. Work," Brian said. "But I got someone else to take a surveillance gig Saturday night so I can spend some time with you." The lies were coming more easily now.

"Dinner sounds great. Left Bank?"

"Sure," Brian said. "What time?"

"Eight o'clock?"

"See you then."

Chapter 27

Ebby

Monday, January 12

Chloe Jeffers had her office on the ground floor of a Victorian house that had been converted to an office building in downtown San Rafael. The house was two-storied, with bay windows on either side of the main entrance door. The walkway up to the house was paved in old brick and weaved through a garden. When Ebby reached the front door, he was surprised when a gamine woman with shoulder-length black hair and bright-red cat-eyed glasses opened the door for him. She was dressed head to toe in black, with the exception of a pair of well-worn purple cowboy boots.

"Mr. Engstrom?" The woman held out her hand. "I'm Dr. Jeffers. Follow me. I'm on the second floor. No elevator, I'm afraid."

Her office was at the back corner of the house, overlooking a large backyard, complete with a grove of eucalyptus trees. "Have a seat." She indicated a comfortable-looking couch. The room was austere: the couch, a chair, and a small computer desk with a printer and scanner, over which Dr. Jeffers' framed credentials hung. On another wall hung one single painting of a seascape, which depicted a foamy green wave, curling against a still gray sky. Unable to resist, Ebby stepped close to it, realizing how much he missed the beach.

"You like the beach?" Dr. Jeffers asked.

"Yes. Love to surf. Been a while though." He sat down on the couch. "Do you prefer that I lie back?"

"Whatever makes you most comfortable," Chloe said. "Thanks for filling out your paperwork early. I have everything to bill your insurance."

"I imagine you got my records from my previous doctors?" Ebby asked. He half expected to spend this first session telling the story of his mother's murder, his subsequent dissociative amnesia, and how it had affected his life.

"Actually, I think we should do things a little differently," Dr. Jeffers said. "I purposefully did not get your records because something tells me you need a fresh start. Would that be a correct assumption?"

Ebby couldn't believe his ears. Historically, his condition had always intrigued medical professionals, and the psychiatrists he had seen over the years had seemed focused on the aspects of his amnesia rather than on how the amnesia was affecting him. "You have no idea," Ebby said.

"If it's okay with you, I'd like you to tell me what's happening now. How you're coping, whatever you want to discuss. I know you mentioned that you want your memory to return, but I think we should just let that go for now, at least until you get to know me. Thoughts?"

"That sounds good," Ebby said. "Honestly, I swore I'd never see another psychiatrist in my life."

"Therapy can get tedious, especially if it's not giving you what you need. So I'd like to discuss your needs and expectations today. First off, I wanted to tell you that I'm a psychologist, not a psychiatrist, so I can't prescribe meds."

"I understand," Ebby said.

"As we go along, you may change your mind and decide that you want to continue taking medication. If that becomes the case, I can refer you to a handful of psychiatrists that I trust. You can always ask a psychiatrist for a regimen that is temporary."

During all the years Ebby had undergone therapy, he'd never been given a choice. He was impressed with Dr. Jeffers' style of communication; it felt like he was having a chat with a friend. There was zero pretense about this woman, and for the first time since he lost his memory, he entertained the idea of getting himself sorted out.

Without thinking, Ebby leaned back on the couch, pleased to see Dr. Jeffers smile. She'd spoken the magic words with her promise of a fresh start. As Ebby lay back and closed his eyes, he suddenly knew that things were going to be okay.

Chapter 28

Olivia

Brian had done some digging and discovered that Olivia wasn't the first female lawyer Seth Woodson had hassled since his hiring two and a half years ago. Although Olivia was reluctant to go over opposing counsel's – or anyone's – head, she knew speaking to Gwen was the right thing to do in this instance. When she finally got through to Gwen Kyleson's personal assistant, she'd been honest and straightforward. "I have some issues with a case with Seth Woodson. Something's happened. I feel like the DA needs to know, and I want to tell her personally before I file an ethics complaint with the State Bar. If she could spare me ten minutes, I'd be very grateful."

When the assistant didn't respond, Olivia crossed her fingers and kept talking. "If I were in Mrs. Kyleson's position, I would want someone to tell me what's going on. Will you at least ask her if she'd meet with me?" The assistant had taken Olivia's number and promised to call back. Sure enough, twenty minutes later, an appointment for 9 o'clock the next morning was scheduled.

Now, Olivia grabbed her briefcase and headed into the civic center toward the DA's office. Given the information that Brian had discovered about ADA Woodson, Olivia had opted to speak to Gwen Kyleson by herself. She reasoned that it wouldn't have been appropriate for Ebby to become privy to the underbelly of the DA's office. With Ebby as a witness, DA Kyleson would be less likely to speak to Olivia candidly. Olivia's strategy was to present her complaints in a professional and unemotional manner. She would say her piece, thank the DA, and leave it all in the hands of Lady Fate.

As far as she could tell, the meeting would go one of two ways. Her accusations would be categorically dismissed, in which case she would move forward with Ebby's preliminary hearing and trial, or Gwen Kyleson would believe her and act accordingly. In any event, if Olivia didn't get a response by Monday, she'd turn her focus to the preliminary hearing, present the exonerating evidence to the judge, and file an ethics complaint with the California State Bar Association. Ebby didn't do it. She was confident she'd win. A solid plan, she reminded herself, as she paused in the corridor just outside the DA's office and took a deep breath.

Ten minutes later, she followed the same assistant she'd spoken with on the phone to Gwen's office. Before the assistant left Olivia, she said, "We were rooting for you last October, Mrs. Sinclair. You were a hero, a credit to our gender."

"Thank you," Olivia said.

Olivia hadn't seen Gwen since the Bar Association Christmas party two years ago. Looking at her now, seated behind the large modern desk, it took all Olivia had to not react to the physical change in the woman. The cancer had ravaged her. She wore a wig, and her round face was gaunt with prominent cheekbones. Despite these changes, Gwen Kyleson's eyes still sparkled with intelligence. When she spoke, her voice was strong and assured. She stood and offered Olivia her hand. "Hello, Mrs. Sinclair."

They shook hands and Olivia sat down in the offered chair.

"Thank you for agreeing to see me." Olivia took a moment and collected herself.

"This is unusual, Mrs. Sinclair. It's not my practice to meet with opposing counsel on any cases pending in my office. You said you had some concerns?"

Yet here we are. Olivia took the ME's report out of her briefcase and held it on her lap. "I represent Edward Engstrom, whose mother was brutally murdered in 1984. My client was thirteen at the time. He is believed to have witnessed the murder, but immediately after, he suffered a severe and persistent case of dissociative amnesia. He's never remembered what happened that night. The police investigated the case and Edward was cleared by the medical examiner, who concluded Edward's height and weight did not align with the stab wounds on the body, based on the angle and location of the wounds. Yet Mr. Engstrom was recently arrested for the crime, even though the police cleared him thirty years ago.

"I've come across evidence that was omitted from discovery that exonerates my client categorically. When I approached ADA Woodson after court, asking if we could meet to discuss the case, he said, and I'm quoting verbatim, 'I don't meet with people off the record, especially old bitches like you with an axe to grind. I know you're on some feminazi crusade. I couldn't care less. I'm coming for you, Mrs. Sinclair. I don't give a shit whether or not your client is innocent.'"

Olivia was pleased when Gwen's eyes opened in alarm.

"As you can imagine, I was totally shocked. I've dealt with my share of bullies, but this was uncalled for. Most importantly, I'm concerned for my client. Seth Woodson left the original ME's findings that prove my client's innocence out of the discovery he produced." Olivia handed Duncan Wymark's report to Gwen Kyleson. "Of course, I'll move for a dismissal at the prelim. Had Seth done his homework, he would never have arrested my client. I'm here today because I feel obligated to file an ethics complaint against Mr. Woodson. If I were in your shoes, I would want to know what my staff were up to."

Olivia waited as Gwen Kyleson took her time reading the report, not once, but twice. When she was finished, she turned the report face down on her desk and said, "If this was left out of discovery, how did you get a copy?"

"After the case went cold, Fiona Engstrom, the sister-in-law of the murdered woman, hired a private investigator. He obtained an entire copy of the file. I met with Duncan Wymark yesterday. He remembers this case and has agreed to testify regarding the report." She met Gwen Kyleson's gaze and saw the flash of anxiety there.

"I don't usually go over opposing counsel's head. Forgive me if I've overstepped, but if I was in your shoes, I would want to be told about this."

Gwen stood, indicating the meeting was over, and extended her hand. "Thank you for coming in, Mrs. Sinclair. I'll look into this and get back to you by the end of the day."

Olivia nodded. As she walked out, she heard Gwen on the speaker to her assistant. "Nancy, get me Cal Lonsdale. I don't care what he's doing. I want him in here within the hour." Olivia knew Cal Lonsdale by reputation – a senior investigator who had been with the DA's office for ages. Joe was known among his peers as a bulldog, a guy who held grudges and was as loyal as they come. Gwen Kyleson, it seemed, was taking Olivia's concerns very seriously indeed.

* * *

San Rafael Joe's has been a Marin institution since the 1940s. Known for its affordably priced Italian food, San Rafael Joe's – in Olivia's opinion – had the best eggplant parmigiana in town. Olivia had a standing lunch date with Stephen Vine, her dear friend, who also happened to be one of the most prominent criminal defense attorneys in the San Francisco Bay Area. They had been friends since they graduated from law school and had referred clients to each other over the years. When Olivia had been accused of murdering her husband's mistress, she'd hired Stephen. Today he waited for Olivia, reading the paper and drinking coffee.

"Sorry I'm late," she said.

"No problem. You look healthy. Seems criminal law agrees with you." The waiter came and took Olivia's drink order. Once he was gone, Stephen said, "You've knocked the DA's office on its head."

"You heard about my meeting with Gwen Kyleson already? I just left there."

"I have contacts. These things get around."

"Well, what else did you hear?"

"Well, Seth Woodson's expected to be gone by the end of the day. Big surprise there, but he had it coming. Was I correct in assuming you wanted the eggplant?"

"You were," Olivia said.

"Good. I took the liberty of ordering for you." The waiter appeared with their lunch orders. He set the ravioli down in front of Stephen, the eggplant parmigiana in front of Olivia. "So, Olivia, tell me why you seem like you're carrying the weight of the world on your shoulders. You've accomplished something monumental for your client. You're back in the game. What's the problem?"

Olivia sipped her wine. "I know this is going to sound ridiculous, but there are times when I feel like I'm past my sell-by date, if that makes sense. I don't know what to do with myself anymore. Part of me regrets getting rid of my practice. The other part of me knows that it was time to slow down. The events of last October still haunt me. I'm still picking up the pieces, still looking over my shoulder when I leave the house for that lone journalist looking for a story. And while I'm glad I was able to help Ebby, I know now that I don't want to practice criminal law."

"So fix it," Stephen said, in his usual direct manner.

"It's not quite that easy," Olivia said. "I have no idea what needs to be fixed. I'm just completely out of sorts."

"Why?"

Olivia bit back her irritation.

"Don't get pissed at me, Liv. But here's the thing: you don't know what to do with your life. You're questioning who you are and how you can be of service. Am I right?"

"That would be an accurate statement."

"So do what you know, on your own terms. You could go back to family law," Stephen said. "Just make it work for you."

"What do you mean?"

"Well, word on the street is that Claire Montreaux is struggling a bit. She assumed she could fill the void you left just by getting referrals from me. She's a good lawyer, don't get me wrong. But she doesn't have the people skills you have, for lack of a better word."

"I'm sure Claire doesn't need me to tell her how to do her job."

"No, but it seems to me you two could come to some arrangement. The way I see it, you could do the research and writing, handle the clients, and let Claire be one who steps into the arena. One thing we both know, Claire Montreaux enjoys the fight." Stephen gave Olivia a knowing look. "I know you're finished being a litigator. I get it. That part of the job can chew you up and make you crazy. When we're young lawyers, we're hungry and ready to argue and fight and get ourselves out there. It stands to reason that attitude would shift as we age."

"It hasn't changed for you," Olivia said.

"Not yet. But it will. I know that and am prepared for that eventuality. You're a good writer, Liv, a good problem solver. You're brilliant at coming up with masterful creative settlement options, and clients love you. You can go back in for one round of glory and then quit practicing on your own terms, not because you were arrested for a murder you didn't commit. Here's one more layer of unsolicited advice: before you make any grand decision about what to do with your life, you should get out of here. Take a vacation. It's been years, Liv. Go someplace warm. Sit on the beach. Have a fruity drink with an umbrella. Heal your soul."

Olivia did a quick calculation. She and Richard hadn't taken a vacation together in at least the last three years of their marriage, and she hadn't been anywhere since their divorce.

"I think I'll go and see Denny."

"Brilliant idea," Stephen said. "When you get back, you can make some decisions … or not. And take Brian with you."

Olivia shot Stephen a look.

"What? You think it's not obvious? You two are made for each other. You both know it. What are you waiting for? No one's getting any younger."

Olivia smiled in spite of herself. Stephen was right, Olivia did need a break, needed to get away for a while. With any luck, some distance would give her some much-needed perspective.

Chapter 29

Seth Woodson

Tuesday, January 13

When Seth Woodson went back to his office after spending the morning in court, Blair, his paralegal, was at the reception desk, drinking a cup of coffee and chatting with the lady who answered the phone. He'd hired Blair because she was easy on the eyes – tall, nice boobs. When she'd interviewed for the job, she'd worn a skirt that showed off her long legs. After a few weeks of working for Seth, she'd caught him staring at her while she was bent over a stack of files.

"Looking good," Seth had said, pleased that he'd chosen this moderately intelligent but extremely attractive girl out of the dozen or so who had applied for the job.

She stood up and wheeled around to face him, her cheeks flushed. "What did you say?"

"I was just complimenting you," he'd responded, not feeling the least bit guilty.

Blair had never worn a dress after that incident. As the weeks went by, their relationship had become more and more strained. He'd asked her out for drinks a couple of times, but she had always flat-out refused. After her thirty-day probationary period was over, Blair had come into his office.

"Can I talk to you?"

"Of course," he said.

"I want you to stop sexually harassing me. If you don't, I'm going to report you."

"What are you talking about?" he'd said.

"Just stop," Blair had said. "I don't like ratting people out. But you've got to stop asking me out, stop staring at me. Do you understand?"

Seth didn't say anything.

"Good," Blair had said, before she stormed out.

Since then, Seth had been looking for a reason to fire her. Unfortunately, he couldn't just let her go at will. Procedures needed to be followed. And, as fate would have it, Blair's work performance was excellent. Now, as he caught her gossiping when she should be working, he wondered if he could use this to his advantage.

"Do you need me to find something for you to do?"

Seth expected Blair to hurry back to her desk and pretend she was busy. Instead she smirked at him. "No," she said, her tone curt. "Mrs. Kyleson wants to see you right away."

When Seth started toward Gwen Kyleson's office, Blair said, "They're in the conference room." Seth switched direction, wondering who *they* were, realizing that Blair had fallen into step behind him. "I know the way, Blair," he said over his shoulder.

"Go to hell, Seth."

He came to a stop in front of the door that led to the conference room. "What did you say to me?"

"You heard me." Blair pushed past him, stepped into the conference room, and took the empty seat next to Gwen Kyleson.

Seth's stomach clenched as he walked in the room and saw

Gwen Kyleson, and her devoted guard dog Cal Lonsdale, along with the lady whose name he couldn't remember who was in charge of human resources. Wearing a smug look on her face, Blair took the empty seat next to Gwen. *What the hell is this?*

"Ah, Seth," Gwen said.

"What's going on?" He swallowed, his mouth suddenly dry.

Gwen Kyleson didn't meet Seth's eyes as she spoke; instead she opted to keep her eyes on the papers in front of her.

She's weak. Whatever she's trying to do to me, she's just a woman. Weak, stupid. Inferior. When he met Cal's eyes, Seth nearly recoiled at the cold, hard stare.

"I'd like to talk to you about a conversation you had with Olivia Sinclair last Friday, after your motion to suppress hearing." Gwen looked up and looked at Seth straight on. He had a flash of what it would be like to be on the opposite aisle of Gwen in court, and realized he might have made a fatal miscalculation in judging his boss's intelligence. "Do you remember that altercation?"

"I wouldn't call it an altercation," Seth said. "She wanted me to dismiss the case. I refused."

Gwen cocked her head for a moment before she rifled through the file and pulled out a stapled document. "You're confident you have sufficient evidence for a conviction?"

"Working on it," Seth said. "I'll have it before trial. I have confidence in this case, Gwen. We arrested the right guy. I'll get a conviction."

"Okay. And have you been forthright with your discovery?"

Seth caught Blair's eye and tried to convey the message that he would deal with her later. She smiled at him.

"What's going on here? Why the interrogation?"

Gwen turned the stapled document over and pushed it across the table to him. "Do you recognize this?"

Oh, crap. Seth felt his face go flush with heat at the realization that he'd been caught out. He knew Gwen wouldn't take any malfeasance regarding discovery lightly. One of his colleagues had been fired just a month ago for pulling a report that should have been provided to opposing counsel.

"This is evidence that exonerates Mr. Engstrom. Why was it not given to Olivia Sinclair?"

"But it was." Seth turned his attention to Blair. "You screwed up and you're blaming me? I told you to fax this over."

"You're a liar," Blair said. "You pulled it out of the documents I was photocopying to produce in discovery and you said you would fax it over yourself. The receptionist heard you. She was standing right there, you idiot."

"This is a misunderstanding," Seth said. "Blair and I can sort this out."

"No, we can't," Blair said, her voice tight with anger. "I'm not your scapegoat, Seth."

"You seem to be missing my point," Gwen said. "This report exonerates Mr. Engstrom without question. Have you read it?"

"Of course I've read it. I read it before I had him arrested. The science from 1984 is dated, Gwen. I'm waiting to hear from another expert whose opinion contradicts the 1984 ME."

"Which science precisely is no longer applicable?" Gwen asked.

Seth squirmed in his chair. The walls started to close in on him. White-hot fury at his bitch of a boss tightened in his stomach, as he fumbled for a cohesive answer.

"Do you understand my question?" Gwen asked again.

"Of course I understand your question. I'm not stupid," Seth snapped.

"Then explain your position."

"This is total bullshit," Seth said. He stood and turned to go out of the room, only to discover Cal Lonsdale had stood up to block his way.

"Sit down, Mr. Woodson," Gwen said. She waited until he was seated. "Olivia Sinclair came to me."

"Oh, so she's the reason we're having this little conversation.

She has no criminal experience, so she goes over my head because she doesn't want to face me in court? This is unreal."

"So did you call her an old bitch, or a feminazi with an axe to grind? Did you tell her that you didn't care if her client was innocent or guilty because you were coming for her?"

"I most certainly did not say that. Surely you don't believe her."

"Actually, I do. Olivia Sinclair has a stellar reputation. I know her as a woman of integrity and honor. And I assure you, she wouldn't withhold discovery."

Seth shot Blair another dirty look, and was once again surprised that she didn't react to it. He shook his head. "That figures."

"What figures?" Gwen asked.

"Of course you women stick together," Seth said. "I can't win here. If you don't like the way I'm handling the Engstrom case, I'll dismiss it. Is that what you want? Fine." Seth started to stand again. He had paid leave coming. He was going to call in sick tomorrow. Let someone else worry about his case load. Or he could even go to the doctor and ask to go on stress-related disability. His parents had a house in Squaw Valley. Maybe he'd just go the mountains and let all the losers he worked with cover his responsibilities.

"I heard you," Blair said.

"What?" Seth asked, as a feel of doom washed over him.

"I heard everything you said to Mrs. Sinclair. I was coming to have you sign some pleadings. I heard you call her an old bitch. Your words stopped me in my tracks. Geez, Seth. All she wanted to do was talk about the case. You were horrid to her."

Seth looked from Blair to Gwen, conscious all of a sudden, of what was coming.

"You lying bitch," Seth said.

"I'm not lying—"

"Enough," Gwen said. "Blair, that will be all. Thank you."

Blair stood up, glared at Seth, and walked out of the room. Once she was gone, Gwen cleared her throat and fiddled with the folder on the table. When she looked at Seth, there was no mistaking the disgust in her voice. "Your services will no longer be required, Mr. Woodson," Gwen said. "We'll leave you with Mrs. Scofield, who will go over your exit pay and have you sign some papers."

"I'll need to clear my desk. And hand off my files."

"Already taken care of. You're no longer authorized to be near the employee-only area. Cal will have your belongings ready and help you to your car." Gwen stood and so did Cal Lonsdale. Without a backward glance, the two of them stepped out of the room, leaving Seth alone with Mrs. Scofield.

Ten minutes later, Seth Woodson stared straight ahead, his hands clenched in fists as he was not only escorted out of the DA's office, but also escorted out of the Civic Center. Cal Lonsdale walked him all the way to his car and watched him drive away. By the time Seth was heading south on 101 toward Sausalito, where he lived in his parents' basement, he was furious. There were no grounds to terminate him. He hadn't done anything wrong. He'd lost his job thanks to Blair Davis, Gwen Kyleson, and Olivia Sinclair.

Chapter 30

Olivia

Tuesday, January 13

Ebby was waiting outside for Olivia when she returned to the office after her very enlightening lunch with Stephen Vine. He had a canvas tote under his arm and a smile on his face.

"What's in the bag?" Olivia asked as she unlocked the office door and stood aside, so Ebby could enter ahead of her. Once they were in, Olivia locked the door behind them and headed to her office.

"I've been cooking pretty much non-stop since moving in with Felicity. I've made you a couple of things, namely a chicken curry and a large batch of chicken noodle soup." Ebby set the bag down on Olivia's desk.

"Thanks, Ebby. That's really thoughtful."

"To be honest, I think Felicity's neighbors are tired of me knocking on their door with food." He gave her a sheepish smile as he sat down across from her. "For all I know, they're just throwing it away. How did it go today? What did Mrs. Kyleson say about the medical examiner's report?"

"She was stoic but receptive. Said she was going to look into the matter and get back to me about the best way to proceed. I made a strong case for dismissal and left her with the medical examiner's report that was left out of the discovery we received from the DA. Worst-case scenario is that we ask for a dismissal at the preliminary hearing. We can call the medical examiner to testify."

"And if the case isn't dismissed at the preliminary hearing?"

"We go to trial. The evidence is incontrovertible, Ebby. There's no way you could have killed your mother in 1984. You should never have been arrested. Remember, all we need is reasonable doubt. I've got way more than that."

Ebby sighed. "I know. I just want it over."

"I understand." Olivia kicked off her shoes and stared at her client, noticing that the dark circles under his eyes had diminished and his color had come back. "You're looking better. How are you feeling?"

"Honestly, I'm feeling hopeful for the first time in ages. I had my first session with Dr. Jeffers yesterday. She's going to help me."

"I am glad you like her. She's very direct and utterly without pretense. I've used her on a fair share of custody cases. She's one of the few expert witnesses I've known who turned down a job because they didn't agree with my position. I respect that. She's irreverent and unorthodox and I figured she'd be perfect for you."

"Have you spoken to Elodie?"

"No," Olivia said. "Why?"

Ebby hesitated a second. "I recently discovered that Felicity is my half-sister. You're not going to believe this, but my father and Allegra – our housekeeper – were very much in love. Felicity is their love child."

Olivia opened her mouth and shut it again – she didn't quite know what to say.

When Ebby said, "I'm actually very happy to have Felicity as a sister," Olivia breathed a sigh of relief, then had another thought.

"Have you and Felicity discussed the night of the murder?"

"No," Ebby said too quickly.

He's lying. Olivia knew it, and she wondered why. They were interrupted when the phone rang.

"Olivia Sinclair."

"Mrs. Sinclair, Gwen Kyleson. I've just reviewed Edward Engstrom's file, and I'm afraid I owe him an apology."

"Mrs. Kyleson, Mr. Engstrom is here with me now. May I put him on speaker?"

"Please," Mrs. Kyleson said. "Mr. Engstrom?"

"I'm here," Ebby said.

"I've reviewed the medical examiner's findings from the original file, and must concur that his findings were conclusive and accurate. There's no way you could have killed your mother. As such, I'm going to see that your case is dismissed by the end of business today."

Ebby's face broke into a huge grin as his eyes welled with tears, and he and Olivia gave each other a high five.

"Mr. Engstrom?"

"I'm here. Thank you so much, Mrs. Kyleson," Ebby said.

"Had Mr. Woodson done a more thorough investigation, you would never have been arrested."

"Thank you, ma'am," Ebby said.

"And, Mr. Engstrom, I should tell you that we'll be taking a fresh look at your mother's case. These cold cases are so difficult to close, especially after all this time. But I promise you I'll put some fresh eyes on it and report back. Please accept my apologies with regard to this matter."

"Thank you," Ebby said.

"Mrs. Sinclair, I'll send you an email confirming the dismissal of Ebby's case within half an hour or so. Look for the dismissal to be filed first thing tomorrow morning. If the judge wants to see us in person, I'll call you. And, Mrs. Sinclair, I'm glad you came to me. You did the right thing."

"Thank you," Olivia said. She hung up the phone and faced Ebby, who looked as though the weight of the world had been lifted from his shoulders. He exhaled as his expression became serious.

"That was close, wasn't it? I could have gone to trial, the jury could have not liked me or believed me, and I could have wound up in jail."

"But you didn't," Olivia said. "We had good evidence, Ebby."

"Still."

"How can I ever thank you, Olivia?" Ebby said.

"Your chicken curry is all the gratitude I need. But I do have a question."

"Ask it," Ebby said."

"Why do I get the feeling you're holding something back with regard to Felicity?"

Ebby sighed. "I am. And I'll tell you this in confidence because you're my attorney. Felicity saw something the night of the murder. Her mother made her promise never to tell a soul what she saw, a promise that was reiterated when Felicity's mother lay dying. Felicity confided in me, and I swore that I would carry her secret. For now."

"She witnessed something that night?"

Ebby nodded. "I think if it becomes necessary, Felicity will talk to the police. But I'm not going to push her."

"Your case is going to be dismissed, so I've held my side of the bargain. Could Felicity's secret help you find the real killer?"

"I don't know," Ebby said.

* * *

Olivia arrived home just as the afternoon sun was slowly setting. It bathed her living room in long slivers of light that did little to dispel the chill. Now that Ebby's case was complete, she was back where she started. As she changed into comfortable clothes,

Olivia realized she had arrived at a fork in the road. Choices needed to be made. She'd successfully defended Ebby, which was evidence in her mind that she could still maneuver in the courtroom. But the situation with Ebby had just proved to Olivia that she really didn't want to litigate cases anymore, having long grown tired of unethical shenanigans. But she did like to write and research, and she'd always had a soft spot for the clients who needed her help.

Dressed in yoga pants and an oversized sweater, cup of chamomile tea in hand, Olivia booted up her computer and drafted an email to Claire Montreaux: *Claire, I'm looking to pick up some freelance work and am wondering if you have any you'd be interested in throwing my way? Even if you don't have any work, we could meet for lunch. I'd like to hear how things are going.* Olivia hit send before she could change her mind. She sipped her tea, and thought about Brian, about how she missed him, especially now that she knew their feelings were mutual. What was stopping them from being together? Nothing. Not one thing.

Olivia got up to prepare dinner. She chopped veggies and put a salad together. As she moved to the kitchen sink to rinse her teacup, she saw Brian's car pulling up. When he got out of the car and met her eyes, any doubts Olivia had about their feelings for each other vanished. She opened the front door. Their eyes locked and everything Olivia needed to know about Brian and his feelings for her were clear. Without speaking, she took his hand and led him to her bed.

* * *

Later, when they were lying in each other's arms, Brian said, "I'm sorry, Olivia, for not communicating with you like an adult. I should have told you how I was feeling ages ago."

"I should be apologizing to you," she said. "I was an idiot to push you away. I regret it every day."

Brian turned on his side and faced Olivia. He touched her cheek and ran his fingers over her lips. "What happened to us?"

"Grief and betrayal." Olivia didn't hesitate. "I pulled away from you because you are still in love with your wife. You pulled away from me because you're not ready for a relationship."

"I admit to still holding Maureen in my heart, Olivia. I always will. But I'm finding there's room there for you. I've missed you. Being here with you, knowing you've got my back – had my back – especially now, means the world."

A flood of unchecked emotion washed over Olivia. She swallowed the lump in her throat and said, "I feel the same."

Brian pulled her close. "I know."

Chapter 31

Ebby

Tuesday, January 13

By unspoken agreement, Ebby and Felicity had been lying low together, not discussing the situation at hand, and spending most of their time putting the finishing touches on Ebby's cookbook. He'd sent it to his agent on Monday, and she had gotten back to him after two hours with a handful of minor changes for him to make before she started shopping it. "I've got three publishers interested, Ebby. I'm going to sell this book." Under normal circumstances, the idea of people around the country – maybe even around the world – cooking the food he loved would have filled Ebby with joy. But the question of who murdered his mother, and his desire to remember what he had witnessed, still consumed him.

It had been difficult, but somehow he had managed to refrain from cross-examining Felicity about the night of his mother's murder. Dr. Jeffers' suggestion that he just let it go wasn't terribly helpful. She had suggested hypnosis, but when Ebby had visibly tensed, she had quickly dropped the subject. There was nothing else to be done, at least on Ebby's part. He and Brian Vickery would meet after the dismissal came through to discuss a plan of action. Ebby would find out who killed his mother. He'd never give up.

Meanwhile, he and Felicity had fallen into a quiet comfortable routine, made even sweeter to Ebby's mind now he knew that Felicity was his half-sister. This newfound knowledge was the one bright light that came out of this horrid ordeal.

He rolled out the choux he would use for the batch of chocolate eclairs he was making, enjoying the comfortable tapping sound of rain on the windows. Cooking was his therapy. Not only had he filled Felicity's freezer and fridge, he had taken to baking for Felicity's neighbors as well, and Olivia, who had all accepted the food with surprise.

He moved into the living room, reached his hands over his head and took a deep breath, slowly bending forward to stretch his back. Through the door he saw Felicity sitting on her bed, sketching some flowers, taking instruction from of a how-to book of botanical drawings.

When the doorbell rang, Ebby said, "I need to deal with this pastry, can you get it?"

"Sure," Felicity responded.

They were both surprised to find Fiona and Elodie standing outside, Elodie holding a houseplant, and Fiona holding a bottle of Perrier-Jouët.

"We've come to see you both," said Elodie, always the master of the obvious, as she stepped into the room. She set the houseplant on the bench near the front door. "We're so relieved that you've been cleared, dear."

"Olivia took a chance going straight to the DA." Not wanting to worry his aging aunts, Ebby hadn't given them the details of the missing discovery and that Fiona's records had given Olivia something to approach the DA with. Now, he kept his answer short and concise. He didn't have any interest in a play-by-play recap of the situation. "Thanks to the records Fiona kept, we had evidence to prove my innocence." Fiona grabbed onto the back of the sofa, just as Elodie wrapped her arms around Ebby and kissed him on both cheeks. Once she was finished with him, she moved on to Felicity, pulling her close and holding her tight. "I'm so sorry, Felicity. I've always known you were my niece. I should have spoken up on your behalf. Fiona and I are both very sorry. Can you ever forgive us?"

"Oh, Elodie," Felicity said, her voice breaking with emotion. "Fiona, there's nothing to forgive."

Elodie and Felicity sat down on the couch, while Fiona followed Ebby into the kitchen and put the champagne in the refrigerator.

"Should I get glasses?" Ebby asked.

"No," Fiona said. "We can't stay long. We need to talk to both of you. You two need to be aware of what's been going on at the house."

"I want to make something clear. Neither Felicity nor I will ever step foot in our family home again. Melinda has been horrible to Felicity. It's time for me to leave my childhood home and those memories behind. Time for me to turn my back on the past and face the future. I'll be glad to see it sold."

"I know, dear." Fiona patted Ebby's arm. "You bore witness to something horrible there. Elodie has agreed to come and live with me at the beach. You're doing the right thing."

"Should I make tea?" Ebby noticed Fiona's coloring was off. She'd lost enough weight to make her cheekbones even more prominent than usual. Ebby wondered about her health. "Aunt Fi, are you okay? You look pale."

"Fine, love. Just old. And tired. Let's sit in the living room. Elodie and I need to talk to both of you."

Ebby had always loved and admired his aunts. As he watched them today, he couldn't help but worry about how much they'd aged, how frail they looked. If he hadn't asked Olivia Sinclair to help him find out who murdered his mother, they wouldn't be in this situation. Should he have tried to deal with the nightmares and flashbacks on his own? Funny. He'd been so focused on his arrest and legal issues that he hadn't had a flashback of the murder or a nightmare since he'd moved into Felicity's apartment.

"We just came to tell you that Mark has been questioned by the police. He's in some serious financial trouble," Fiona said.

"He's in a foul mood," Elodie said. "And don't look at me like that, Fi. He's been bullying both of us." She looked at Ebby. "He wants us to bail him out financially."

"And we said absolutely not," Fiona said. "Mark's had everything handed to him. He's an entitled fool, who's made his bed."

"He's family," Elodie said, her cheeks flushed.

"We are not going to bail him out," Fiona said with finality. "Elodie, dear, please. Give it a rest. We just wanted you to be aware of the situation. Mark is being investigated for money laundering and a host of other financial crimes. He in all likelihood will be arrested. We wanted you both to be prepared."

"What about Melinda?" Felicity asked. "Is she okay?"

"No," Fiona said. "She's in a foul mood too."

"I feel guilty for quitting and running out on her," Felicity said.

Elodie squeezed Felicity's hand. "Don't. She was horrid to you all these years. You owe her nothing."

"I know," Felicity said. "But I still feel sorry for her."

"We should go," Fiona said.

Elodie rose and put an arm around her sister. "Lean on me, sis."

Once the aunts were gone, Ebby and Felicity sat on the couch, sipping their tea.

"I should have told them that I'm still looking for my mother's murderer," Ebby said.

"I wouldn't worry about that," Felicity said. "They'll find out soon enough."

Chapter 32

Brian

Thursday, January 15

Brian entered the last of his time into his billing software and shut down his computer. His PI business was growing at a solid pace. He had a handful of good corporate clients, who needed employee background checks and other work of that nature. Today, he'd caught up by spending the afternoon writing status-update emails to the clients he had been neglecting since Ebby had hired them. He'd been jumpy all day, plagued by worry about his upcoming date with Leanne. There were a hundred ways it could go south. To make matters worse, he was worried about Olivia and their involvement with the Engstroms. There was something about that family that didn't pass the smell test, as far as Brian was concerned. He was sure one of them had committed a perfect murder.

Brian grabbed his keys and was ready to walk out the door, when his mobile rang. Rathman.

"Hey, Brian. Are you at the office?"

"Just getting ready to leave. What's up?"

"We have a situation."

What now? Brian sat back down at his desk.

"Leanne's been watching you. Her car was parked outside Olivia's house last night. If she thinks you're in a relationship with Olivia, she's hardly going to believe she's making you fall for her."

"Does that matter?" Brian asked.

"I think so. She wants something from you, something more than your wife's identity. She's already got that. Why stick around? She's grooming you, probably for marriage, maybe access to your bank accounts. Who knows? In any event, if she knows you're romantically involved with Olivia, she could get suspicious of your interest in her. Detective Summerville's thinking maybe we should call off the dinner Saturday night, and he should arrest her before she goes on the run."

"Let me think for a minute." Brian wanted Leanne convicted, and he needed to play a role in the process as a form of penance for his own stupidity. "I think I can fix this," he said, thinking fast. "I'll call Leanne right now and tell her that Olivia's been harassed by the husband of an old client, and that I'm staying with her until a restraining order is in place."

"Do you think you can pull that off?"

"I'll consider it a dress rehearsal for Saturday."

"Call me back." Rathman hung up.

Brian took a moment to collect himself. His mobile flashed with a text from Olivia, which he ignored, keeping his focus on Leanne. She answered on the first ring.

"Hello, beautiful," Brian said.

"Brian. I wasn't expecting to hear from you. Thought you were busy with work," Leanne said.

"I am. Just making sure we're still on for Saturday night. I've had a brutal week, and I'm looking forward to seeing you."

"Me too. What are you up to?"

"Well, I have a situation. Olivia's being harassed by a rather aggressive husband of an ex-client. I told her I'd stay with her until the restraining order is in place. It's taking longer than it should because we can't find him to serve him the paperwork. Anyway, long story. But if they don't find him by Saturday night, maybe we could just have dinner at Olivia's house? It will be the three of us, but I want to see you," Brian lied easily.

"What does Olivia say?" Leanne asked.

"She'll be glad to have us. I think the whole situation has her a little on edge. I know it's not the romantic evening we planned, but at least we can see each other. We can do our dinner for two as soon as we get this guy served with paperwork."

"Okay," Leanne said. "Tell Olivia thanks. Can you text me her address?"

"Will do," Brian said, once again impressed by how well Leanne lied.

On Saturday morning, he'd call Leanne and tell her the man had been served, the restraining order was in place, and dinner would take place as originally planned.

"Are you at work?"

Knowing that Leanne could very well be parked somewhere watching him, Brian said, "Just wrapping up at the office. I am behind on paperwork. Hope to finish up tonight."

"Okay, hon. Don't work too hard."

"I'll let you know about Saturday," Brian said. Once they hung up, he sent a text to Rathman. *All went well. Saturday is a go.* The minute he sent the text, Rathman called. Brian declined the call, grabbed the bag that held his laptop, and headed to Olivia's.

Chapter 33

Olivia

Thursday, January 15

Since Ebby's case was wrapped up and Olivia didn't have anything pressing at the office, she opted to spend the day cooking before she sat down at the computer to search for a house to rent for a couple of months in Tahoe. She hadn't told Denny of her plans to visit yet, but as she searched for houses and thought of the logistics, the idea of getting away became more and more appealing.

She heard the front door open and Brian's voice. "Liv?"

"In here." She stood up and said, "I've made soup for dinner. And I have an idea—"

Brian wasn't paying any attention to her. He'd moved into the kitchen and closed the curtains. After that, he moved around Olivia's living room, shutting the curtains over the large window.

"What's going on?"

"We need to talk," he said.

Olivia followed Brian around the house, watching as he

double-checked all the doors and windows, and pulled the curtains. After he had cocooned them in, they wound up back in the kitchen. Olivia poured them each a glass of wine. "It's Leanne, isn't it?"

"Rathman called. They have a tracking device on her car. She's been watching you, watching us."

"Which means she knows you're staying here?"

"I can't believe I didn't think about that. I've put you in potential danger and made a tactical error that could have blown the entire operation." Brian swallowed his wine.

"You don't have to go through with this," Olivia said. "Can't the detectives from Minnesota just arrest Leanne now?"

"Rathman suggested that. But I want to sit across from that bitch and let her know that I know what she's done. She murdered a man. I want – no, I need – to get her to confess and see her led away in handcuffs." He looked at Olivia with tired eyes. "I called Leanne and told her you were being harassed by the husband of an old client, and that I agreed to stay with you until the restraining order is in place."

"Did she buy that?"

"Think so."

After spending decades as a homicide detective with the San Francisco Police Department, Olivia imagined how difficult it must be for Brian to admit he had been sucker punched by an experienced con woman. Even though he wasn't an ego-driven man, his self-esteem surely had taken a hit. If Olivia were in Brian's position, she would be beating herself with an emotional cudgel.

Olivia refilled their glasses and raised hers in a toast, "Better days."

"Better days," Brian said. "Whatever is in that pot smells delicious."

"Can you tell me what the plan is for Leanne?"

"I'm taking Leanne on a romantic dinner, where I will charm her and get her to confess."

"How are you going to do that?" Olivia stirred the butternut squash soup.

"I have a plan."

* * *

Later than evening, Brian and Olivia were sitting by the fire. Brian was reading the newspaper, while Olivia was continuing her search for a vacation rental in Tahoe. "How are you able to act normal when you're around Leanne?"

"It's a challenge," Brian said. "She's smart and probably a little suspicious."

Olivia shook her head. "Does she try to kiss you and be intimate with you?"

Brian hesitated. "Yes. And the only way I can get through it is to pretend I'm with you."

"Oh, Brian," Olivia said.

"I know. It's a mess."

Olivia's ringing cell phone interrupted their sweet intimacy.

"It's Vonnie Wilson," she said answering the phone and putting the call on speaker. "Hey, Vonnie. Are you still in Hong Kong?"

"I am. Won't be home for another week or so. But I found something out that I thought you might find a bit interesting. Is this a good time?"

"It is. I'm here with my business partner, Brian Vickery. You're on speaker."

"Thanks. Hey, Brian. Nice to meet you," Vonnie said.

"Hello," Brian said.

"I was at a dinner last night and just happened to be seated next to a man named Cary Carlton. Very charming. Widowed. Has a son who plays for the Vienna Philharmonic. Cary has a rare coin shop in Palo Alto. Or he used to. He's recently retired and his son has taken over the business. On a whim, I told him a little bit about your situation with the Engstroms. I didn't go into detail, but I asked him if he had heard about the 1984 murder and alleged theft of a quantity of gold sovereigns. These stories tend to become legend among collectors. I call it the *buried treasure syndrome*. Once a collector gets wind of the theft of a cache of anything, they become obsessed with chasing it down.

"Anyway, Mr. Carlton hadn't heard of it because he emigrated from Ireland in the early Nineties, but he did tell me that every year since 1992 – that's when he opened his shop – a woman has come in to sell a quantity of sovereigns. And I'm talking a large quantity, Liv. But get this. The last four or five years, the woman has been bringing double the usual number of coins. And it turns out she was just at his shop in November. He'd always wondered about her and had even tried to start up a conversation, but she wasn't very talkative. The last few times she was there, she requested the proceeds from the sale be wired to an account in the Caymans."

"Did he contact the authorities?" Olivia asked. Brian grabbed the pad of paper by Olivia's landline and started writing.

"No, but he reported the transaction as required by law," Vonnie said. "This is on the up and up."

Brian pushed the pad toward Olivia, who asked the question he had written out. "Vonnie, does Mr. Carlton happen to have video in his shop?"

Vonnie chuckled. "He does. And he's got clear footage of the woman."

"I love you, Vonnie. Really," Olivia said.

"Glad to be of help," Vonnie said. "Anyway, Mr. Carlton is happy to help. He won't be back in the US for a couple of weeks, but he told his son what was going on. I'm texting you the son's contact info right now. He's expecting to hear from you, Liv."

"Thanks, Vonnie."

"No problem. You can fill me in on the details when I see you in February. This was a long shot, and I can't believe it paid off. Anyway, we've got some catching up to do."

"We do. Safe travels," Olivia said.

After she hung up the phone, she turned to face Brian. "We may have just found Cynthia Engstrom's murderer."

"Agreed. And it's a woman," Brian said.

Olivia called Cary Carlton's son, who agreed to send the video footage to Brian and Olivia first thing tomorrow morning.

Chapter 34

Olivia

Friday, January 16

The next morning, Olivia called Gwen Kyleson and told her what Vonnie had discovered. Gwen was surprised and asked Olivia and Brian to contact Detective Rathman. Rather than have her own investigators work the case, Gwen had kicked it back to the Central Marin Policing Authority. The case had in turn been assigned to Detective Rathman, who was the senior detective. As for communicating with Ebby, Olivia left it in Brian's hands.

At 10:30, Detective Rathman came to the office. After Olivia briefed him on Vonnie Wilson's discovery, he said, "That's a long shot that paid off."

"Olivia likes the long shots," Brian said.

"Just being thorough, Detective," Olivia had said.

"I heard that you went to the DA about Seth Woodson," Rathman said. "He got fired. Did you know that?"

"I'm once again amazed at the way information travels in this county," Olivia said, refreshing her email. They'd been waiting since 8:30 for Cary's son to send them the surveillance video. "It's here."

Brian and Detective Rathman went to stand behind her as she downloaded the video and hit play. At first, the video was grainy, and for a minute Olivia worried that the quality would be so bad, they wouldn't be able to see much. But after a few seconds the film became clearer and depicted an empty store, with glass cases along two walls and an unobstructed view of the front door. The front door opened. A woman stepped inside, dressed in a long black coat and a floppy hat. A disguise? She carried a duffel bag over one shoulder. Given the way she struggled to lift it up to the counter, Olivia bet it was heavy. When an elderly man – presumably Cary Carlton – came into the frame, the woman took off her hat and extended her hand, which the elderly gentleman shook. When Mr. Carlton slid the duffel down the counter, the woman moved in the same direction. Soon her face was lined up with the camera lens. Olivia, Detective Rathman, and Brian all gasped in unison.

"It's Melinda Engstrom," Olivia said. The wheels in her mind turned, as she mentally sorted through the evidence, rearranging it like a puzzle to fit this scenario.

"I need to move on this. Can you send me an email of that footage?"

"Sure," Olivia said. But Detective Rathman didn't hear her. He was hurrying out of the office, barking orders into his cell.

"What should we do?" Olivia asked Brian.

"Nothing," Brian said. "We stay right here and let Rathman do his job."

Chapter 35

Ebby

Friday, January 16

Ebby valued his employees and knew that he especially owed his success to his friend Javier. Not only had Javi and his father helped Ebby build his cottage, Javier had worked tirelessly with Ebby, putting in long hours without complaint, while they built up The No Name Diner. It had been two weeks since Ebby had collapsed at the restaurant and Javi had driven him home. Since then, his friend had been running the restaurant single-handedly. Since The No Name Diner opened at 7 o'clock for breakfast, Ebby and Javier had met at the restaurant that Friday morning, sitting at a table, sharing a big breakfast, while the business they had built together bustled around them. The meeting had been fruitful. Ebby had made an offer. Javier had said he'd think about it.

With a feeling of cautious optimism, Ebby had gone for a long walk on the Corte Madera Larkspur bike path before heading to Felicity's apartment. By the time he got back home, it was 10:30. Felicity's bedroom door was still shut. Unusual for her, as she was one of those women who rose with the sun and slayed her to-do list before lunchtime.

Ebby put his ear to her door, listening for any sign that she was awake. "Felicity?" he called out. No answer. The door wasn't locked, so Ebby slowly pushed it open, only to discover not only was Felicity's room empty, but her bed had been made, and her purse and laptop bag were gone. Worried now, he dialed her number, but the call went straight to voicemail. Something wasn't right. Felicity wouldn't have left so early without telling him. Ebby didn't know what to do. Call the police? And tell them what? Felicity was an adult. There was no evidence of foul play.

Had she gone back to the Engstrom house for some reason? No. Felicity wouldn't have gone back there, not without telling him first. Not after she'd made it so clear that she was tired of Melinda, tired of the memories. What to do? He decided to call Elodie and ask her if by chance she had seen Felicity, when his phone beeped, signaling a new text. When Felicity's name popped up as the sender, he started to breathe a sigh of relief, until he read the message.

Went to collect my paycheck from Melinda. My car won't start. Can you come and get me?

Without thinking, Ebby grabbed his keys and headed toward the house he swore he would never set foot in again. On the way over, he couldn't shake the unexplainable feeling that something just wasn't right. His heartbeat quickened when he reached the family property. He slowed when he reached the gate to the driveway. The winter trees bare of their leaves gave Ebby a view of the Engstrom house, which stood in shadowy relief against the gray winter sky. As he headed up the drive, he remembered that Felicity didn't get paychecks. Her wages were automatically deposited into her account. Pushing away the panic that threatened to take away his reason, Ebby turned into the drive and headed toward the house. Without thinking, he hid his car behind an old, dilapidated shed and headed up to the house on foot. Cell phone in hand, he crept up the driveway, staying in the shadow cast by the tall shrubs that grew along the way.

The house was seemingly empty when he let himself into the kitchen. A knot of fear had formed in his stomach. He wanted to call out to Felicity, but he stayed silent as he stood in the center of the room, heart pounding. Unable to shake the feeling that he had stupidly walked into some sort of a trap, Ebby took out his cell phone and dialed Olivia.

"I was just about to call you," she said. "It's Melinda."

"What do you mean?" Ebby asked.

"We've got video of Melinda selling the sovereigns. Where are you?"

"I'm at the main house."

"Ebby, listen to me. Turn around and leave. Right now. The police are on the way—"

Ebby held the phone away from his ear. He was so engrossed in the vivid memories, bright and clear as a spring day as they ran before his mind's eye.

"I can't. I'm remembering. I'm remembering everything," Ebby said before he dropped his phone.

Chapter 36

Ebby

Friday, January 16

Head pounding, Ebby woke up on the kitchen floor, the hard tile cold under his cheek. He kept his eyes closed for a moment, wanting to hold on to this last bit of time before he faced his past, faced the events he had witnessed that had nearly destroyed his life. He had finally remembered. Everything. The blood, his mother's lifeless eyes staring at him.

"Ebby, you've remembered, haven't you?" The voice was kind, as it had always been. He rolled on his back. "Let's get you into the living room. Felicity is waiting for us."

Mind racing and unsure how to process his memories from the night of the murder and his current situation, Ebby followed Fiona into the living room. Felicity sat on the couch, looking terrified. Her cell phone was in her lap, and Ebby wondered why she hadn't called the police. "What's going on?" he asked.

Felicity gave a subtle shake of the head, a silent request that Ebby not speak, while Fiona sat down on the couch, lifted up

The Wall Street Journal that had been left open. A gun sat on the table. Fiona picked it up and leaned back.

When Ebby's mother died, Elodie had stepped in as his guardian and had loved him like a mother. She could always be counted on to provide emotional support and a soft spot to land. She made his favorite cookies and knew just to what to say when he felt the expected loneliness any child would feel at the loss of their parents. Meanwhile, Fiona was in the background, supporting her sister in the care and raising of a vulnerable young boy. As the family tomboy, it had been Fiona who taught Ebby to throw a curve ball and build a fire in the rain. Fiona, the fearless soul, who had taught him how to swim in the ocean and dive under the waves to swim past the breakers. Fiona, who took him surfing, paddling out with him on a long board, encouraging him to "Put your hands on the deck and stand up, Ebs." He'd never forget riding that first wave, that feeling of freedom, as though he had harnessed the ocean. All due to Fiona.

When his brother and Melinda had scorned him for his love of cooking and feeding people, Fiona had encouraged him to take over the diner and start his own restaurant, even providing the seed money he needed. She had been a career woman, a successful stockbroker in a male-dominated industry, a ferocious warrior with an eye for numbers and a knack for sports. She had always been there when Ebby needed her.

But the aunt he revered had murdered his mother in an unspeakably violent way, and Ebby had seen it happen.

Ebby turned to Felicity, and with a quavering voice asked, "Are you all right?"

"Of course she's all right. I'm not going to hurt either you or Felicity. I'm sorry for deceiving you both to get you here."

"Then why do you have a gun?" Ebby demanded.

Ebby watched his aunt as she stood, took the gun, and moved to the window, where she stood with her back toward him, staring into the gray winter day, the gun held loose at her side. The swell of the dowager's hump between Fiona's shoulders served as a stark reminder of the years that had passed. He should have been furious at this woman who had killed his mother. He should hate her. But he didn't. As he inventoried his feelings – a trick he had learned in therapy – he realized that all he felt now was exhaustion.

"The police will be here soon," Fiona said, as she moved away from the window.

"What are you up to?" Ebby asked, eyeing the gun.

"I'm going to confess." Fiona turned to Felicity. "Are you ready?"

Felicity gave Ebby an uncertain glance before she nodded.

Fiona reached in her pocket with her free hand and tossed Felicity her cell phone. "Say the words, Felicity. Just how we discussed."

"What's this about?"

"You'll see, Ebby. I'm clearing the way for you to be free of us. You and Felicity can start afresh, with Elodie." Fiona turned her attention to Felicity.

"Are you ready?"

Felicity nodded.

"And you give me your word that you will email this to the reporter at the *Marin Independent Journal*? You need to promise me you'll send it before the police confiscate your phone."

"I will," Felicity said. A lone tear ran down her cheek.

"Go ahead. Say it just as we discussed."

When Felicity spoke, her voice was wobbly. "Today is Friday, January 16th, 2015. We are here to film the confession of Fiona Engstrom for the murder of Cynthia Engstrom."

"Fiona, wait," Ebby said, his eyes flicked to the gun as he realized how this scenario was going to end.

"No. Now is the time, Edward. I've carried this burden all these years and it's broken me." Fiona walked over to Felicity and reached out to tuck a stray strand of hair behind her ears. When Felicity cowered, Fiona pulled her hand back. "I'm so sorry, Felicity, to bring you into this. Once this is over, you can begin healing. Elodie and Ebby will take you into the fold." She turned to Ebby and said, "I lured you and Felicity here because I want you both to know what I did and why I did it."

"I would have come voluntarily," Ebby said.

Fiona shook her head. "No, you wouldn't have. You made it very clear that you were never going to set your foot in this house again. Ebby, dear, you were a stubborn child and you are a stubborn man."

Ebby didn't need to hear Fiona's confession now that he'd remembered every word she had uttered to his mother on the night of her death, when Fiona had unleashed a litany of accusations that made Ebby's mind reel. He wanted to believe Fiona's accusations were a misunderstanding, that his mother wasn't capable of the horrible things his aunt had suffered at her hands. But as the events of the evening sprung unbidden into Ebby's mind, he knew in his heart that his mother had provoked Fiona, had hurled a litany of insults, like arrows to the heart, in response to the accusations. He knew because he had borne witness, and the horror of it all had caused his amnesia.

"Don't confess," Ebby said. "The police don't have any evidence."

"I never in a million years thought I would get away with it. You saw me, Ebby, and I'm sorry about that. Your mother pushed me to madness. God, we hated each other. Sometimes I think she married your father just to spite me. Your amnesia, though a tragedy for you, was a blessing for me. I'm ashamed of that, but it's true. And I felt so guilty, that I almost turned myself in. But then I decided to wait it out, wait for the police to arrest me, but they didn't."

"How did you come to be at the house that night?" Ebby asked.

"Bertie and I went to dinner at the beach—"

"Who's Bertie?" Felicity asked.

"Bertie was my lover of many years," Fiona said. "That night, he had to get home, so he left my house early. Cynthia called me just after he left and told me her brother was going to move into the house after he was released from jail. I was so furious at her. I got in the car and drove here to confront her. I was so angry. I don't know what I was thinking."

"My uncle raped you," Ebby said.

"Your uncle ruined my life. He took everything from me." Fiona took a step toward Felicity.

"Let me start at the beginning. Cynthia North and I became friends when we were thirteen years old. We met at summer camp, when we both snuck out of our bunks in the middle of the night to raid the refrigerator. After that we were inseparable, like sisters. Cynthia usually came to our house. She was impressed by the trappings of wealth. My mother didn't trust her, and I felt like such a hero defending her."

The room was cold. Fiona moved to the fireplace, striking a match and tossing it into the pile of shredded newspapers and kindling, while Felicity tracked her with the phone. "We were juniors in high school when she did something terrible, the worst kind of betrayal. Elodie and I went to the movies. Cynthia was there with her older brother, Gary. He was seventeen years old and had a car. It was good to see her. We got to talking, and when the movie was over they offered to give me a ride home. I left Elodie to ride home with Mom and Dad and took a ride with Cynthia and Gary instead."

Over Fiona's shoulder, Ebby saw a policewoman in the doorway between the entry hall and the living room, quiet and as unobtrusive as shadows. Fiona didn't notice as the detective made eye contact with Ebby and Felicity and put her fingers to her lips.

"I knew something was wrong when they missed the exit for my house and kept going. I'll never forget sitting in the front seat between the two of them. They looked at each other, and Cynthia nodded. I recognized the unspoken communication between siblings. They had a scheme, and I was the target. I felt like a field mouse with two hawks circling above." Fiona stopped narrating long enough to throw a log on the kindling that had caught fire. When she spoke, her cadence was flat, her emotion clearly spent. "When we arrived at Cynthia's house, I asked to use the telephone. I wanted to call my parents and have someone fetch me. Of course, they told me to go on in and use the phone in the kitchen."

Fiona closed her eyes and with her free hand, she reached up and clutched at her blouse. "I sensed Gary behind me. When I turned around, the look in his eyes …" Fiona shivered. "I can still remember it to this day. Positively demonic. I pushed him, somehow managing to knock him off his balance, and started to run. Cynthia tripped me. Sent me sprawling on my belly. Then she held me down and pinned my arms, while her brother raped me."

"Oh, Fiona," Ebby said. He started to go to her.

"I was so ashamed. They drove me home. I remember locking myself in the bathroom. I took a shower and tried to scrub Gary North out of my body." Fiona spoke in a monotone, as she stared straight ahead. "Elodie knew something had happened, but I couldn't tell her. I thought if I didn't talk about it, the memory would fade. If I pretended nothing happened, I could go back to being that innocent, trusting young woman who went to the movies with her sister." She laughed, a dry mirthless sound that broke Ebby's heart. Tears flowed down her wrinkled cheeks unchecked. "Life went on. I graduated from high school and moved to Boston to attend college. I was about to start my senior year when I discovered that Elliot, my brother with the most gentle soul, was dating Cynthia, that they had fallen in love, and that somehow Cynthia North – the girl from the wrong side of the tracks – had managed to charm my parents.

"And I'm sorry to say this to you, Ebby, because your mother loved you, in her own way, but she was an odious woman. The brother who raped me ended up going to prison for bank robbery. I came to find out that he had a history of rape and violence toward women. I did my best to stay away from the family. I couldn't stomach watching Cynthia in the home that had been my sanctuary. I bought my house at Stinson Beach and was tactfully polite in public. But the truth hung between us. Things like that never go away. After Elliot died, I thought she'd move on, marry someone else. I prayed for it, to tell you the truth. But she didn't.

"It took me years to regain a sense of normalcy after the rape. But I will never forget the smirk on Cynthia's face when she told me her brother, the man who had raped me violently, was going to be living in this house. My God, I lost my mind. We fought, but she wouldn't back down. When I told her that I would go to the police and tell them what she and her brother had done, she laughed in my face. Called me a liar. Told me I had it coming to me. The letter opener was right there. I picked it up and started stabbing her. And God help me, the act was cathartic. Once I started, I couldn't stop." Fiona pulled a handkerchief out of her dress pocket and wiped her eyes.

"When I was finished there was so much blood – I was covered in it. I hurried out of the house. I'll never forget the feel of the adrenaline as it pumped through my veins. My intention was to call the police and confess. But as I stood in the dark night, under the winter stars, I realized, as far as I could tell, no one had seen me, no one knew I was there. I knew Felicity and Elodie were upstairs with Allegra. I couldn't bear to go back in the house, and figured I'd just wait outside until the police came. Then I would confess. I didn't realize you were in your cubby, Ebby, I must have walked right past you. I watched through the window as you walked through the door into the office and found your mother's body. I realized you'd seen the whole thing. You heard me argue with your mother, and saw me kill her. There was nothing I could have done. I couldn't get to you fast enough from where I was standing. God, I've never felt so helpless. You ran to her and held her in your arms. The way you screamed …" Fiona wiped her eyes on her sleeve. "I don't deserve your forgiveness, but I am truly sorry that I did that to you. You didn't deserve it. I watched Elodie come down the stairs in her bathrobe. She swept you into her arms and carried you away, back upstairs. When I heard the crunch of footsteps on the gravel drive, I ducked into the bushes. I was surprised to see Melinda come walking up the driveway. She was dressed head to toe in black, like a cat burglar. From my hiding place I watched through the window, fully expecting her to scream bloody murder when she saw Cynthia's body. But she didn't scream. She grabbed the bag of coins and slipped out of the house with no one the wiser. I have to give her credit for composure under pressure."

Fiona started to sob. Ebby moved toward her, but she held up a hand. "Don't. Please.

"I was going to drive to the police station and turn myself in before you could tell them what you saw, but something made me drive home to the beach. I had my revenge, I reasoned that I deserved one night of freedom near the ocean before I went to jail for the rest of my life. The next morning, Elodie called and explained that Cynthia had been murdered, the sovereigns had been stolen, and that you had been found holding her body, and were now suffering from amnesia. No sooner did I hang up from speaking to Elodie, than I heard on the morning news that Bertie had driven his car off Mt. Tam on his way home from my house. It seemed as though the graces had given me an alibi. I decided not to confess, until such time as your memory came back. I spent the morning burning my clothes and cleaning the blood out of my car before I came back to the house to support Elodie. When the police questioned me about my whereabouts when Cynthia was killed, I told them I was in bed with Bertie, which couldn't be verified, of course. Bertie was dead. But I knew my freedom was a temporary gift. When you remembered what happened, I was going to confess."

Ebby tried to wrap his mind around Fiona's story. "Why did you hire an investigator, Fiona? Weren't you worried you'd get caught?"

"That's exactly why I did. I wanted to see if I'd left a trace. I couldn't believe the police didn't figure out it was me. Apparently, I'd committed a perfect murder. Truth be told, my life was over after I was raped. And I'm ready to end it now." Fiona nodded. "You can turn off the recording, Felicity, and hit send."

Felicity fiddled with her phone. "Okay. I sent it."

"But why—"

Fiona smiled. "I know what you're trying to do, Ebby. I'm finished talking. I'd like you to leave."

"Go ahead, Felicity," Ebby said.

Felicity didn't have to be asked twice. She hurried out of the room, just before the policewoman stepped in, her gun drawn.

"Put the gun down," she said.

Fiona laughed. "Do you realize how ridiculous you sound? I'm ready to die."

When she held the gun up to her temple, Ebby cried out, "No!" and charged her.

The gun went off. Ebby and Fiona landed in a heap on the floor.

Ears ringing from the gunshot, Ebby watched as chaos broke out around him. A squad of uniformed and plainclothes policemen charged into the room. Time seemed to move in circles, and before long, bright lights flicked through the living room window as an ambulance pulled up to the front door.

"Fiona," Ebby cried out. She lay under him, not moving. Careful not to crush her, he gingerly lifted himself off her body, eventually coming to a squat next to her. Taking her hand, he said, "Fiona, I'm so sorry. Please don't die."

His aunt was lying on her back now and was so still, Ebby thought she was dead. He stood and made room for the paramedic, who started to poke and prod at Fiona, all the while talking to her. "Miss Engstrom? Can you hear me?" When his hands moved down to her lower back, Fiona yelped.

The paramedic said, "I think her hip's broken."

A uniformed policeman asked Ebby to wait outside. He stepped out into the cold January day and saw Felicity sitting in a police car, a blanket around her shoulders, looking at him with worry and concern. As he made his way toward her, Olivia, Brian, and Elodie came rushing up the driveway to him.

Ebby took Elodie's hand and pulled her away from Brian and Olivia. "Felicity explained why you lied to me."

"I hope you'll understand that I was forced to make a decision. Leave you holding your mother, covered in her blood, and have you go through hell to explain what you saw to the police and maybe to a judge in a courtroom. Even if you didn't remember, they would have interviewed you, cross-examined you. You would have carried that stigma with you for the rest of your life. I couldn't let that happen to you, Ebby. You were already a young man without parents, an orphan. Allegra and I made a choice that night to lie in order to protect you. I don't regret it. Not one bit. And I would do it again in a New York minute. You may not be able to forgive me. I'll respect that. But I stand by my actions that night."

"Did you know Fiona killed my mother?"

"No. I had no idea. No idea at all. I can't hardly believe it."

As Elodie stood before him, he saw the worry and concern – for him – in her eyes. He'd been a witness to a horrible tragedy. For the first time, he was able to grasp the blind love that motivated his aunt. The time had come to let it all go. The time had come for Ebby to be free. With a breath and a sigh, he let his anger go and pulled Elodie into his arms. "I realize why you made the choices you made, and I thank you for them." As he uttered those words out loud, he felt his burden lift, felt the weight of what he had carried leave his body. Elodie leaned against Ebby and wept.

He held her and tried to soothe her, catching Felicity's gaze. She nodded at him, as if she sensed the chains of the past slipping away. Ebby knew that all was now well with the world.

241

Chapter 37

Brian

Brian chose The Left Bank for his fated date with Leanne, reasoning the outdoor seating would provide the necessary privacy for a murder confession. He had a role to play and didn't need an audience. To assert control, he had arrived early and ordered a dry martini, extra olives. Resisting the urge to down the drink in one go and order another, Brian watched the other diners through the window as he forced himself to sip, intrigued by the scenarios he imagined playing out at the different tables. Six well-dressed professional-looking women had commandeered the corner booth and were celebrating something with a bottle of Dom Perignon. At the small table next to them, two men were in earnest conversation while they ate steamed clams, Brian's favorite dish, dunking their crusty bread into the savory saffron-infused broth. At another table, a man and a woman ate dessert, not speaking to each other. At first glance they seemed like an ordinary couple who had fallen into the quiet routine that comes with familiarity. Brian smiled when he saw the woman's foot slide up the man's pant leg under the table.

Two men sat at the long wooden bar. Solitary diners. Widowers? Lonely? One of them read the paper, while the other simply stared into his drink, cognac from the looks of it. Brian's heart galloped with anxiety when Leanne walked into the room. He took a deep breath and forced himself to remain calm, to stay in character. He watched as both men at the bar turned, surveying her in that way men do. Brian had to admit that Leanne – Andrea, he reminded himself – was a beautiful woman. She took pride in her appearance and dressed to impress. Initially Brian had fallen for Leanne's flashy good looks. Now he found them garish. What had he ever seen in her?

He stood as she approached the table. When Leanne rose onto her tiptoes for a kiss, it took everything he had to respond with feigned passion.

"I'm glad to see you," Leanne said.

Brian took Leanne's hand and met her eyes. "We need to talk."

She furrowed her brow, and for the briefest second Brian wondered if the Minnesota police were wrong, if this whole situation wasn't some horrible mistake.

"I know who you are," he said.

"What are you talking about?"

"Leanne – or should I say Andrea?"

She froze at the mention of her real name, at the hint that Brian could know her real story. She looked around, a calculating look on her face. "Is this some sort of a set-up?"

"Of course not. But I do know about you. About your husband." The waiter came over. Brian ordered another martini.

"Same for me," Leanne said. Once the waiter left, Leanne said, "You need to let me explain. It's not what it seems. I was scared for my life."

To his surprise, Brian found himself wanting to believe this woman. Not because he cared about her, but because he was looking for exoneration, some indication that he hadn't fallen victim. "Why did you run? If you didn't have anything to hide, you could have cooperated, helped them clear things up."

"I tried to cooperate. My husband worked for the DA's office. The police weren't going to take my side. Surely you know how the old boys' network operates."

Brian realized that Leanne's husband had a few different jobs, a few different backstories. They were all a lie, and Brian hadn't picked up on the inconsistencies. He let that irritation at himself go. Her confession would go a long way towards his redemption. She stopped talking when the waiter brought their drinks and left them with their menus.

"He used to beat me on a regular basis. Once he threw me down our basement stairs and locked me down there for two days. He broke my jaw and dislocated my shoulder. I went to the police after that, but they didn't do anything."

"Did you kill him, Leanne? Just tell me the truth. I'm not going to judge you." While Brian spoke, he thought of Maureen as she lay dying of cancer. He knew his love of Maureen and his grief for her would show in his eyes. He told himself the emotional toll for this exploitation of his beloved wife's memory would be worth it.

She fiddled with the two skewered olives in her martini, not meeting Brian's eyes. "I did. And I would do it again. That man abused me. It was only a matter of time before he killed me." Leanne reached for Brian's hand over the top of the table. "I swear to God, I killed him in self-defense."

Andrea Seaton was a cold-blooded murderer, a sociopath. He knew she was lying about her husband. Detective Summerfield had let him read the entire investigation file, along with the police reports. A slow, planned poisoning was not the same as killing someone in self-defense. And there was no record of abuse, no broken jaw, no dislocated shoulder.

"You believe me, don't you?" Leanne asked.

"Of course. I can't believe you have to ask me that," Brian said. "I was a cop for a long time. I've seen families torn apart by abuse."

He saw Detectives Summerfield and Daniels across the street. *Thank God this charade is nearly over.*

"You're a compassionate man, Brian. Thank you for listening." Leanne said. "Will you come away with me? We could start over. I've got money. We could go to Mexico or Canada. You love me, don't you?"

"I'm not ..." Brian said.

"What?"

Detective Summerfield approached their table. He stood behind Leanne, a pair of handcuffs in his hand.

"I'm not a compassionate man. Your husband never abused you. You dosed him with antifreeze and caused him a slow and painful death. You're a monster, Andrea or Leanne – whatever your name is. You belong in prison so you can't hurt anyone else. And guess what, sweetheart? I'm going to testify to make sure you go away for a very long time."

"Mrs. Seaton?"

Leanne turned around, startled.

"Did you get what you need?" Brian stood and buttoned his coat.

"We did. Thanks, Mr. Vickery," Detective Daniels said.

A white van was parked in the lot across the street from the restaurant. Brian saw Olivia get out of the back. Resisting the urge to run to her, he wheeled around to face Leanne. "You picked the wrong mark. Once I discovered you stole my wife's identity, I volunteered my cooperation."

"Liar. I had you convinced, and you know it," Leanne said, venom in her voice. "We would have been married in six months."

"Don't think so," Brian said. "Olivia was onto you from the beginning."

When Detective Daniels pulled Leanne to her feet, she started to scream. Brian turned his back on her and walked out of the restaurant, toward Olivia, who waited for him on the sidewalk out front.

"You were great. Rathman said he'd give us a ride to my house—" She furrowed her brow and stared at him. "Are you all right?"

"I don't know," he answered honestly. "Let's walk back to your house instead. I need to clear my head."

"Sounds good. I'll just go tell them, okay?"

Brian nodded. He watched Olivia speak to Detective Summerfield, just as Leanne was led from the restaurant. What would have happened if Olivia hadn't been suspicious? If she hadn't pushed him to see Leanne from a different perspective? As they headed up the hill toward Olivia's house, Brian realized his relationship with Leanne could have turned out so much worse.

Chapter 38

Olivia

Saturday, January 17

The walk to Olivia's house under the waning crescent moon went a long way toward relieving Brian's anger at Leanne. Once they got home, they ordered Chinese food and opened a bottle of wine. As they ate with chopsticks out of the cartons, they talked about future travel plans and the anticipation of Denny having her child.

At least it was over. Leanne was out of their lives for good. All that was left was for Brian to testify at Leanne's trial. Olivia would go with him to Minnesota. After the trial, they would travel north and make a vacation of it.

She put on the kettle for tea, and tossed the takeout containers into the garbage, which she tied shut and then took to the bins outside. Shivering in the cold, Olivia heard footsteps crunching on the gravel behind her. She turned and for a minute didn't recognize the woman who stood under the halo of the streetlamp.

"I want you to give them a message for me."

"Melinda?" She'd cut her hair short and bleached it blond. She wore jeans and industrial-looking boots with thick rubber soles. Wire-rimmed glasses completed the look. Olivia wouldn't have recognized her if she saw her on the street.

"We thought you'd be long gone," Olivia said.

"Not yet. I'm getting ready to leave. Right now, I'm hiding in plain sight."

"The police will find you, Melinda."

"I haven't done anything wrong. I'm not hiding from the police," Melinda said. 'I'm hiding from Mark. He'll be arrested soon. He's up to his ears in felonies. Once he's in custody, I'll slip away."

"You stole the Engstroms' collection of gold coins," Olivia said.

"I'm considering it my divorce settlement. This family owes me for putting up with Mark all these years."

"Did you know that Fiona killed Cynthia?"

"I had a suspicion. They had an interesting relationship. I overheard arguments between them over the years. Fiona had zero respect for Cynthia. Cynthia was horrible to her. I overheard them fighting once. Fiona was furious, yelling at Cynthia. Cynthia was taunting Fiona, saying her brother, Gary, was going to move into the house. Fiona lost it. I don't know what happened between those two, but Cynthia was evil, and as far as I'm concerned, she got what she deserved. She tortured me from the minute I started dating Mark. I'm not going to give you a recitation of my grievances, as I don't have time. But Cynthia insulted my hard-working parents, called them white trash, and did her best to keep Mark and me apart.

"On the night of her death, Mark was in Tahoe on his ski trip. Cynthia invited me over. Mark had proposed and I thought Cynthia wanted to bury the hatchet, if you will, make friends. We both loved her son, or so I told myself. Instead, she called me a whore and offered me money to leave him. Of course, I turned it down. I stormed out of the house and went home and cried for an hour. But then I got so angry with her, I wanted to talk to her, try to reason with her. She came from humble beginnings, too. Did you know that?

"When I got back to the house, she was dead. I swear to God. I heard Ebby crying upstairs and Elodie barking out orders to Allegra." Melinda shivered. "It was awful. I felt someone watching me. When I looked outside the window, I thought I saw the glow of a cigarette. The bag of sovereigns was right there behind the desk. I couldn't resist. The idea that I could have my own wealth was irresistible. I honestly had no idea what I would do with them. Over the years, I thought about mysteriously giving them back, but the situation never presented itself."

"Where did you keep them?"

"At first I kept them in my parents' garage in an old suitcase. When my parents sold their house, I buried them in the woods." Melinda laughed. "I had my own buried treasure. When my marriage started to fall apart, when I realized that I'd married an abusive son of a bitch, those coins were my security blanket. I realized I had made a huge mistake marrying Mark. He was abusive and cruel, but I felt stuck, so a little over twenty years ago, I started cashing them in and stashing the money, knowing when the time was right, I'd leave.

"I want you to tell Ebby that I'm sorry. Tell him I didn't mean to hurt him—"

Both women froze at the sound of footsteps crunching on the gravel.

"Olivia?" Brian called out.

Olivia turned to see Brian in his pajamas, walking barefoot on the gravel. "I'm here. Just taking the garbage out," Olivia called.

"Who are you talking to?"

"Melinda—" But as she turned around, Melinda Engstrom was gone.

Chapter 39

Olivia

Six months later

Olivia stood in the doorway between the dining room and the kitchen, taking in the crystal glasses, the used napkins set beside the delicate china plates, and half-empty wine bottles glimmering in the candlelight, in her mind the perfect tableau of a successful dinner party. She and Brian had been surprised when her long-time friend Lauren showed up with Detective Rathman. Apparently the two had met at a mutual acquaintance's dinner party and had started dating. Conversation had flowed, along with the wine and the laughter. Lauren regaled them with stories of her life in the music business. When she passed the baton to Rathman, he told them stories of his life as a cop in New York that even Brian couldn't match.

As the group moved into the living room and settled in front of the television, Olivia scooped coffee into the French press and put on the kettle. At this very moment, all was right with her world. She savored the feeling. For the first time in decades, she felt a deep sense of peace. That feeling of being lost without a career had slipped away, as she reflected on how she would step back into family law and – as Stephen had suggested – exit on her own terms.

"Hey," Lauren said, carrying the empty wine glasses to the sink. "You okay?"

"Never better," Olivia said and meant it. "There's brandy to go with the coffee, if you want to carry it in?"

"Sure," Lauren said. She stepped close to Olivia and spoke in a whisper. "I like him, Liv. Do you think it's weird that I'm dating a cop?"

"Not even a little."

"We're going hiking tomorrow," Lauren said. "He's nice, isn't he? He reminds me of James Bond."

Olivia laughed out loud. "Grab the brandy, would you?"

They carried the coffee and brandy to the couches where Brian flipped through the channels with the sound muted.

They had all come together to watch a true crime show about Cynthia Engstrom's murder. Although actors had been hired for the dramatization of the events surrounding the murder, Detective Rathman and various members of the Engstrom family had given interviews, providing the audience with a firsthand account.

The story of Cynthia's murder and Fiona's role in it had captured the headlines. As the details came forth, especially those surrounding Cynthia's brother, Gary, and Fiona's accusations, the story garnered interest. Melinda's theft of the famed bag of gold sovereigns and slowly cashing them in, so she could run away from her husband, had added an extra layer of intrigue. Just as the sensational news of Fiona's video confession started to lose steam, Mark Engstrom was quietly arrested at a hotel in Southern California near the Mexican border. He was charged with securities fraud, wire fraud, mail fraud, money laundering, and for filing false claims with the SEC. When the extent of his crimes came to light, he was catapulted into the spotlight. The news channels were reporting there was so much evidence against Mark Engstrom, the case was a slam dunk, and his lawyer was trying to negotiate a plea. Mark's arrest kindled interest in the disappearance of the Engstrom sovereigns and his wife.

"Some of these shows are really dumbed down," Lauren said.

"This one won't be," Martin Rathman said. "They'll be putting a lot of emphasis on the hunt for Melinda and the coins."

"They won't find her," Brian said. "She's long gone."

"Have either of you heard from Ebby?" Lauren asked.

"We talk occasionally," Olivia said. She pushed the plunger in the French press and poured out the coffee. "He brought me a copy of his cookbook. He's going to focus on writing now. Last I heard he, Elodie, and Felicity were in upstate New York."

"Probably trying to get some privacy," Lauren said.

Brian put his arm around Olivia, and she leaned into him. She thought about loose ends and her need to have things tied up and tucked away. Prior to Leanne, her relationship with Brian was a tangle of unsaid words and half-spoken promises. All that was in the past now. They had talked about their feelings for each other, both expressing their fears, worries, and expectations for the future, an act of intimacy that bound them together. She looked around at her friends and honored this moment, grateful that she and Brian were now free to weave their own story. Together.

Chapter 40

Ebby

Six months later

Elodie was already at Fiona's grave when Felicity and Ebby came walking up the sloping grassy knoll, a huge bouquet of tulips under Felicity's arm. As they drew close, they saw Elodie was on her knees, working a trowel and planting a small rosebush near Fiona's headstone. Ebby smiled to himself. The groundskeeper had given them strict instructions against planting anything. Elodie had scoffed at him and promptly ignored his warnings.

"She's spry as a teenager," Felicity said.

"Until she stands up, and then she'll complain about her aging knees," Ebby said.

When Fiona had held the gun to her head, Ebby hadn't thought about her fragile bones as he had tackled her to the ground. The fall had indeed broken her hip and wreaked havoc on the alignment of her spine. Once she arrived at the hospital, she was whisked off to surgery for an immediate hip replacement. She didn't survive the anesthesia, and Ebby Engstrom was given yet another burden to shoulder. Because if he hadn't tackled Fiona, she would have never broken her hip. It she hadn't broken her hip, she wouldn't have needed the anesthesia that killed her – so he thought.

It wasn't until the autopsy was completed that the family discovered Fiona had been diagnosed with an aggressive form of breast cancer four years earlier. At the time of her diagnosis she had – against her doctor's vehement advice – refused all forms of treatment, thereby signing her own death sentence. During the autopsy it was discovered that the cancer had metastasized and spread throughout Fiona's body, and that she was literally at death's door. The medical examiner had taken the time to speak with Ebby personally. Based on his findings, he doubted Fiona would have lived another month. "I don't want you to feel the guilt of her death, Mr. Engstrom. If my aunt held a gun to her head, I would have done the same thing."

Ebby believed his aunt had wanted to die. Maybe Fiona felt she owed her life for the one she had taken. Now, he stood before her grave, ready to say a final goodbye before he moved to Italy.

"I had no idea what Cynthia and that brother of hers had done to Fiona. If only she had told me." Elodie stood now, her head bowed before her sister's grave. "But times were different then. Women who came forward with accusations of rape were often ignored or told it was their own fault."

Felicity put her arm around Elodie. "Remember we agreed that it's time to say goodbye to the past. We Engstroms need to move forward. Ebby's moving to Italy, where he's going to write a new cookbook, and you and I will be very happy at the beach. We can remember Fiona there."

When Elodie touched Felicity's cheek, Ebby knew everything was going to be okay with his little family. They didn't talk about Mark. Ebby had tried to reach out to his brother after his arrest, but Mark didn't want to see him and specifically forbade his family meddling in his business affairs. Ebby had no problem honoring

Mark's wishes. He had broken free of his jealous older brother who had controlled the family narrative to suit his purposes, who had used the Engstrom name and reputation to garner the trust and favor of his clients, only to turn around and cheat them.

"She's right," Ebby said. "It's time to move on."

"I'm so proud of both of you." Elodie looked at Ebby and Felicity and said, "We're family now, the three of us. No more secrets, okay? Family's the most important thing. I want you both to promise me that you'll never forget that."

"Promise," Felicity said.

"Promise," Ebby said.

"Very well. Ebby, be good. We love you and will look forward to seeing you at Christmas." They hugged their goodbyes. Felicity would ride to the beach house with Elodie, while Ebby would head to the city to celebrate with all The No Name Diner staff, who had pulled together to purchase the restaurant. Ebby would turn in his rental car and spend the night at a hotel near the airport. By 10 o'clock, he would be on an airplane bound for Rome. The time had come for Edward Engstrom to make his own way in the world.

Acknowledgements

Whenever I finish a novel and send the final copy in for publication, I am always amazed by the generosity of the many people who help along the way. I would like to thank Erica Galvan, the property and evidence technician at the Central Marin Policing Authority for answering a myriad of questions with regard to evidence and investigations, especially as they relate to a murder that has long gone cold. Jim Beaty of Backstage Music in Starkville, MS, for answering technical questions regarding a plot line that was intriguing but ended up being left out of this story. (Stay tuned – it may show up in the future!) Patti Swensen Pedroli gave me an accurate summation of identity theft and how someone could get away with it – at least for a while – in these days of complete connectivity.

Kasey Corbit and John F. Prentice get massive thanks for double-checking my legal procedure and helping me fashion my plot in a way that is realistic and accurate. Thanks to both of you for reading the courtroom scenes, addressing procedural issues, and – mostly – for assuring me when I thought I'd written myself into a corner. Big thanks to Detective Adam Richardson at The Writer's Detective Bureau Q&A Facebook page and thanks to the Forensics and Flowers Facebook page. Both pages provide

257

a cornucopia of information about police procedure and forensic science.

Thanks to Abigail Fenton, Dushi Horti, and Helena Newton, HQ's fabulous team, whose editing acumen never ceases to amaze. I owe a debt of gratitude to all of these women, whose insights have made me a better writer. And I must give giant kudos to the art department at HQ Digital UK, whose book covers have played such a huge role in my success.

A warm thank you to my beta readers, Kim Laird and Gloria Rowland, for going through *The Witness* with a fine-tooth comb. Thanks to Jennifer Young, Angela Baxter, and Suzanne Simonetti for helping me flesh out that ever-important opening paragraph.

Special thanks to all the social media gurus who have helped me get the word out about my books over the years. Susan Peterson, Sharlene Martin Moore and Bobbi Wendel Dumas, Novels and Lattes, Book Nook Reviews and Fun, Suzy Weinstein Leopold, Linda's Book Obsession, The Historical and Timeslip Novels Book Club, The Write Review, Laura Pearson at Motherlode Book Club, Wild Sage Book Blog, High Society Book Club, The Napping Bibliophile, and Bookworms Anonymous. All of these pages are chock full of wonderful book recommendations and conversations around books. Social media connects readers and writers, so if you're looking for your next great read, I recommend any of the above pages.

And a final heart-felt thank you to all of my readers. When I sit down to a blank screen to tell a story, I do so with you in my mind and heart.

Happy Reading!

Terry

Keep reading for an excerpt from *The Betrayal* …

THE
BETRAYAL

Marriages are
built on trust.

This one's built
on lies.

THE *USA TODAY* BESTSELLING AUTHOR
Terry Lynn Thomas

Prologue

When the alarm blared the Sunday financial recap, the woman woke with a start. She didn't care about the Dow Jones Industrial Average, nor did she care about market volatility. Fumbling, she unplugged the old-fashioned clock radio and tossed it under the bed. Her thoughts, as they often did, went to her lover. She rolled over and pressed her face into his pillow, taking in the scent of him, that strange concoction of vanilla and citrus that made her senses reel.

Rolling over on her back, she took a deep breath, and cradled her belly, thinking of the baby that grew inside her. The positive pregnancy test lay on the table next to her, its vertical pink line a source of unimaginable joy. She snuggled under the duvet as the automatic coffeemaker kicked into gear, filling her apartment with the aroma of the dark roast coffee her lover preferred.

She saw the card on the doormat just as she poured her first cup of coffee.

I've rented a beach house for us tonight. I'll send a key and the address by messenger. Meet you there around ten?

261

Leaning back against the counter, the woman closed her eyes, anticipating their rendezvous. Dear God, she craved him.

She did not know she had less than fifteen hours to live.

Chapter 1

Friday, October 10

Olivia Sinclair's life fell apart on the day of her sixty-second birthday. The morning started with promise. She and Richard lay entangled in the sheets, their limbs intertwined and glistening with sweat. Olivia marveled – as she often did – at the way their passion had withstood decades of marriage. Somehow, she and Richard had managed to keep passion alive.

"Happy birthday, beautiful." Richard ran his fingers along her side, taking his time at the curve of her hip. "I've got something for you."

Olivia watched her husband, his body still athletic and strong as he moved to the dresser and opened the top drawer. When he turned to face her, he held a familiar blue Tiffany box.

"This is for you, for your birthday and your retirement, a celebration of your accomplishments, if you will. I don't tell you this enough, but I'm proud of you, Liv." Richard always gave Olivia jewelry from Tiffany's at birthdays and Christmas. This year's gift was a platinum necklace, the pendant an antique skeleton key studded with diamonds.

"It's beautiful," Olivia said. She held up the platinum key to the morning light, the sunbeams making the diamonds dazzle.

Richard took it from her. "Let me help you put that on." He hooked the clasp and kissed the back of her neck. "When do you and Claire sign your paperwork?"

"She's coming in today. I'm going to ask for all the changes you suggested. Assuming she agrees, we'll wrap things up.

"She's got the capital?"

"She does. I think she's probably borrowing the money, but she'll be fine."

Richard ran his fingers through Olivia's thick hair. "I hear she's a go-getter. Are you okay with walking away from all that success, the notoriety?"

"Notoriety? That's your department. You're the television legal guru. I just help beleaguered women get their fair share."

Richard laughed.

"At least we can travel now, or at least I can come with you when you go away for weeks on end for depositions and trials," Olivia said.

"That's great, honey."

"We need to talk about your plans, Richard. Do you have any idea when you might walk away from Rincon Sinclair?"

Richard turned to Olivia. "I'm not ready, Liv. Not now. Maybe a year or two?"

"That long?"

"We'll talk about it later, okay?"

Olivia recognized this ploy. *We'll talk about it later* meant they wouldn't talk about it again until Richard was good and ready. She was about to push him, wrangle a commitment to retire out of him, when the alarm by his side of the bed started blaring the morning news.

"You shower first. I'll make the coffee." Richard tied his bathrobe around his waist and turned off the radio. "Are you sure you don't mind cooking tonight? It's your birthday."

"I'm sure," Olivia said. "I want to cook dinner for my family."

"Maybe you can strike a truce with our son-in-law," Richard said.

Olivia held her hand over her heart. "I swear, I'll try."

As she headed into the shower, she thought of the promise of freedom, and the time she would have to garden, travel with Richard, and tackle her toppling To-Be-Read pile of books.

After Richard left, she took her time over the morning paper and was going over her calendar when the front door opened and Denny called out, "Hello? Anyone here?"

"In the kitchen," Olivia said.

Her daughter stepped into the kitchen, a sweet smile on her face, her golden hair cascading around her shoulders, a huge bouquet of flowers in her hand.

"Happy birthday, Mom." Denny kissed Olivia's cheek before pouring herself a cup of coffee.

"Thanks, honey." Olivia watched her daughter over the rim of her cup, trying to ignore the dark circles under Denny's eyes and the tight lines around her mouth.

"How's David?"

Denny smiled to take the edge off her words. "Come on, Mom. We both know you don't care a bit about my husband. But he's fine, thank you very much."

She set her coffee cup on the table and pulled her hair back into a ponytail, a gesture that reminded Olivia of Denny when she was an outspoken, opinionated little girl. Richard and Denny would debate at the dinner table, Richard subtly teaching his daughter to argue like a pro. Olivia suspected that those arguments were Richard's attempt to get Denny interested in the law.

Olivia loved that irreverent spark in her daughter and had been dismayed to see it diminish when David Grayson came into her life. Now Denny watched what she said, and if David was around, she would cast anxious glances his way, worried – to Olivia's mind – that what she was doing would make David angry. Denny never argued, never expressed an opinion these days. That impulsive, no-filter child had married a man hell-bent on putting out her fire.

265

"Honestly, Mom, I don't mean to sound harsh, but I wish you two could spend some time together. If you got to know David, you'd come to realize what a good man he is. You're just not used to his traditional values. You're a modern woman, Mom. I'm not."

Olivia longed to ask her daughter about her marriage, to make sure she was okay, but she was afraid that her inquiry would be seen as an intrusion, which would push Denny even further away, so she let it go. For now. "Honey, I'm never going to believe that women need to be told what to do by their husbands or boyfriends. Marriage should—"

"—be a partnership." Denny laughed as she finished the sentence. "You look nice. Court today?"

"Very tactfully done, Den. I see how you changed the subject. No court today. I'm meeting with Claire Montreaux about selling my practice."

"Somehow I can't see you retiring, Mom. Are you sure you're ready?"

Was she ready? Her small practice was nothing compared to Richard's illustrious career, but Olivia and Richard had planned it that way. Olivia's office was close to home, so she had been able to care for Denny, freeing up Richard whose relentless litigation schedule kept him away from home. While Denny was young, Olivia had attended her plays, piano recitals, and pageants. As Denny got older and became more independent, Olivia turned her attention to the vast sloping hillside behind her house, turning the wild grassy area into a terraced garden. She did all the backbreaking work herself and soon had fruit trees, a large plot dedicated to vegetables, and a vast picking garden, which kept Olivia and her friends in fresh flowers all summer long.

Olivia had spent a lot of time alone in her marriage. Even though she kept herself busy, she missed her husband and looked forward to spending more time with him, even if that time was spent traveling for his work.

"So to answer your question, yes, I'm ready. I can travel with your father now."

"I don't see Dad retiring anytime soon. He likes the limelight. I honestly don't think Dad would know what to do with himself if he retired."

And therein lies the problem.

Richard worked long hours and each week spent a night or two in their condo in the city, with its galley kitchen and an even smaller bathroom. Nestled on the top of California Street, the condo had a beautiful view of San Francisco, and since it was the first place they had purchased – mortgaging their souls after Richard passed the bar – they kept it out of sentimentality. That was thirty-two years ago. Olivia consoled herself with the knowledge that after all these years, despite him sometimes seeming married to his career, she and Richard still loved each other. *Thank goodness for that*, Olivia thought.

"I'm hoping I can get him to slow down a little bit. As for me, I'm happy in the garden. Maybe I'll take up painting or something." Olivia sipped her coffee. "Den, tell me the truth. Did your father plan a surprise party for me?"

"Of course not," Denny said. "You made it perfectly clear you absolutely didn't want one."

Olivia sighed with relief. She was looking forward to an intimate family gathering. Maybe tonight she would come to see her son-in-law in a new light. For Denny's sake she would try.

"Are you having your birthday lunch with Lauren today?"

"I am," Olivia said.

"Tell her I said hello. Maybe the three of us could meet for lunch sometime?"

"That would be great," Olivia said. "I know Lauren would love to see you." This wasn't the first time Denny had mentioned lunch with Olivia and Lauren, but despite half a dozen invitations, Denny always had some excuse.

"Are you sure you don't want me to bring anything besides the cake? It doesn't seem like much of a birthday with you slaving away in the kitchen."

"It's not slaving when you enjoy the labor. Anyway, I've got it all under control. Shopping's complete, most of the prep is already finished. I'll come home early and get the lasagna in the oven. Want to come and keep me company while I throw things together?"

"Can't. We're going to struggle to get here by 7:30 as it is. David's busy at work right now." Denny hoisted her purse onto her shoulder and kissed Olivia's cheek. "Love you."

Her conversation with Denny left her troubled. Olivia had meddled in Denny's life behind the scenes, hiring an investigator to follow Denny's husband. The investigator had reported back, worried that David had spotted him. Of course, Olivia had terminated the relationship, but it left her unsettled. If Denny knew what she had done, she'd feel so betrayed, and David wouldn't miss an opportunity to exploit Denny's anger. After all, Olivia had no concrete evidence that David was having an affair, but her years as a family law attorney had honed her intuition to a sharp edge. She knew a cheater when she saw one. David Grayson was a cheater.

"Love you, honey," Olivia said. She walked Denny to the door and stood for a moment in the cold October sun, watching the daughter she loved with her heart and soul drive away.

Fifteen minutes later, Olivia pulled into her reserved spot in the downtown Larkspur municipal parking lot and headed on foot down Magnolia towards her office. It wouldn't do to be late for her meeting with Claire Montreaux, the young lawyer who was going to buy Olivia's practice. After her meeting, she had a lunch date with her best friend, Lauren Ridley. Although the two women had lunch once a week, birthday lunches were always special and often involved champagne.

Situated in a store front and snuggled next to the historic

Lark Theatre, the Law Office of Olivia Sinclair had no sign in the window. Given the incendiary nature of the divorces she litigated, the front door was kept locked at all times, and clients were seen by appointment only. Digging the key out of her coat pocket, Olivia let herself into the office, taking in the thick carpets and the comfortable sofa with fresh eyes. She had done her best to make this part of the office welcoming. A huge bouquet of flowers rested on the waiting room coffee table.

"There you are." Mary Chadwick, Olivia's assistant since she started her practice, hurried to her desk, a stack of files in her arms. "Happy birthday, Olivia."

"Thanks. Who sent the flowers?"

"Blythe Harden dropped those off. She said to tell you they were a small testament to her gratitude. I'm also to tell you that if you ever need any favor from her, not to hesitate." A small slip of pink paper was tucked into the corner of Mary's blotter. She set the files on her desk, pulled it out, and waved it in the air, a sly smile on her face.

"There's a west wind today, a portent of big change."

After twenty-seven years of working with Mary, Olivia knew that in good time Mary would tell her what the west wind had brought them today. Her assistant – a trusted, intelligent woman who masterfully found needles in haystacks – was driven by age-old superstitions handed down from her equally superstitious grandmother.

"I've found Roland Rainwater."

"What?" Olivia didn't bother to hide her surprise. Certain that Roland Rainwater had vanished into thin air, Olivia had planned to hand the whole Rainwater file, along with its hefty retainer, over to Claire once she came on board. Claire could hire a private investigator to track down the deadbeat husband and get him served with a summons.

"How did you find him?"

Mary giggled. "On an Internet dating site."

"Do I want to know about this?"

"It's legit, don't worry. I put up a fake profile of a woman who is very similar to Hetty. You know, bohemian, artsy. I made sure to hint at wealth untold. Sure enough, Roland was looking for a new meal ticket."

"Well, where is he?"

Mary looked at her watch. "Probably on his way to Peet's. I'm meeting him for coffee in twenty minutes." The Rainwater file sat on the corner of her desk. She pulled the summons out with a flourish and grabbed her purse. "Back soon."

Olivia laughed. "Just make sure he doesn't follow you to your car."

"Don't worry. I've got my pepper spray. Oh, Claire Montreaux will be here in ten minutes or so. Want me to get some sandwiches for your birthday lunch with Lauren while I'm out?"

"Thanks, Mary. Use the company card. Get something for yourself, too."

"Will do. Back soon." Mary waved and headed down the street, walking as purposefully as a bloodhound who had picked up a scent.

Olivia surveyed the small office, the home base of her work life for the past twenty-seven years. Her eyes roamed over the various diplomas and certificates that hung on the wall, the bank of filing cabinets, the stacks of files and papers. She had worked hard for all of this, but the time had come to pass the baton. There was a gentle knock on the door.

Claire Montreaux waited while Olivia unlocked the door.

"Good morning," Claire said.

"I always keep the door locked," Olivia said. "I had an angry husband come after me with a baseball bat once."

"Really?"

"Yes. I was lucky there happened to be a policeman down the block. But I wound up with a smashed-in window, so lesson learned."

Claire was young and fresh and very much like Olivia had been when she started practicing law so very long ago. A tiny thing with black hair that hung down to her waist, Claire looked like a fifteen-year-old cheerleader. Although Olivia had never been opposite Claire in court, word on the street was that the young lawyer was whip-smart, had a photographic memory, and could out-argue the best and most seasoned litigator. Today Claire wore a very short skirt along with stiletto heels so high Olivia's lower back threatened to spasm at the very sight of them. She felt old all of a sudden. Out of touch with this new generation of lawyers.

Claire stood in the reception area, surveying her surroundings. She turned a slow circle. "This office has a really nice feel to it. Uncluttered with lots of light."

"Thanks. Of course, you can change things as you see fit," Olivia said.

The women didn't waste time with small talk. Once they were situated in Olivia's office, Claire reached into her spanking new Mark Cross briefcase and pulled out the partnership proposal that the two women had hammered out a month ago, when Claire first approached Olivia with the idea of coming on board as a partner. Several pages had been tagged with Post-its. Claire opened to the first one and said, "I need your assurance that Stephen Vine will still be sending referrals from his criminal practice this way." She leaned back, confident and in charge, and continued. "My position is that Mr. Vine's influence will be needed, especially since I'm new to the area—"

You're new to the profession, darling. Olivia didn't say the words out loud. Everyone had to start somewhere, and she couldn't find fault with Claire's attention to detail. Granted, Claire was taking a risk, sinking her time and capital into her own firm so early in her career. Stephen Vine, Olivia's long-time friend and well-respected criminal defense attorney, didn't take family law cases and had been referring clients to Olivia for years. Claire would need those referrals, especially in the beginning.

"—so will that be a problem?" Claire said.

"Not at all," Olivia said. "I've already spoken to Mr. Vine. He's agreed to meet with you alone or with me, whichever you prefer."

Claire exhaled. "That's great. Is he easy to get along with? I've heard rumors that he can be prickly."

Olivia settled back into her chair. "Stephen doesn't like liars. Be honest and genuine and you'll get along fine. Pardon my French, but he can spot bullshit a mile away." She thumbed through her copy of their agreement. "And I have an issue I would like to change. I'm looking to be out of the practice in six months instead of a year. I'm willing to adjust the financial aspects accordingly …"

And so the meeting went on. For an hour Claire and Olivia negotiated, easily agreeing on changes and amendments. By 11:35 Claire was gone, off to type up the agreed changes. Next week Olivia would sign it. After Claire left, Olivia turned her attention to her computer, methodically sorting through the thirty-plus emails she had received overnight, making note of things that needed her attention and forwarding the rest on to Mary.

"I'm back," Mary said. Olivia heard her putting food in the fridge. She came into Olivia's office and sat on the couch. "Dear Roland wasn't very happy. Silly ass. I got you sandwiches and a bottle of champagne. Will you be back after lunch?"

"Nope. I'm going to check my email and head out."

"Good. How did it go with Claire?"

"Well. She's agreed to everything."

Mary kicked off her shoes. "Today I feel like a tired old woman. I have really enjoyed working with you, Liv, but won't deny that I'm looking forward to retiring."

"Hard to believe, isn't it? We've had quite a run, haven't we?"

"That we have," Mary said. "And I don't mind admitting that I'm a wee bit exhausted."

Olivia had just deleted the last email, when a new message from an unknown sender popped into her inbox, with a subject line that read: *Check out your husband!*

"I've got an anonymous email. It mentions Richard and looks like it's coming from someone's phone," Olivia said.

Mary put her glasses on and leaned close to the computer as Olivia opened the email. The body said, "You think you know everything, don't you? You stupid bitch."

Olivia didn't think twice before double clicking the attachment. Grainy footage slowly came into focus. Thinking there was an error with the download, she started to close the file just as it popped into focus, revealing a nubile blond, younger than Denny, astride her lover.

The couple went at it like rabbits, and Olivia was just about to exit the video, when the man – hidden by the camera – flipped the girl, so she was underneath him. From this new angle, Olivia recognized the man's face. Richard. Her husband. Screwing someone young enough to be his daughter.

"Oh, God," Mary gasped, stepping away from Olivia, her hand over her mouth.

Olivia closed the laptop and pushed it away from her. The sound of crashing waves filled Olivia's ears. She pushed her chair away from the desk, as if distance would make the wretched thing go away. It didn't. Her stomach clenched into a painful cramp. She picked up the glass of water that rested on her desk, but it slipped from her shaking hands, drenching her lap in water.

Ignoring the mess she'd made, Olivia said, "Mary, would you excuse me. In fact, why don't you take the rest of the day off."

Mary waited, her embarrassment balanced by a look of worry and concern. "Are you sure?"

Olivia nodded. She waited until Mary had left and locked the door. Taking deep, steadying breaths, she pulled the laptop towards her, and ignoring the cold water that puddled in her lap, she forced herself to watch the video, this time with the sound on. When it finished, with Richard and his lover satisfied, Olivia sat at her desk, numb and unable to move, her stomach feeling as though she had eaten a bag of rocks. Olivia couldn't quite catch her breath.

When the office walls started to close in, she snapped the laptop shut and tried to stand, and despite her weak knees, somehow managed to find her way to her car.

Dear Reader,

Thank you so much for reading *The Witness*, the second book in the Olivia Sinclair series. If you are so inclined, a review on Amazon, BookBub, and/or Goodreads would be very much appreciated.

I'm busily writing the next phase of Olivia's journey, and I can't wait to share it with you. If you would like to be notified when I have a new release or when any of my books go on sale, you can sign up for my mailing list here: http://www.terrylynnthomas.com/

I enjoy connecting with you, so feel free to find me and introduce yourself on Twitter and Facebook. I do lots of promos and giveaways on social media and would love to hear from you!

Facebook: https://www.facebook.com/terrylynnthomasbooks/

Twitter: https://twitter.com/TLThomasBooks

Thank you again for taking the time to read my books.

Happy Reading,

Terry

#ReaderLove

Dear Reader,

We hope you enjoyed reading this book. If you did, we'd be so appreciative if you left a review. It really helps us and the author to bring more books like this to you.

Here at HQ Digital we are dedicated to publishing fiction that will keep you turning the pages into the early hours. Don't want to miss a thing? To find out more about our books, promotions, discover exclusive content and enter competitions you can keep in touch in the following ways:

JOIN OUR COMMUNITY:

Sign up to our new email newsletter:
http://smarturl.it/SignUpHQ

Read our new blog www.hqstories.co.uk

𝕏 https://twitter.com/HQStories

f www.facebook.com/HQStories

BUDDING WRITER?

We're also looking for authors to join the HQ Digital family!
Find out more here:

https://www.hqstories.co.uk/want-to-write-for-us/

Thanks for reading, from the HQ Digital team

If you enjoyed *The Witness*, then why not try another gripping thriller from HQ Digital?